THE AUDREY HEPBURN HEIST

A CHARLOTTE DONOVAN MYSTERY

MOLLIE COX BRYAN

❀ Created with Vellum

CHAPTER 1

How the hell did I get here? Here I am throwing a party, surrounded by Hollywood folks, which I never would have believed a year ago, heck, even six months ago. And throwing a party like this? Not my cup of tea, at all. But then again, Justine Turner's will obligated me to do certain things. Throwing a huge party was one. At first, I chaffed. Here Justine was, wanting to leave me her money, but it had strings attached. I should have known. I was still in the clutches of my famous dead boss.

The saxophone's sound reached into my chest and curled around in a deep vibration as the jazz band played a 1940's smoking tune in what was once Justine's living room. The trio played in a corner of the apartment with a makeshift stage plopped down on the black-and-white marble floor. Heavy crimson-velvet drape-covered windows provided the backdrop. Funny how easily the room became a stage—or at least a corner of it did. Bronze sconces, dimly lit, sliced the light and shadow against the walls. I drew in a breath: Hard to believe this apartment was mine now.

Clutches of people scattered about the place. This apartment was made for parties. The L'Ombrage was one of the oldest and grandest Art-Deco apartment buildings in the city; it spoke of elegance and graciousness.

I gazed around at the party-goers, not recognizing many of them. I wiped my sweaty palms on my fancy dress and lowered my eyes to the floor. I felt like I was inside someone else's life. The agency had taken control of the guest list, insisting security would be top-notch. But—how did some of these people get in?

A man wearing white pants, a glitter shirt, with pink hair swung his hips to the beat. A tiny frumpy woman circled him as if getting ready to pounce. A woman's horsey laughter broke out over the music. A ridiculously handsome man draped his arm across her shoulders. A group of men huddled on the couch. They were probably making some kind of multi-million dollar deal. I recalled the words of my agent, Natalie, a few minutes ago. "Everybody in this room has deep ties with Hollywood, Audrey Hepburn, and Broadway."

"Someone ought to give that woman laugh lessons," Kate, my best friend, said with a flat note.

Gemma Hollins, an actress up for the role of Holly Golightly in *Golightly Travels,* a new production, leaned closer. "It kind of ruined the song, didn't it?"

Kate cackled. "If you weren't from London, I'd swear you could be from Cloister Island."

Big compliment coming from Kate. She was right—Gemma fit right in with the two of us Cloister Islanders masquerading as Manhattanites.

Den's wide shoulders and narrow waist captured my gaze. I couldn't look away, picturing the sculpted muscles and contours under the fabric. He winked. Caught. I grinned. Rented tux or not, I was ripping that off later tonight. "Hey there, the party is going well."

"So far so good." I kissed his cheek. "I'm glad you could make it."

"You were right. This place is full of beautiful people. Just caught one a little lost coming out of Justine's bedroom. Lots of plastic in here if I'm not mistaken." He laughed and rolled his eyes.

Gemma laughed a sparkling tingling sound, as she wrapped her arm around me. The woman glowed. She had the air of a young Audrey Hepburn. She was definitely the favored actress on the audition reality show. Just being close to her made me feel like anything was possible. "How are you holding up, friend? This is so not your scene."

"You know me so well." I smiled and wrapped my arm around her. "I'm fine. For now."

She rubbed my back and pulled me in for a hug. "I'm so proud of you."

My heart fluttered. If I had a "type" of friend, Gemma would not be it. Yet, I adored her. Her with her plastic surgeries and constant diets. Exactly the kind of woman Kate and I loved to hate. But Gemma was genuine.

She was open about her surgeries—lips and nose done like Audrey's and a breast reduction. She wanted this role, lived to play the part of Holly in the new mini-series, focused on what happened to Holly after *Breakfast at Tiffany's*—the movie, not the book.

She wore a little black dress similar to the one Audrey wore in the movie and she also sported the long gloves. I lent them to her from Justine's private collection. If you allowed yourself, you could imagine it was 1961 and you were in the company of Holly Golightly.

Justine would have loved her, too.

The other two actresses up for the role had yet to show, even though they were invited.

A server came along with a tray of drinks. We each took one.

"Where is the restroom?" Gemma asked.

"I'll show you," I said. I needed to head that way, too. She followed me back the long tiled hallway, past the life-size painting of Greta Garbo, Justine's favorite. ("A lesbian icon, kinda like me," she'd say and laugh.) Her heels clicked on the tile, echoing. We sat our drinks on the table outside of the restroom.

She slipped inside and shut the door and I hurried into my private bathroom.

Private bathroom. The words rolled around in my head. Me. Charlotte Donovan, a Cloister Island girl, living in a swank apartment in the Upper East Side, partying with folks from Hollywood. It was a cool twist in my life.

I walked back out into the hallway and grabbed my drink from the table. Gemma had already taken hers. I found my way back into the crowd where Kate was holding a group rapt with one of her stories. I waited for the end. Cue: laughter. I stepped into the loose circle, realizing more guests had arrived since I'd left. More people I didn't know. The room filled with chatter and music, glasses brimming with champagne.

Not too bad, I told myself. I tried not to look at my sparkling new watch. Only a few hours left. One server brought over a tray of tiny slices of bread, spread with glistening caviar. I reached for one, just as Gemma squeezed between Kate and her date—a dashing wealthy gentleman, Roger, who adored her. But then again, how could you not adore Kate?

Kate wore a sky-blue sleeveless cocktail dress, which brought out the blue in her eyes. Sparkling necklaces draped her neck. She dazzled.

She had stuffed me into a cocoa and pale pink floral original Vera Wang, which she said suited my small curvy frame and brought out my brown eyes. I was prepared to feel uncomfortable, but my feet throbbed, and I felt as if a boob might pop out of my dress at any moment, so I moved around stiffly, which added to my discomfort. I took in Kate and her relaxed, elegant self, and then glanced over at Gemma, also a fashion inspiration—beautifully put together and comfortable in her skin.

But something was wrong. I squinted at her. Gemma's complexion had taken on a sickly pallor. She wobbled and Kate held onto her.

I stepped forward. "Are you okay?"

Kate grabbed her by the elbow and tried to steady her. But Gemma collapsed. Some drama queen's scream pierced the room. "What is that?" Gemma muttered, attempting to point.

I crouched down beside her. "What is what?" She wasn't making any sense.

Den took over. "Okay everybody back up, give her some room."

"Can we take her into a bedroom?" I stuttered.

"It's best we don't move her until we see what's going on." Den's voice held authority and experience.

"She passed out," Kate said. "That's what's going on."

Den held her wrist. "I said to stand back!" Curious onlookers backed away, and a hush fell over the room as the music stopped. "Call 9-1-1."

He started CPR.

My focus zoomed in and out from the scene in front of me to the other guests gathered around. Zach, the director of the reality show the three wannabe Holly Golightly's were in, edged his way to the scene. "What's going on? Is she okay?"

"She passed out. Maybe she needs to eat," I said, ignoring that Den said she had no pulse. That couldn't be right. She didn't eat enough. I told her that all the time. Of course she never listened to me. Now, look at what she's done to herself. Passed out from a lack of eating. "Do you know if she has any health issues?"

He shrugged. "None."

Den continued the CPR. Everything else around me faded out. Time moved in drips and waves.

Finally, a man came over to Den and stopped him. Den's rhythm stopped as the other man took over. He sat up, sweating, flushed. He stood and put his arm around me and whispered. "There's nothing I can do."

My mouth felt like sandpaper as I tried to form words. My throat stuck and itched. I coughed and sucked in a breath, "Den? What do you mean?" Trembly. Hushed. But I pushed the words out.

Blood drained from his face and his eyes caught mine. "She's gone."

Air whooshed out of my chest. "What do you mean?" I stammered, gripping my chest. "She's not—"

Stern-faced Den nodded at me and eyeballed Kate. "Secure the doorway. Don't let anybody out. Do ya hear?"

Kate nodded and dragged Roger with her to man the door.

My heart thudded against my ribcage. A stone-cold chill swept through me. Leaving me shivering, teeth chattering. Someone draped a blanket over me. Rubbed my shoulder. Kate, who must've left Roger alone at the door. Ever by my side. "Are you cold? Let's get you some whiskey and take you out of here." She attempted to lead me, but my legs were frozen to the floor.

"Charlotte, look at me." She held my face. I blinked. And blinked again. "Let's go in the next room." Her voice sounded as if she were in a tunnel. "Can you hear me?"

I nodded as best I could and let her lead me, one step after the other.

A young and healthy woman had just collapsed and died at my party. A woman I adored. An actress, a friend, a bright spark in this dark, dark world. A welling sprang up inside of me when I reached the chair in the next room, a welling rising through my guts, burning through my chest and throat, exiting as a wail. I collapsed into the chair and sobbed.

Three shots later of the best gold-label bourbon I ever tasted and I found my sea legs and talked myself into going back into the party room.

Kate helped me stand. "You don't have to go back out there. There's nothing for you to do."

"It's my party." Surreal. Tragic. But still, my party. I had to at least show my face. And I couldn't leave it all up to Den and god-knows-who else.

I WAS TRYING to keep it together, now, back in the main room. My throat burned as I tried to swallow back the sorrow. I blew my nose on a linen handkerchief.

"Someone poisoned her," Den said into my ear. "I smelled and almost tasted something on her." He turned to the party crowd. "Get comfortable folks. It's going to be a long night. Uniformed officers will take your names and numbers, along with statements about where you were in the place when this happened."

I stifled a groan.

"This is a hell of a party," Natalie whispered into my ear. "People will remember this."

"Yes, I suppose they will."

"But you've filled your obligations. Killed two birds with one stone, so to speak. And now you're off the hook."

So says Natalie.

Kate came up to us now. "There's a so-called actress at the door. Holly number two." Kate smirked. "As if."

It must be Jazz Wilson, who the viewers (and Kate), loved to hate. I tried not to waste too much energy hating her, but she was obnoxious.

"Tell her she can't come in," Den said.

The party crowd parted, as Jazz entered the room A stunning blonde, with an Audrey-Hepburn neck and doe-like brown eyes, she stood with her hands on her round, lush, hips.

"You tell her," Kate said and flung her silky cobalt-blue scarf over her shoulder.

"Who says I can't come to the party of the century?" She opened her arms as if to display her perfect figure—more Marilyn Monroe than Audrey Hepburn. In truth, Capote's choice first to play Holly was Marilyn, which I never understood. "Since you're inside, please take a seat and wait for my uniformed officers," Den said.

As if she just noticed the paramedics, her eyebrows shot up. "What's going on?"'

I sniffed. "It's Gemma. She's dead."

The actress's face fell and drooped, before she picked it up, while everybody looked on. "What? What? How could she be dead? I don't understand." She leaned in. "I just spoke with her. She was fine."

It was as I suspected. The two of them were friends. Their rivalry was a part of the Hollywood smokescreen. The spin.

Jazz wobbled, but tried to compose herself. As hard as she seemed to fight it, she hit my marble floor with a sickening thud.

As I rushed to her, a dark presence loomed behind me, which I couldn't deal with now. Now, I focused on Jazz. Patted her perfect face. "Jazz, come on, get up."

I cranked my head around as some of the partiers gathered. There stood actress number three—she was the looming darkness I'd felt, no doubt. Arms crossed. Hip extended. "Such a drama queen." Was she trying to be funny? Nobody laughed. Tone deaf didn't begin to describe her statement.

Jazz moaned and tried to open her eyes, as I held her head up, I spotted the one last acting rival—Zoe Noss. She blinked away a cold glare when my eyes caught hers. The depth of it made me shiver.

Perhaps I was still paranoid over the ordeal of Justine's death. But I had gazed into the eyes of the man who killed her, and Zoe's eyes, in that brief moment, held that same cold, empty guise.

CHAPTER 2

Would an actor kill because of the role of a lifetime? It seemed absurd to me, like much of Hollywood, but the mini-series would be a career maker.

Gemma had once told me she became an actress because of her passion for Audrey Hepburn. Gemma and Audrey shared common traits, starting with their birthdays. Same day and time, right down to the minute. Weird.

I stepped off to the side, choking back a sob, as the paramedics carried her off in a milky-gray body bag.

Kate came closer. "Are you okay?"

"Depends on what you mean." Sometimes Kate could be a mother hen. My chronic Lyme Disease hadn't flared in ages —and she always watched out for it. No. My Lyme seemed so far away as I held back the tears threatening. My throat burned. Oh Gemma.

Kate flung her hair over her shoulder. "Poor Gemma. I wonder what happened?"

I swallowed hard, balled my sweaty hands into a fist. "Den suspects someone poisoned her."

"As in on purpose? So, that's why they're questioning people." She snapped her fingers.

Jazz, recovered and sitting on a chair across the room from us, laughed with a tall woman standing next to her.

Kate raised her chin in Jazz's direction. "My money's on that bitch."

I wanted to agree. I wished it were as simple as Kate suggested. I eyeballed Jazz, confused as to who she really was beneath her carefully tended facade. "She wasn't here yet. Besides, she and Gemma might have been friends."

"What? They're arch enemies on the reality audition show."

"That's Hollywood," I said with a sarcastic tone.

Kate grunted. We sat in near silence for a few beats. The two of us grew up together on Cloister Island, off the coast of New York City. We had big dreams of moving to the city —him as a woman, and me as a writer. Karl was Kate now, and me? As for my writing, I penned a bestseller, but I shared a byline with the famous Justine. I'd yet do it on my own.

I'd been Justine's assistant for years, longing to write my own books. She kept promising to let me pen a whole book, instead of bits and pieces. Now I had a couple of book contracts of my own, but I had yet to deliver. Sometimes when I sat at my keyboard, the words wouldn't come. A paralyzing fear tugged at me. Whispers of doubt. Was this my voice or Justine's? How would she handle this paragraph and should I handle it the same way?

This party and this Hollywood gig were an awful idea. I should have listened to my gut.

Another group of people exited the flat, and a few walked over to Kate and me to say thank you for the lovely party. "Really?" I wanted to scream. Lovely? Gemma died, Jazz passed out, and Zoe continued to spew evil.

This party was a nightmare. More of a nightmare than I'd

imagined. I could have had another kind of party and it would've met the will's requirements. Instead, my agent talked me into inviting the cast and crew of reality audition series. So out of my league. And it showed,

As if he read my mind, Fitz Wellston, one of the few people I knew at my own party, winked at me. "It will be okay."

Fitz's husband cleared his throat. "All publicity is good publicity." He grinned as his hand twisted into a flourish.

A murder in my home is not publicity, I stopped myself from spatting. A strenuous exercise for me.

Fitz kissed my cheek, said thank you for everything, and left.

"I don't like that guy. Slick bastard," Kate said

I agreed, scanning the room. The police made headway, with a few people left to interview. Den sat next to Zoe to question her. He was all business, but she batted her eyes and flipped her hair. I couldn't blame her. My man was hot. A Daniel Craig lookalike, with a Brooklyn accent, and a broad chest that left me breathless. And he liked me.

Was I in an actual relationship? After years of hopping from cop to cop? Den had shattered my record. We'd been together six whole months. But I was not one to get my hopes up. Nah, they'd been dashed too many times. But I continued to see him and hold my hopes in check. Den was more than steady and good, he was a mix of passionate and funny and genuine New Yorker. Irresistible. He moved me in ways I was still trying to name.

"Is that the woman playing Gigi in the play?" Kate glanced toward the petite, painfully thin actress.

I'd read that it annoyed her fans she wasn't in the running for *Golightly Travels*. But she lacked interest in TV of any kind. Usually bubbly and vivacious, Ginger Pence drooped against the wall. "Yes, and she's not looking so hot."

I flew toward her. "Are you okay?"

She managed a smile. "It's been an interminable day."

"Can I bring you a glass of water?" And a steak? Or even a hot dog or two?

She nodded. Pale, big-eyed, and made up like a Broadway star, she resembled an antique porcelain doll. As I left her to go to the kitchen, her date turned to her and slipped his arm around her slim waist.

I retrieved her water and returned to a room of people circling something. Where was Ginger?

I elbowed my way in and discovered her flat on the floor.

"She's passed out," her date said.

My heart lurched in my rib cage as I rushed to them.

I hoped that she had passed out and not expired. Two dead actresses at my party would be unbearable.

Her date patted her face with a gentle touch. "Ginger."

Her eyelids flickered. Oh, thank god. Not dead then. Just passed out— which was going around tonight.

He frowned, "She's not eaten today. And she's been rehearsing like crazy." He took the water from me.

Den came up to me, serious-faced. "I've interviewed her. She's free to go as soon as she feels up to it."

Her date nodded, and Ginger sat up, with him cradling her. "What a party!"

Scanning the sparse crowd, some of whom laughed and others stood by stone faced, I wished all of them gone— except for Kate and Den. The only people I liked to have around for any length of time. I could get out of this dress, take off the make-up, and flop down on the couch with them.

"The party was great!" Natalie said, leaning in closer, whispering. "It'll be okay. I assure you."

She was still here? I'd forgotten about her.

Kate grabbed my elbow. "Come with me."

We stole away to the library where a bottle of chilling

champagne and two glasses waited. "You needed out of that scene. Let's have another drink. Or two."

I exhaled. "Sounds good." I sat as Kate poured. A dark, sinking sentiment niggled at me. The sparkling glass and bubbly liquid triggered a nagging sense of a memory. A whisper of something important.

I lifted the glass to my lips and remembered that Gemma and I walked to the lavatory together and had set our drinks down on the same stand. I had wondered if we may have switched drinks.

"Damn." I sat my drink down. "I need to talk to Den."

CHAPTER 3

"Let me get this straight," Den's placed hands on his hips. "You and Gemma got drinks at the same time. You both took them back to the restroom, sat them on the table outside, she went inside and you went to your private bath."

I concentrated on responding to his words, when falling into his arms is all I craved. His warmth. His heartbeat. "That's right."

"You think maybe the drinks were switched. Why?" He emphasized the word, think.

I picked up my half-filled champagne glass, hand trembling, and sipped. "I'm not sure. It's just that I remember thinking Gemma might have taken the wrong glass, but then, I didn't consider it a big deal. Neither one of us had taken a drink at that point."

A uniformed cop walked into the room. "We have Gemma's glass, on its way to forensics. Should give us something." He lifted his chin. I wasn't sure, but I might know him. *Know* in the Biblical sense. My face and chest heated in a flush. I turned and ducked my head.

"Thanks, Lou," Den said.

Lou. That's right. Yes, I recognized him. My face heated more, so hot it might erupt. *Please don't notice me, Lou. Please.* If I had magical powers, I'd snap my fingers and disappear. Right now.

When he left the room, my body sighed a deep private exhaling relief. Whew. What were the chances that my boyfriend and a past lover would be on the same case? What would I do if Lou, or someone like Lou, told Den about my history? Would Den care about my reputation as badge bunny? I owned it. That was me. For years. But, I've not dated anybody else since I met Den. It shouldn't matter to him or me. The past was the past. I shrugged it off.

Perhaps Kate was right. Maybe my penchant for cops stretched back to my wayward cop father, who abandoned us. Didn't make much sense. You'd assume I'd stay away from them. I was in a new relationship with one of the finest people I'd ever known. I should divulge it all to him before he finds out another way. I resolved that's what I'd do. At the right time.

"So, maybe the poisoner was after you." Kate sat down her champagne glass. "Seems like we need to figure that out soon."

Den nodded. "Right away."

"We're being paranoid. Who'd want to kill me?" I said.

"Six months ago you were a target. don't forget about that," Den said.

"Paranoid? Who wouldn't be?" Kate said. "You were almost killed!"

MY MIND RACED, buzzing with memories. I sat my champagne glass down. No more alcohol tonight. I needed a clear mind.

"You're getting to be a famous writer," Kate said. "Maybe a whack-job writer wannabe? What was his name? The one who wanted to write the Harlow book? Hartwell?"

Sweat beads pricked on my head. I reached for a tissue.

My eyes met Den's. "I'll find out where Hartwell is these days," Den said.

I shivered as I patted the sweat from my head and face. A wave of nausea threatened to creep up my throat.

Den paced. "No offense, but it's more likely that Gemma was the intended victim with all this reality show *Golightly Travels* business. One of her competitors?"

I recalled the distant stare of Zoe's eyes when Gemma was on the floor dying. "Could be. If there's one thing I've learned about actors over the past few months, it's that most of them are desperate and insecure beneath the carefully tended facade." ("Just like writers," Justine would often say.)

Gemma was different. She had the rare quality of humbleness, yet she radiated confidence. She'd had a positive upbringing in London and was a solid sort. My stomach roiled. Poor Gemma, killed at the start of a brilliant career. They hadn't made the official public decision yet—but surely she'd be the next Holly Golightly. She had my vote. She seemed to have a link with Hepburn, even though she'd never met her.

"Nothing to do but wait on those results," Den stopped pacing. "In the interim, we investigate both probabilities. We're aware of Hartwell. We know Gemma's two enemies. Are there others?"

I sorted through memories of my conversations with her. "I don't think so, Den. I've not known her for long." I blinked back a tear. "She was respected and loved."

"Do you have other enemies?"

"Judith Turner," Kate said.

Den's head tilted, chin lifting. "Justine's cousin?"

"Yes, that bitch has been causing many complications—or at least trying to." Kate never minced words. And she always had my back.

Judith wasn't happy that Justine willed me the apartment. Nor was she happy that she left me money. As always, the money part had conditions. Justine's order I throw a party was just one in a litany of obligations. "She's threatened me a few times. But she's an old woman, and she lives in Florida. I don't see her trying to kill me."

"I do," Kate said and crossed her arms. "I mean not getting her hands dirty. But she'd hire someone."

Den shook his head. "Unlikely. Pros rarely poison." One eyebrow lifted. "But I won't discount that theory, yet."

Could someone be trying to kill me again? How likely was it? Did lightning strike twice? I inhaled, exhaled. It was one-hundred percent more likely that Gemma was the intended victim.

Yes, I'd cling to that idea.

I wasn't up for another chase down Fifth Avenue, or attack in Central Park. I wanted to get on with my life. I'd keep my nose out of police business, as long as it didn't involve me. I believe in our justice system and realized the NYPD was the finest force in the world. And I should know —having "dated" my way through several of them. But as I took Den in, observing him move through my apartment, writing things down, barking orders at the uniforms, conducting phone calls, I understood my preoccupation with other cops was long gone.

CHAPTER 4

The first 24 hours after a murder case were the most important. So I kissed Den goodnight, hoping he'd find answers soon. Kate insisted I stay with her because my apartment crawled with police. It was a crime scene. My new apartment. Justine's grand dame of a home. Leaving it was akin to ripping off an appendage.

"It's a majestic place," Kate said. "But you spend too much time there. You need to get out more often."

Non-writers didn't understand. I couldn't gad about town and get words on the page.

"Whatever," I muttered, as I threw a couple of things in an overnight bag. "I'm sure Roger isn't happy with the situation."

"Roger is a fine man. He's more worried about you than getting laid tonight, I assure you. What else do you need?" She looked around the room and spotted the box of Audrey Hepburn memorabilia sitting on my chair. "Did you leave that out like that?"

I shoved a few more things in my bag. "Yeah. Nobody knows about it and who'd be coming into my room?"

"Right. Exactly like who'd be killing Gemma Hollins at a party. Sometimes I wonder about you." She picked the box up and shoved it into my closet. "When we come back, we'll put it back where it belongs."

"The secret closet." I zipped up my bag. "I hope I get the gloves back from Gemma. I need to mention that to Den. They're the real deal."

"I'm sure everything in Justine's secret closet is the real deal. Ya have to wonder how she acquired it."

"One of these days, when I have time, I'll research all those pieces and donate them to a museum. What good are they doing here? Why did she hoard them away?" Justine had loved her things. (What's this crap about living lightly on the planet," she said. "I adore my things. Don't take my things away.")

"And hoard them in secret, in a room behind her closet, like something out of a novel," Kate said. "When are we going to start going through everything?"

I yawned, exhausted, not thinking clearly. "Soon. I promise"

Kate and I left the police and apartment behind. We grabbed a cab because nobody wanted to take the subway at 1:30 a.m.

"I still can't believe Gemma is dead," Kate said as we rode. The blare of the backseat screen played loud, upbeat music. My hands balled into fists. "I wonder what will happen now."

"I suppose the producers will have to choose between Zoe and Jazz." I leaned forward. "Can you shut this thing off?"

The cabby smiled. He didn't understand a word I'd said. "Off!" I made a turning motion with my hand.

He nodded, and the screen blanked. A hush came over the cab.

"My money was on Gemma. She had the most Audrey-like quality, don't you think?" Kate glanced at herself in a mirror she'd pulled out from her bag. "God, I look tired. More lipstick, please."

"Kate, we're just going back to your place."

"No excuse to look like death."

A few beats of silence.

"Yes, I suspected Gemma would be Holly Golightly. She was perfect for the part. Quality." My throat squeezed. I didn't want to cry. I was not a crier. I bit my lip and swallowed. It had worked since I was a kid, not wanting the others to see me cry about my dad. A wave of fear and sadness would come over me and I'd start crying as school. On the bus. At lunch. In music class. Until I finally learned to bite my lip and swallow hard,

But as we drove along, I processed the evening. I couldn't do anything else but cry. Unravel in the safety of a cab, next to my best friend. Again. I sank into a big ugly cry, with Kate shoving tissues at me.

I blew my nose and took a breath. "I hope they find who killed her.'

"But what if they meant it for you?" Kate said, eyes slanted, chin tilted. "What then?"

I sniffed and shrugged. What if? I'd feel ten times worse if Gemma died because of me. If she didn't die by accident, and she was the target, the other two actresses up for the part were the primary suspects. Not a cool scenario either. I'd spent hours with them on set and would spend more once the filming of the new series started. I'd rather not hang out with killers.

"If someone was trying to kill you, they ain't going to be happy that you're still alive."

My head hurt. The muscles in my neck tightened. Why did Kate point that out? I'd gotten through the earlier ordeal, but I didn't want to go through that again.

Kate sighed. "Now that I consider it, Gemma was doubtless the person targeted."

I cracked open a window. The cab smelled of stale body odor and Kate's perfume of the day—something floral and lovely, but mixed with the BO, it made me queasy. The breeze blew over my face and I drew in the cool air. Autumn in the city was one of my favorite times—after the stifling heat of the summer and before the stone cold of the winter.

It was different on Cloister Island, where I grew up and my family still lived. The seasons were more forgiving without the concrete and high rises. I closed my eyes and recalled the view from my bedroom window at home—the waves rolling on the rocky shore, gulls flying, landing on the rock and earth. I closed my eyes even tighter, calming my racing heart and throbbing head. I could practically smell the sea air.

CHAPTER 5

Every time I shut my eyes, Gemma's face sprang in my mind. After tossing and turning, I untangled myself from the blankets and tiptoed into the kitchen for a glass of water.

I sat at her kitchen table drinking a glass of water. The events of the evening left me spent, but wired.

"Can't sleep?" Kate asked as she entered the kitchen.

"I guess you can't either."

"I'm here to fetch my sleeping pills. You want one?" She reached into a cabinet and pulled out her bottle.

I held out my hand. She plopped two pills into it.

Kate's kitchen was one of my favorite places. All her wonderful cooking odors lingered in the walls and cupboards. It smelled like home.

"Are you smelling my kitchen again?" An eyebrow lifted.

"Guilty."

"Is that a compliment? I mean, I do clean the place from time to time." She smiled and sat at the table.

"It doesn't smell dirty. Just nice."

"That's what he said." We laughed. Big fans of *The Office*

and the character Michael's jokes. In fact, we had analyzed him and the other characters on the show multiple times. It might be the closest thing to a hobby we had.

The sleeping pills worked fast, and I rolled off to bed, longing to drift off into a sea of nothing. Sleep might be my favorite thing. Well, next to my other favorite thing. Which prompted thoughts of Den, my absolute favorite thing.

I dreamed of a party. A technicolor *Breakfast at Tiffany's* party held it at my place. Loud music. People dressed in bright pink and orange 1960's garb. Beehive hairdos and eye-patches. A woman stood at the mirror—it might have been Kate, laughing and sobbing. Just like in the movie. Also, like the movie, someone yelled "timber" and another fell straight down, like a tree. It was Gemma that fell.

As I awakened, vivid images of my dream played in my mind's eye. There was more chalky blue eye-shadow at my dream party than is even manufactured these days.

When I'm working on a biography, I often dream about my subject. The line between my writing and real life blurs. When I awaken from these dreams, I lie there and try to connect the dots.

I mulled over my dream, hesitant to get out of bed. I'd been writing about the party in *Breakfast at Tiffany's* and had a party, so it's forefront of mind. But to dream about it? Was I that deep into this book?

Gemma's face became Audrey's face in my dream. A hollow pang erupted in my chest. She was gone. Another longing came over me, I craved Den's arms, his calming voice, all of him.

A knock interrupted my morning thoughts. Um. Perhaps they were noonish thoughts.

"I've made omelets," Kate's voice came through the door.

"Be right there."

I sat up, stiff and pained, hoping my Lyme wasn't flaring

from the stress of yesterday. Maybe my bones were tired from all the work I'd done for the party. Still, I made a mental note not to forget to take my pills this morning.

My phone buzzed. When I saw the caller's name on the screen, I let it go. It was Ian Matthews, the IT guy I'd inherited from Justine. He knew his stuff, and had just "fixed" my computer, but said he needed to do more to the anti-virus something or other. I'd put him off because of the madness of the party. And I let my phone go into voicemail. Justine liked him, but he kind of creeped me out and I had to gird my loins before dealing with him again.

The divine scent of the cheesy omelet lured me into the kitchen. "God it smells so good in here."

"Sit down and eat," Kate said.

She topped the omelets with avocado, salsa, and cheese, and when I took my first bite, I almost drooled. She slid a cup of hot, black coffee my way. I sipped and my brain pinged.

"Any word from Den?"

"Not yet. He'll call when they know something." I didn't want to think about yesterday. Not at all. Gemma died at my party. It was too much to unpack at the breakfast table. I wanted to tuck into the delicious breakfast and fly off on an eggy cloud.

My phone buzzed again. It was Matthews. He was persistent. I picked up and rolled my eyes at Kate.

"Yes?"

"Ah, Ms. Donovan?"

"Yes. what can I do for you?"

"Can we set up a time for me to work on Justine's computer? There're new patches and antivirus software I need to upgrade."

"I'm sorry. I'll call you back. We can't get into the place

right now. It's a crime scene. There was an incident at my party last night."

"But it will only take thirty minutes." What was with this guy? Didn't he hear what I said?

"I'm sorry, but the cops aren't even letting me in." I gestured to Kate, pointed to the phone and shrugged.

"Will you call when it's cool? I mean, I really need to get this work done for you."

He sounded desperate. He was being paid a retainer fee, so I didn't get his desperation.

"Sure, I'll let you know."

After we hung up, Kate turned to me. "Persistent little bugger, isn't he?" She paused. "Your party is all over the news this morning."

"Speaking of parties, I had the wildest dream. What was in those sleeping pills?"

Kate laughed. "You always have weird dreams when you're working on a book. Don't blame that on the pills."

I recapped my dream for her as we ate, which was just what we both needed to keep our minds off Gemma's death.

"An amazing scene." Kate was a huge *Breakfast at Tiffany's* fan. "Blake Edwards was brilliant, wasn't he? That party was one sentence in the script and he took it and ran with it, with real actors, not extras."

I swallowed my bite of toast. "Yeah and he gave them mini-arcs and he hired a choreographer to help fit the pieces together of the scene, even though there was very little dancing, and the scene was almost completely improvised. Which is why he wanted actors. He gave them very little direction—only that they had to hit their marks."

I wondered if Kate needed this distraction as much as I did—although discussing my books had become so much a part of my writing process that we joked that Kate should get a byline.

"I read that the party scene, just that scene, inspired the movie *The Party*." Kate buttered her toast..

"True! The scene took seven days to shoot. The very last day, the party-goers were drinking actual champagne, with the direction "The trick to playing drunk was to play the scene intending to seem sober." I paused. "We both know that only too well." We laughed.

"But Audrey was a bit of a tightass. She drank very little for the scene, said it would make her lose her focus—and she needed it to keep up with Blake's direction," I added. "She was always so serious."

"Speaking of serious, is it too early to ask how the biography is going? Is it as much fun as the Harlow biography?" Kate grinned.

I almost choked on my coffee. "Are you kidding?" She gave me a look that said she wasn't. "Okay, then." I sat forward. "The Hepburn biography is uncomplicated. Harlow's was more difficult because of the time she lived. But Harlow did almost nothing but work. That part of her life was easy to write. The personal stuff challenged me."

Kate guffawed. "I was just thinking here we are comparing Jean Harlow and Audrey Hepburn. Two very different women.'"

"But they had a lot in common." I forked my eggs. Kate cocked an eyebrow. "All they both really wanted was to get married and have children. After several miscarriages, when Audrey finally became a mother, she said it was the greatest joy for her because it was all she really wanted in the world."

"Please," Kate said, with a dismissive wave. "All that 1950's bullshit of womanhood messed up a lot of women. Including her."

I took the last bite of my eggs. "Then there's whole Bill Holden thing. He was married when they were having an affair—"

She slammed her hand on the table. "Not very 1950s of her—or was it?"

"It's the one thing I don't understand and don't like about her. She dumped him because he had a vasectomy? Could she not have married Holden and adopted children? Breaking up with someone ready to leave his wife for you because of his vasectomy? Really?" I stood and took my plate to the sink, rinsed it.

My phone rang again. I glanced at the screen. Mom. "Shit." I let it go into voicemail. My voicemails were piling up.

"Your mom?" Kate poured cream into her coffee.

"Yes, I'm sure she's heard. I need to sort through this before I can talk with her."

"She's just checking on you." She lifted a forkful of egg to her mouth.

"Maybe. More likely she wants the scoop. And I don't have one to give her."

Mom and I were barely speaking. My long-lost father had reached out and asked to see me. She considered it an excellent idea, and I did not. Why should I see the man who abandoned my mother and me? I didn't even have one ounce of compassion or curiosity toward him. No matter how deep I dug.

"But—"

"Nor do I want to talk about it. Not today."

CHAPTER 6

My phone rang and I saw Den's number on the screen, I couldn't pick it up fast enough.

"What do you know about Gemma?" Den asked, while I sat at Kate's kitchen table,with yet another cup of coffee.

"She was British, trained in London, worked for awhile as an extra there, then moved to LA to break into Hollywood."

"That's what I thought, too." He breathed into the phone —which I had learned was something he just did. He wasn't flirting. Weariness edged his voice. "Fake."

"What do you mean?"

"A: she's not British. B: never trained there or anywhere, and C: she's from Jersey, as in New Jersey." He said the word Jersey with attitude, typical, but my mind was still swimming in the rest of it.

"What?" All the hours I'd spent with her and she lied about being British. I swallowed to keep from crying. Or screaming. Perhaps both.

I should have known, or at least suspected. I didn't make friends easily and women like her never glanced my way. A sharp, squeezing pang moved through me, stopped in the center of my chest— the wrong person to let my guard down with.

"A creation of her agent," Den said with a flat note, as if he'd heard it all before. "It got her an audition with *Golightly Travels*."

I bit my lip, as I wondered what else she hid. "So this all came up in your investigation. Is she clean? Any record?"

"Last name is DeSantis."

If I was a dog, my ears would have twitched. "As in—"

"He's her uncle."

I blew out air. "Sylvester DeSantis? Thank God he's in prison, The plot thickens."

Rustling noises sounded in Den's background. Maybe he was shuffling paper. "But it still doesn't look like a professional hit. We're waiting on the tox reports."

I pictured Den sitting back in his chair, four o'clock shadows on his chiseled face, hands running through his hair.

Which reminded me. "Please make sure I get those gloves back? They're the real deal." And to think I almost told Gemma about the secret closet. For a woman who prided herself on street smarts, and a hard shell, how gullible was I?

"Sure." He paused. "I gotta go. I just wondered if you could add more to Gemma's background. I hate the way this smells."

The niece of a mobster had been struck down in my home. I didn't like it either. Either it was a hit on her for crime-family reasons or because she was in the running for this important part. In either case, the DeSantis family would take revenge.

Perhaps we were off. Maybe the killer was after me. Funny, none of the scenarios comforted me. At all.

"Was Gemma her actual name?" Please let her have one true thing. One thing I can hang on to.

"Yep. Gemma DeSantis."

At least there's that. "When can I go home?"

"Maybe tomorrow. I'll reach out later."

Working a case, Den was laser-focused. I preferred his focus on me, but understood. I was the same way when writing. Perhaps that's why we got along. After we hung up, I pulled out my laptop and researched on my own. I keyed in her name. Nothing came up on her. A few Gemma DeSantis's popped up but they were older or way younger and not in Jersey. But then again, if your family is a crime family, you don't use your name on the internet. You tried to live a quiet life. Unless you wanted to be a famous actress. She most likely paid a hefty sum for her past to disappear, and her ties with her family.

With enough money, I suppose you could do anything. Even disappear without an internet trace.

I sucked in air: were we ever friends? She seemed so genuine, compared to the other two actresses up for the role. Perhaps she couldn't tell me her truth. I closed my eyes, conjured her face, with its doe-like eyes, and wide Audrey-Hepburn smile. I hadn't considered her ethnicity before, having assumed she told the truth about being British. But now, I spotted the Italian in her beautiful features.

"What are you doing? Meditating?" Kate said, walking into the kitchen, wrapped in a robe, smelling like lilacs after her shower.

"You know better than that." I drank from my coffee cup. "Den just called."

"And?" She stood with her hands on her hips, a gesture that reminded me of her mother.

I revealed the entire story to her.

She dropped into a kitchen chair; eyes wide. "I'm in shock. I liked her."

"Me too." I drummed my fingers on the table. "If they

meant the poison for her, it presents us with several unpleasant scenarios."

"Well, it's looking more like you weren't the intended victim."

"Still, it happened in my home." It had taken a few months for me to even think of that apartment as my home. When I first stayed there, I lived in one room. Eventually, I took the guest room, after a dream about Justine telling me to stop sleeping on the couch.

"Will you have a hard time going back there?" Kate's voice softened. "Are you going to be okay? I mean, this party wasn't just about you getting a part of Justine's money. It was about your career. The show. The book. The gift book."

So the party was a complete failure on that end.

"I'm okay. I just hope the cops find out who killed Gemma and they also find out it wasn't meant for me."

If that was the case, everything would turn around on me. Shock-like pulses rippled through me. "Kate, if I'm the person the killer meant to kill, we need to come up with a plan. I can't stay here. That would put you in danger. We need to come up with a plan. Like now."

"Let's not talk about this right now. You need to get into the shower and didn't you say you needed to get work done?" Kate cleared away the rest of the plates on the table and rinsed them off.

"I'm serious Kate. If the mob is involved in this . . ."

She wiped her hands on a dish towel. "We don't know what happened yet. Let's not panic."

My cell phone interrupted me. "Hello."

"Natalie Vega here."

"What's up?" Was she calling to check on the book? I was still writing about *Roman Holiday*, Audrey's first actual movie. She was in love with James Hanson, learning how to act, and was unaware, but heading straight for superstardom.

"Emergency meeting today at the office." She paused. "Now that there's only two actresses left, and with the murder of Gemma." Her voice cracked. "I'm very sorry to bother you on a Sunday. I know you're busy writing the book. But if you can make it to the meeting, you should."

I stared into my coffee cup. Writing the book? Hunh.

"Why do they need me? I'm writing a book. I'm a writer. I keep telling them I don't know anything about film or TV." They just ignored my protests and kept asking me questions. "Would Audrey have done this? Or that? Is this hat authentic for *Breakfast at Tiffany's*?"

"You're a part of the inner circle, dear. They need you to help make suggestions. It's a crisis. A lot of money is riding on this. The whole reality show audition concept was ill-advised. I wished they'd listened to me."

I agreed with her, and I was no reality show fan, either. But the Hollywood powers-that-be guessed the public would eat it up. "Okay. I'll be there."

Kate's eyebrows shot up.

I disconnected from Natalie. "I have to go into the office today. Emergency meeting."

"You need me to go with?"

"Nah, I need to get some work done. Unless you're hoping for your big break?"

Kate snorted, clicked on the dishwasher, and danced across the floor, singing, "Getting to Know You." One of her usuals. Also, as usual, she kept at it until I exploded in laughter.

I SETTLED into my seat on the train and keyed in my thoughts about the mythology of the big Hollywood break. Laptop on my knee, leg crossed, a position I used often, if my sometimes Lyme-addled joints allowed it. I clicked at my keyboard and followed my musing into the "break" that Kate and I teased about earlier. Both Jean Harlow, my earlier subject, and Audrey Hepburn had this in common. An important person spotted them, and their lives changed. For a lucky few, a break like this happened. Like all myths, a grain of truth existed.

The train halted. A young man wearing baggy jeans hopped on and sat across from me. I barely looked up from my laptop.

More thoughts:

Audrey, in fact was a working actress when the famous French writer Collette spotted her at the Hotel de Paris. When she viewed Audrey, by accident, as she had rolled herself in her wheelchair right into the middle of the portion Audrey was in, she said, "Voila c'est Gigi."

What she glimpsed in Audrey, perhaps nobody had until that point. She carried herself like a ballerina, and Audrey had an awkward beauty of a young woman on the precipice of something more. Collette took her by the hand and they stole away into the hotel foyer, where she immediately called her producer and agent, who were on the lookout for someone to play Gigi.

Audrey's reaction was, "I can't. The truth is, I'm not equipped to play a leading role. I've never spoken onstage. I'm a dancer."

Jean Harlow's discovery happened when she while waiting for a friend to audition at the studio. She also had the same reaction—she knew nothing about acting.

But both women learned on the job, taking advantage of the opportunity offered to them.

The subway lurched and came to a stop. I glanced up to get my bearings, A girl entered the train carrying books. I love the subway on Sundays. More room when commuters and tourists seemed to be taking the day off. Some man sat next to me and I pulled my knees in closer. A heavy breather. Jesus Christ.

I snapped shut my computer. Two more stops. I could do this.

* * *

The meeting was in progress when I entered the room. I took a seat, but nobody noticed.

"Let me be clear," one of them said. "Zoe is not taking part until they find the killer." *Must be Zoe's agent.*

"Neither is Jazz." Another stranger said.

"We have contracts. The show must go on." Biz Adams, the director, looked out over his glasses.

"Your contracts mention nothing about murder."

"That's an extenuating circumstance, it's under 12 b." Another strange person said.

"If anything happens to either of them, we will hold you responsible."

Biz sighed. "I'll increase security. We can't stop production because of this."

Just then, a group of others entered the room. Lawyers. I can smell them a mile away. One whispered into Biz's ear.

Biz's face reddened. "Okay. Here's what we'll do. We're shutting down for a week and will reconvene. Hopefully by that time, the NYPD will have our killer."

The director, Jess Renquist, stood. "Well, that's that." He gathered his belongings and left the room.

Biz smiled up at the two agents sitting across the table from him. "Your clients are not to leave the city."

Of course, they couldn't. They were probably both number one suspects in the case. I kept that nugget to myself.

"Jazz has an engagement in LA next weekend," her agent said.

"Cancel," Biz said, with an edge in his voice that sent

chills up my spine, even though the remark wasn't directed at me.

The agent rose in a huff, started to walk away and turned back to Biz. She pointed her finger at him. A long sharp, coral fingernail at its tip. "You're going to pay for this."

I locked eyes with the other agent who shifted in his seat, looking at the table.

"I don't take to people who threaten me. Especially agents." Biz turned to me, red faced, almost hysterical. "Do you have any idea who killed Gemma?"

My face heated. How would I? Just because the murder happened at my party? In my apartment? "No. The police are investigating." I kept my voice smooth, belying the silent scream swimming just beneath my skin.

The agent grunted. The others around the table started packing up their papers, files, and computers.

I wondered if the police told them about Gemma's identity charade. Tension in the room sizzled and just one more spark could set someone off.

"Can you get me a list of all the guests?" Biz asked.

"Sure. But the police were there and questioned everybody already. What do you hope to accomplish?"

He was not a man who wore stubble well. The bags under his eyes even more pronounced as he took me in. "I'll hire someone to look into this. I don't trust the NYPD. I want answers. Gemma and her family deserve that." His voice cracked.

I liked Biz. He was one of the most un-Hollywood people involved in *Golightly Travels*. "It can't hurt to hire another investigator. It's a good idea. I'll get that list to you." I reached in my briefcase and pulled out my laptop, placed it on the long metal table. Others in the room were leaving and soon I was alone with Biz, and his assistant. My computer fired up slowly. Too slowly, given that I'd just paid Matthews for an upgrade. I found the file listing the party guests and emailed it to him.

"Done," I said. "Is there anything else I can help you with?"

He sighed, wilting. "She was my Holly. Now what?"

I suspected they had already chosen her. "Will one of the other two work?"

He shrugged and gestured with his hands. "Neither one of them are right. But I suppose we have to choose between the two of them. Contractual obligations."

I recalled Zoe's dark vibes at my party. She was difficult but has the physical type. Jazz was much more Marilyn Monroe-ish to me. "I don't know. It's a tough choice. Knowing that Capote wanted Monroe, I've always thought it would be interesting to see that type play Holly."

He propped his elbows on the table, chin in hand. "But in the popular mind Holly Golightly *is* Audrey Hepburn. I'm afraid that would be a mistake. But I hear you. I need to mull this over and discuss."

"I think either of them would be good," I said. "It'll be fine." It was easy to say. But with all the publicity, now, about Gemma and her death, I wondered if some enterprising reporter would find out about her actual family and it would somehow sour the entire production.

(Justine always said readers and viewers are a fickle bunch. Don't try to second guess them.)

"I never understood why Capote wanted Monroe," Levi, Biz's assistant, spoke up. "I mean, in the book Holly is described as 'A skinny girl, with a flat little bottom, hair as sleek and short as a young man's. A face beyond childhood, yet this side of belonging to a woman.'" That's Hepburn, not Monroe. And it's Zoe, not Jazz."

"It was Gemma," Biz said, stood and left the room.

Levi shrugged. "I was just trying to help."

"I know." I placed my laptop back in my bag and stood. This meeting was weird and stressful and I just wanted to get out. This was studio business. I was only there as an advisor.

* * *

I CAUGHT the subway back to the Upper East Side. I wasn't much of a cafe writer. But I loved the tea at the cafe across from my apartment building and, dang, I needed a cup or two. Gemma loved it, too. Sometimes, I caught a glimpse of something deep and sad in her eyes. Was it the burden of her secret?

When I considered the possibility of a mobster in my place the night of the party, it made no sense. While I didn't know everybody personally, someone did. The powers that be. But then again, I would never imagine Gemma having ties to the De Santis family. Perhaps someone else at the party was a fraud.

The subway stopped, and I elbowed my way to the exit, finally entering the sun and air of the city. The L'Ombrage loomed ahead of me and my heart skipped a beat or two. And home was a crime scene. So I walked toward the cafe and situated myself at my usual table. Laptop and steaming peppermint tea, with a lemon scone.

I rarely glanced up from my work, intent on writing about *Roman Holiday*. How fabulous Gregory Peck had been to Audrey. So generous in the billing. He recognized her talent and knew she'd be a star. He supported her. In my brief encounters with Hollywood actors, I didn't know anybody quite that magnanimous these days. Of course, Hollywood had changed so much since those days, it was barely the same entity.

I tried to focus, but someone stood between me and the window, blocking the light, Just standing. So I looked up.

A large man, almost as wide as he was tall, dressed in a black suit. "Are you Charlotte Donovan?"

I could have lied. But he knew me. A cold tingle of suspicion creeped along my spine. "Yes. Can I help you?"

He stood behind the chair across the table from me and drew in a long breath. There was something familiar about his eyes, the way he moved.

"I'm Gemma's brother," he said. "Name's Vincent. And I want you to tell me exactly what happened last night."

CHAPTER 7

I'm uncertain how much time passed as words rolled around in my mind. Like wobbly marbles. Gemma's brother. Crime family. Standing right there. How did he find me? I glanced at the door—no way I'd make it past him. Heart racing, knees shaking. Him standing there like a thick wall. I searched for air and words. Words to come out of my mouth.

I gave up and gestured with my hand. He sat down.

A server arrived to take his order. "Nah," he said. "I'm good." He turned his attention back to me with a startling laser focus in his eyes, sending chills through me. Mafia guy. Right across the table from me. As he made himself comfortable, I glanced at the door again. If I tried to run away from him, and he caught me, I was a goner. I blinked as if I could blink him a way.

"I can see you're shocked." He shrugged. "Maybe shocked that sweet little Gemma had a big brother like me. One with a Jersey accent to boot." His lips curled into a smile. But his eyes remained unsmiling.

I drew in the air. My heart thundered. "I found out about her fake name this morning."

His elbows went on the table. "So, what happened?" His voice cracked. He looked away and batted his eyes several times. He was trying not to cry. I breathed. Had I been holding my breath?

Vincent cared for Gemma. So did I. We had that in common. Big mobster aside, he was a guy wanting answers about his sister's death. I could relate. "It looks like someone poisoned her. But the police are still running tox reports." I paused. "I'm so sorry for your loss. I'll miss her."

"Poisoned?" One of his dark wiry eyebrows lifted.

I kept the rest to myself. He didn't need to know about the possibility it was meant for me. "Yes, that's the theory."

He drummed his sausage-like fingers on the table. "Cops ain't saying shit to us. We didn't hear that."

Perhaps I screwed up. Maybe I shouldn't have said anything. Why hadn't the police told her family this? It was early in the investigation. And the only reason I knew about it because Den questioned me about her past.

"So how does poison get into my sister at a party and nobody else?"

"Good question." My heart raced so hard I imagined it bursting from my chest at any minute.

"Who was at this party?" He leaned forward on his elbows.

My mouth was so dry. I eyeballed my tea, but I was too shaky to lift the cup. "The cast and crew of the show."

"What about the house staff?" He placed his elbows on the table, chin cupped in his hands.

"Catered."

Both of his bushy eyebrows lifted.

I hadn't considered that possibility. Perhaps a catering staff member slipped something into the drink. But why?

"Who catered?"

I hesitated.

"Ms. Donovan, let me assure you I don't go around beating up people. Or killing them. I'm not involved in the family business at all." He leaned across the table, closer to me.

I had no reason to believe a word he said. I also didn't have a reason not to. Something told me he'd find out, anyway. I just wanted him to leave. He was creeping closer and closer to me. "Okay. The caterers were Joliet."

"Never heard of 'em." He smiled, leaning back in his chair. "That's probably a good thing. I'm going to send someone to talk with them. An investigator."

"But the police are investigating."

He shook his head and laughed. He stood, reached into his pocket and handed me a card. "That's my personal number. If you find out anything about my sister's murder, please call."

He left before I had a chance to say thank you or goodbye. Or even, "Thank you for not offing me."

I held my lukewarm tea to my lips, trying to stop shaking. My cup trembled. I managed a drink of the tea and sat the cup down.

What should I do? Warning Joliet seemed the right thing to do. I'm certain he'd want to know if someone on his staff poisoned Gemma. I also needed to tell Den.

A tingling moved through me, followed by the feeling that someone was watching me. I glanced around the cafe. A group of women sat laughing in the corner. A couple shared a plate of scones. One man sat reading a book, with a cup of coffee in front of him. He looked like an ordinary guy. But it didn't look as if he was really reading that book. His eyes weren't moving.

He was watching me. I've been called paranoid, but I'm a survivor.

I shut my computer and slipped it into my bag. I tried to memorize the guy's face, but he was as nondescript as it came. White. Large nose. Beady motionless eyes. He was not a good reading-faker.

Perhaps he wasn't interested in me at all. Maybe he'd been following Vincent.

I hooked my bag on the back of my chair and finished my tea and lemon scone. What was going on here? I reached into my coat pocket and pulled out my phone. Another message from mom. One from Den. I pushed the call back button.

"Hey there," Den answered.

"Hey yourself." I turned my face toward the wall and leaned my shoulder against it. "I'm at the cafe across the street from my place. Do you know what I'm talking about?"

"Yeah, why?"

"Vincent DeSantis just left here, and another man is watching me."

"What did DeSantis want with you?"

"He asked about Gemma."

"What did you tell him?"

"I told him everything I know. He suspects the caterer might've had something to do with it."

"Christ, Charlotte."

"What? What was I supposed to do? In the meantime, there's this guy here creeping me out. Can you meet me here?"

A long silence. "Hold on," he finally said. "Yeah, I'll be right there."

I slipped my phone back into my pocket and waited. The man still sat, fake-reading. The women rose from their seats and started to leave. One marched after the other in the narrow aisles as they passed by my stalker. Something fell with a thud and his book went flying. A shrill scream pierced the air. I stood to see what was wrong. A crowd gathered around the man and the woman. He was on the floor. "Call 9-1-1," A voice said from behind me.

"How awful!" A woman's voice said. "He's dead! He's not moving! Not breathing!"

"What?" I said out loud. My chest squeezed. I elbowed my way through the crowd. Sure enough, the man was dead. The man who appeared to be stalking me wasn't stalking me at all. He was dying while sitting at his table. Flashes of Justine's death at Layla's popped into mind—and my heart.

Sounds of sirens erupted and got closer. I scanned the area until Den's face came into view. Drawn, tired, he shook his head. This was all he needed—another suspicious death.

"Who is it?" Someone asked, while another person searched him and pulled out his wallet.

A hush fell over the space, with the friends getting closer. "Antonio Joliet. Anybody know him?"

Antonio Joliet? Wasn't he the owner of Joliet Catering? I'd never met him, but had dealt with his managers. My mouth dropped open. We'd just been talking about Joliet.

My eyes met Den's across the gathering of people. What I saw there sent waves of fear through me. Yes, this man owned Joliet Catering and, no, this could not have possibly been a coincidence.

CHAPTER 8

Den was at my side, arm around me. "Was that the guy eyeballin' you?

I nodded. The room tilted.

Den would take charge of the scene, but uniformed police had the matter at hand. He led me outside. "You're so pale. You need some air. I'll deal with these uniforms later."

"I don't understand what's going on." We walked along the street, my arm through his, and my shoulder leaning on his. Weariness threatened and I realized I needed to get back to Kate's for a nap soon. Living with Lyme, preventative measures had become a way of life.

He cupped his other hand over mine. "Looks like the DeSantis family is on the warpath. Looking for revenge. One man dead and it's only one day after her murder."

"Have you found out anything else?" Wind picked up and my hair blew in my face. Den stopped and tucked it behind my ear, reached down, and kissed me.

"How about we keep you out of this case?" He lifted me chin, kissed me again.

Fine with me—but it seemed I was in it, whether I wanted

it or not. "They know who I am. Vincent gave me his personal number. Am I in danger?"

"Probably not. I suspect you were a decoy. It only worked so much as they killed Joliet with nobody seeing it—and they confused you. Now, if you gotta testify, you can tell a judge that Vincent didn't know who the caterer was. You just told him that moment."

I mulled that over. "Would a judge fall for that?"

Den laughed. "Depends on the judge." Den's phone buzzed in his pocket. "Sorry." He pulled it out "Brophy."

We continued to walk toward Central Park, crossed the street, with Den's ear pressed to his phone. As we walked into the park and found a bench, he muttered something into the phone and slid the phone back into his pocket. "Are you staying at Kate's again tonight?"

"I'd rather stay with you."

He grinned that sideways grin that usually made my heart pop, along with a few other body parts. But right now, I was too weary to pop. He leaned in and pressed his lips to mine. And by the time we came up for air, I was a puddle of steam. "Sorry," he breathed. "I'm on the case. I shouldn't even be here. You know how it is, babe. I need to go."

"You're a tease, Den Brophy," I said, with a raspy voice.

He grinned. "So they tell me." He paused. "Want me to call you a cab?"

Such a sweet offer. But even though I was getting tired, I needed to move. The park called to me. "No."

"You need to get some rest."

"I will, but I'm going to get some air and stretch my legs a bit first." I'd been sitting too long. My joints were tight.

"Okay." He kissed me again. "I gotta go." He turned and pointed. "Get home soon. Don't make me call Kate."

I nodded. "Okay." Those two were in cahoots when it came to watching over me.

Den walked away—always a splendid view. He was a cop who took his physical conditioning seriously. He disappeared into the crowd and walked further into the park. As I walked along, I mulled over the past 24 hours. My party. Gemma's death. And now the death of Joliet at the cafe I frequent. I didn't go to the cafe every day. They must have had a tail on me--and maybe Joliet. I wasn't as sharp as I thought, which troubled me.

I walked by the Naumburg Bandshell—a location used in *Breakfast at Tiffany's*. This place is where the characters Doc and Paul have their chat about Holly. I stood for a moment, taking it in, imagining the characters and their conversation, where Doc reveals his marriage to a young Holly. Fourteen. For me, that's when the character's edges turned soft. She was essentially an orphan, and this guy married her. It sickened me to think about it. Fourteen and married to a much older man—and later she'd become a prostitute.

"Capote," Justine had said. "If he wrote that story today, he'd never get it published. If he did, it would have a trigger warning on the cover."

A tour guide came along then with a string of people following. "Yes, there is one of the places the famous movie *Breakfast at Tiffany's* was shot. There are few in the city. The film was mostly shot in Hollywood at a studio."

"I heard there's a remake of the movie," someone in the crowd said.

"No, not a remake," the tour guide said. "A mini-series called *Golightly Travels*. You know, she always left a card at the mailbox when she'd be gone for a few days, alerting the neighbors and the mailman, which said 'Golightly Travelling.' I think that's what the title refers to."

"I bet they don't make it now," one guy said. "Not with Gemma dead."

"Gemma?" Someone else said.

"You know, one of the actresses from the audition show."

My heart pounded in my rib cage. I clasped my hands together and concentrated on breathing. Relax, they have no idea what you know and who you are. ("One of the best parts of being a famous writer is most people never knew who you are." Justine's words, again.)

"Yes, they will. Too much money on the line," another voice said. "Hollywood cares nothing about anyone. It thrives on money and money alone."

"Just like New York City," someone said and laughed.

The crowd moved along, and I sat pondering the smoke, mirrors, and money of Hollywood. I doubted they'd shut down the series. Afterall, the show must go on.

CHAPTER 9

Sitting on Kate's couch, trying to form cohesive thoughts at my computer, my mom poked her way into my mind's eye.

What's the big deal about *Breakfast at Tiffany's*. Or about Audrey Hepburn playing the part? My mom had asked me when she learned I'd be writing about it. But, even though Mom was a young woman at the time, her context was different. It was difficult for her to relate to Holly Golightly. A good Catholic girl who rarely ventured from Cloister Island, mom didn't know any young women who lived on their own, like Holly, let alone one so sexually carefree.

You lived with your parents until you married. "The sixties weren't all about hippies and free love," Mom had chided. "Some of us were raised to believe in the sanctity of marriage."

Mom considered Hollywood's Hayes Production Code appropriate, part of which said, "Adultery must never be the subject of comedy or laughter."

I key some words in. *The creators of the movie faced a challenge when casting the film. Even though the book was explicit in its way, the movie had to be more subtle and the major character could not be all about sex, like a Marilyn Monroe would. They used an actress not automatically associated with sex and make her sexy. They considered Shirley MacLaine, Rosemary Clooney, and even Jane Fonda. The biggest women at the box office were Debbie Reynolds, Elizabeth Taylor, and Sandra Dee. None of them would have been right.*

That left Audrey. Who had a pristine reputation and image.

Thus began her negotiation to sugar-coat some of Holly's hard edges. And it also began a new depth to her acting. Holly had the "mean reds," she went into tirades, and played a long drunk scene.

"*Breakfast at Tiffany's* was the first film I remember where I felt like it was okay for women to have unmarried sex," Kate leafed through *Vogue*, her long legs flung over the side of a purple overstuffed chair.

I glanced up from the computer screen. "I know what you mean. And that's why some people had problems with it. Even Audrey had problems with it."

She flipped the pages. "But men were different, of course. Men were allowed to have sex and enjoy it, right?"

"Has it changed that much?"

"Hell yes."

"I wonder. With you and me and the people we know, for example. Some are more conservative than others. I'm sure some are harsh and judgmental and feel like if a woman sleeps around, she's trash."

Kate grunted. "But now it doesn't matter what they think. In those days, it did."

"That's why Holly Golightly was such an interesting character. So layered. I mean, it appeared as if she didn't have a care in the world. That she enjoyed her work, her life. Until Doc came into the picture and we learn about her past. And you see her in a different light." I needed to key that in. I focused on my screen.

"Holly was so unlike the usual caricature of women. Living on her own at a time that most women weren't. I loved that. She didn't think she needed to live with a man and she could have an active sex life, too. My kinda gal," Kate said.

Visions of a young Kate, named Karl then, dressing up in a little black dress with a plastic tiara and gloves and prancing around my bedroom, danced in my head. Most writers didn't get to have a best friend who's favorite movie was now a part of the biography being written. But then again, the movie meant so much to so many people.

Still, I cherished the conversations with Kate about Holly Golightly. I had talked with so many of the "experts" and Kate's observations were spot on.

I went back to my writing and Kate flipped through her magazine, the quiet only interrupted by sounds of pages turning or by clicking over the keyboard.

My phone startled me when it buzzed. Kate and I had decided not to talk about what happened in the cafe that day. But Den was on the phone and I picked up.

"Hey," Den said. "Are you sitting down?"

"Yes, I'm on Kate's couch. Very comfy, why?"

"Gemma's death was an accident."

My heart danced in my chest. "What?"

"The substance we found in her blood wasn't poisonous. Turns out she had an allergic reaction. A deadly one."

A bubble of sorrow meshed with anger filled my chest. "Why?"

"Yeah, I've no clue. She didn't even know. It wasn't in her records. She'd never been exposed to it before. The ME said it was clear that's what happened."

An accidental death. In my apartment.

"That leaves out me as a possibility." I was thinking out loud.

"Not necessarily," Den replied. "The drug affects Lyme sufferers. Makes them sick."

My breath left my chest in a furious rush.

"Everybody knows you have Lyme."

"Not everybody. Come on."

"Enough people. I can't rule out the possibility you were the target."

"Seriously, Den?" My voice raised a decibel.

Kate looked up from *Vogue*.

"I need to examine that list of your enemies and get cracking."

"Wait, Den. If you weren't my boyfriend . . ."

"Come on, Charlotte. Don't go down that road, okay?" His voice held an edge. "I'm a detective. This is what I do. The fact that we're dating has no bearing."

"No bearing?"

"I've talked with my bosses. I was on-site. Even though I've got personal feelings and connections here, I'm the best man for the job."

Connections. Personal feelings. I warmed.

"You need to stay awhile longer at Kate's place. That okay?"

"How long? One more night?"

"Or two."

"I'm sure she won't mind. But I'd like to get home." I closed my laptop.

"Charlotte, humor me and stay away until it's safe for you."

The tone in his voice chilled me. It was the same tone I heard in his voice when another man pointed a gun at me. I sickened.

After we hung up, Kate lifted her chin. "You've gotten pale. I glean he thinks you're in danger."

"He's just being too cautious. Who would want to kill me?" I concentrated on drawing in air.

"Seriously? Don't be so stupid. There are at least two people who'd love to see you dead."

The room fell silent. "Okay. But to go to such lengths? I'm not sure either have the time, energy, or smarts."

Kate pointed at me with her magazine. "Listen Charlotte, don't underestimate your enemies."

CHAPTER 10

When I closed my eyes that night in Kate's guest bed, my mind kept replaying the scene in the cafe. The man watching me. The mobster who sat at my table. Me, a mob decoy.

I had no idea who any of these people were. If Gemma's poisoning was meant for me, and her family got wind of it, yeah, I guess I could be in trouble with her family. Depending on how they interpreted it.

I rolled over onto my side and stared at the print on the wall. One of Kate's favorites—the Lady of Shalott by John Waterhouse. She sat waiting in a boat for her man. I tried to trick myself into sleeping by recalling the poem written by Alfred Tennyson as I looked at the boat containing the character.

As I studied the print closer, I admired the emotion the woman had on her face. She was waiting for her man, her life to begin with him. I'd like to think women waiting were a thing of the past, but it had played out in my own life, with my mom waiting for years for my father to return.

Finally, he reared his ugly head. I had understood we had

given up and accepted he was dead. Turns out, Mom had saved a part of herself that allowed hope.

Men leaving their families. I remembered parts of my dad —his rough cheek brushing against mine, his large hand cradling mine, and the way he made me feel safe. Audrey Hepburn, also left by her dad, remembered more about her father.

* * *

"IS THERE a connection between Audrey Hepburn's father taking off and her gaping need for a husband and family?" I asked. "I mean, help me out Doc. I need to piece her personality together and you're my expert."

"It's probably not so simple. Hepburn grew up in wartime, don't forget. She was hungry, ate tulip bulbs to stay alive. She probably craved a normal life, which at that time was a husband and family. Of course, her father leaving didn't help matters." I heard her blow into the phone. She hadn't stopped smoking. She kept saying she would. But the last time she tried to stop, her blood pressure soared. "Living through hunger leaves an imprint the rest of your life."

"I imagine." I doodled on my notebook. We didn't have much on Cloister Island, but we always had food.

"I just read a study about malnourished children. They're five times more likely to score higher than normal on tests of neuroticism — a trait that measures negative emotions and a tendency to feel uncontrollable distress— even into their forties, compared to the well-nourished controls. Hunger influences suppressing development of extraversion, or sociability, since the children who had been starved were three times more likely to have abnormally low scores for this trait in middle age than the controls."

I tapped my pencil. "It fits Audrey's personality. Given to nervous bouts. Exhaustion."

"A remarkable woman," Maude said. "Not only was she hungry during the war, but she saw a lot of cruelty. It definitely marked her personality."

"It would anybody's."

"Yes, but Audrey wasn't just anybody."

"You could say that again. Saintly was a word used to describe her time and time again. Yes, she was a kind woman. But no. She wasn't a saint. Just ask Jack Holden's wife," I said.

"I've got to run, Doll. Should we talk Wednesday?"

"Sure."

WE HUNG up and I made my way to Kate's kitchen for a glass of water.

"Do you want to go to lunch with us?" Kate said as she walked into the room.

"I don't want to be a third wheel."

"Puh-lease, girl. It's not going to be a long lunch or anything like that. I've got to head into the office to check on a few things. And he's busy, busy, busy."

"Okay," I said. It would do me good to get out of the apartment. I'd been writing most of the day, then called Maude, who always seems to suck the energy right out of me. "Do you mind if I invite Den? I've not heard from him. He might be sleeping. The case."

"Sure, yeah."

I texted Den and he responded that he could get away for an hour or two.

WE WALKED THROUGH CHELSEA, my old neighborhood. It brimmed with galleries, shops, and interesting people.

Though, now, mostly people who had money, as even Chelsea had gotten to be too expensive for the average person. I saw Den standing outside Rosemary's Eatery, dressed in his black pants and a gray suit jacket and red tie. Since he'd become a detective, he dressed more professionally. My heart pinged. My man.

He reached out for me and hugged and kissed me. "Damn, I miss you." He breathed into my ear.

"Solve the case and come on home, mister." I grinned.

As we four sat and ordered our meal, my cell phone buzzed. Normally I wouldn't pick it up. But it was Natalie, who never called unless it was important.

"Sorry," I said to everyone as I stood. I made my way outside.

"Yes," I said into the phone.

"Hold onto your hat," Natalie said.

"What?"

"The show has lost its biggest sponsor. It's finished. The reality TV show is no more."

My stomach turned. The show wasn't my thing. Books were my thing. I'd been dragged into it. So why did I care? But, in getting to know the people involved, I cared about them. Sort of.

"What will happen?"

"They will still produce *Golightly Travelling,* but have nixed the reality show. You'll still get paid as a consultant. Your contract is solid."

I paced beneath the awning. "What about the leading role?"

"No announcement has been made yet."

Something about this all picked at me. "Why did the show lose a sponsor? I don't understand."

Sponsorship was about money, and the show made tons of it.

"One of the big ones, the foundation. It's all about family values," she said. "Even though she was yet to be chosen, when Gemma was linked to the DeSantis family, the family-values sponsor pulled out."

Gemma had gone to great lengths to distance herself from her family, at least publicly. And yet, she'd be remembered for that one thing, if nothing else. It sucked.

"I'll be in touch," Natalie said. "Any news yet on what happened?"

The energy drained from me as I stood there on the busy Chelsea sidewalk. I didn't feel like going over the story. "Nothing new," I said.

Only that Gemma's brother visited me and probably killed an innocent man right under my nose. And the poison wasn't meant for Gemma. Which meant, of course, it must have been meant for me.

CHAPTER 11

The table quieted when I relayed my news.

"What does this mean?" Kate asked. "Will you still get paid?"

"Yes, and I'll be able to finally pay off my last hospital bill. But I'm sorry for the other people who invested time, money, and heart into this mess." I spooned French onion soup into my mouth. Lukewarm now, but still good. I could barely manage the soup as Den wolfed down a burger.

"I'll never understand the industry. Okay, so she was a DeSantis, but she's gone." Kate shoved her salad around on her plate.

My appetite vanished. I sat my spoon on the edge of the bowl. "Just the whiff of scandal."

"You'd figure that'd bring them even more money. But who knows? As long as you get paid for your trouble, don't worry about it." Den slipped his arm around me in the booth. Black leather seats squeaked with the movement. A server passed by with a tray full of food and a mother and her young son went by—he dragging her to the bathroom.

Kate and Roger's heads drew together. He whispered

something in her ear. She seemed content. She's not had a relationship in a while. Though she wasn't as bad as me, hopping from cop bed to cop bed. I still didn't consider that as a problem, more of a phase.

Kate straightened. "So any word on Hartwell or Judith?"

"Yeah," Den said. "Hartwell is in the city. But he's in St. Jacobs."

"What?" I sat forward.

"Yeah, he had a nervous breakdown. Not your guy." The server sat another beer in front of him. "The only good memory I have of him is him being taken away in cuffs."

"He was such a dirty player, had tried to ruin Justine's career as a Hollywood biographer," Kate explained to Roger. "When she died, he went after Charlotte. The Harlow biography obsessed him and he wanted to write it, even though they already had the contract and were writing the book."

"I'd feel sorry for him—if he hadn't tried to attack me. He was pitiful."

"Hartwell's in the nuthouse." Kate said. "Good place for him. That leaves Judith Turner, who we both know despises you."

A part of me felt like I was sitting outside of my body as we discussed the people who might want me dead. Everything that had happened with Gemma was surreal enough. But to think someone tried to either kill me or just make me very sick, was borderline unbelievable to me.

"I've not been able to track her down," Den said, after a few minutes, sending chills up my spine.

Justine's only living relative wanted all of her money and property—including the luxurious apartment I now lived in and called home. The apartment was left to me, her loyal and trusted assistant. I wasn't sure I'd be able to keep it—as next year, I'd have to pay condo fees, which were more than my mom's monthly house payment.

"I don't understand. The woman is wealthy in her own right. Why does she want Justine's money?" I finished my soup and eyed a roll.

"Greedy," Den said. "I don't know that many wealthy people. But the ones I know are just about getting even more money."

"It's a sickness," Roger spoke up. He would know, as he was from the St. Johns family. "I know it well. But every once in a while you get wealthy people like my Uncle Hiram, who gives so much of it away, he makes other rich people look bad." He cracked a chiseled smile. Kate was right. He was one handsome man, especially when he smiled.

Kate slid her plate away. "Justine wanted you to have it all. Judith needs to back off."

"She wanted me to have her apartment. That's for sure. But her money comes with strings, as you know."

"So? You had the party. You'll do whatever the next thing is and be a wealthy woman."

"She always liked to push me out of my comfort zone. Justine used to say, 'Books are great. But you need to close one once in a while and take a walk. That's where life happens.'"

"I hope I'll be a wealthy woman. I'll need it to stay at the apartment."

Den laughed. "Yeah. Maybe you should sell it."

"Hush your mouth!" Kate said, waving her well-manicured finger at him, grinning. Her purple nails glittered in the soft restaurant lighting.

Kate loved the place—so did I, even though I didn't quite feel like I belonged there. The L'Ombrage was built in the shadows of two other grand Art Deco Apartments in the Upper East Side. But, even though some apartments had been chopped up into three or four condos, there were still some grand ones left that maintained the architectural integrity of the place. Justine's was one of those. There was at least one secret room in her place, and it would not surprise me to find another. The place was almost a living, breathing entity. It smelled of Justine's Topaz cologne; It sighed and moaned with movement across the old floors, and it spoke of another time.

For a woman who grew up on Cloister Island in a rickety house, not able to afford to move out on her own, living at L'Ombrage was like living in a dream. Warmth spread through me, starting in the center of my chest. I squeezed Den's hand. He looked at me and winked.

I refused to let this little thing get to me. Okay, someone had tried to kill me. I would not dwell on it. After all, they failed. At least that's what I'd tell myself. Over and over again.

* * *

LATER, I finished writing the *Roman Holiday* section of the manuscript. Finally. I wanted to go back and visit Audrey's meeting with Collette in a Parisian hotel lobby. That I would do tomorrow. My eyes burned from the blue light of the computer screen. I snapped it shut and slipped into bed.

Kate's guest room was pleasant, but I couldn't wait to get home and sleep in my bed. I was in that place between awake and sleep when my phone alerted me I had a text message. I turned over, ignoring it. It beeped again. Okay. I reached for it.

"Your father contacted me again."

The next message:

"I'm not sure what to do."

Another message:

"He really wants to see you."

I pushed the button to phone my mom.

"Hello." She sounded weary and as if she'd been crying. My tough-love attitude melted.

"Are you okay?" I sat up in the bed.

She paused. "I just don't understand why he's suddenly taken an interest."

"Exactly. And has he answered you about where he'd been all these years?"

"No. He says he'll tell us everything when he sees us."

"I have no desire to see him, Ma. He let us think he was dead. He never sent money, a letter, nothing. As far as I'm concerned, the man is dead."

"That's harsh, Charlotte. Things happen. Maybe he had a breakdown."

"Stop making excuses." I wanted to roar into the phone, but it came out as a harsh whisper. "Tell him you don't want to hear from him anymore. You don't need this in your life." She knew what I meant. She was a recovering alcoholic and had just been through an incredible rehab program in New Jersey. "Have you talked with your counselor about this?

"No. Maybe I should."

"Yes, you should. In the meantime, try to get some rest. And don't respond to him except to tell him to leave you alone."

"But I—"

"Mom, please. Think about this. He was gone for over twenty years. What could he possibly say to justify that?" I wanted to punch my fist into the wall.

"Okay, Charlotte," she said after a few beats. "I'll take your advice for now. But I might just need more closure on the relationship."

The word closure rankled me. My mom had started using words like that since rehab.

"Promise me you'll talk with your counselor before you

do anything. It's up to you. But I don't want anything to do with him."

And I didn't. I was tired of women making excuses for men and their unacceptable behavior. I'd seen it way too much in my life. My dad left us years ago, without a word. Kate's dad beat her up when she told him she was having the sex change operation—and her mom is still with the man. How? How could she be with a man who beat her child half to death?

"Okay, Charlotte." She paused. "Are you in bed? It's late."

"Yeah, Ma, I was almost asleep when you texted me."

"How's the book coming?"

"It's going well."

"Shame about Gemma Collins, isn't it?"

My stomach waved and rolled. "Yeah. She was lovely."

"But they say she was a DeSantis. Grew up in Jersey. She wasn't British at all."

"Yeah." Vincent's face flashed into my mind.

"What a fake."

I loved Gemma and considered her my friend. But what my mom said was true—and it hurt. She had not trusted me enough with her big secret. Maybe she'd planned to.

"It's complicated. I guess she didn't want people to know she was a DeSantis and you can't blame her for that."

"Poor thing." Her voice hushed, reaching into the center of me. "Good night, Charlotte."

"Good night, Ma."

I sat my phone on the nightstand and turned it off. No more messages from her or anyone. I was exhausted and longing for a good night's sleep.

I sank back into the bed. Had Gemma really left them behind when she took on her lifetime role. Judging by Vincent's actions, she must have at least been close to her brother. She was on the cusp of a brilliant career. The press was just beginning to pay attention to her when she was a part of the new reality show. They auditioned thousands of women for the role of Holly and chopped it down to ten hopefuls, then three. The press started following her when she was selected to be in the top ten. Who knows if she would have become famous if she could have gotten away with the charade?

Maybe it would have just added to her fame. I'm a writer and loved to research and dig beneath the surface of a story. But there was a part of me that loved the mystery of old Hollywood. Some of those movie star's stories were so fabricated that we'll never know the truth about them.

I dreamed of Gemma. We sat at the kitchen table, drinking coffee, and she talked with me. But I couldn't understand a word she said. Her face turned white, then sickly gray, and she pointed behind me. All I saw was an enormous blade being thrust into my neck. I awakened with a gasp in a pool of sweat—my neck hurt like a bitch.

CHAPTER 12

The next day, I opened the door to my apartment and found it sparkling clean, as if nothing had happened here. No party. No murder. No crime scene. After I made a pot of coffee, I sat down and flipped open my computer.

I checked my email. Oddly enough, I'd received alerts from some underground art and auction circles I'd found when I was researching the Harlow book. When a long-lost item re-emerged—Jean Harlow's blue star sapphire ring, for example —these boards went crazy. So, I wondered what had been found. I clicked on a link.

"Collette's Jewels Resurface: Yes, the jewels she left to Audrey Hepburn!"

A ping zoomed through me. That can't be right. I had those jewels. What was going on here?

For years, it had only been a rumor the famous writer had left Hepburn her jewels. But I'd found them in Justine's secret room in a thick, gold velvet box, labeled. Nobody else knew about them. Just me, Kate. and Den. And they were tucked safely in the secret room.

I marched back to Justine's room and pulled the clothes in her closet off to the side so I could enter the room behind the closet. We donated most of Justine's clothes to charity, but kept a few, just to help hide the secret room behind the closet.

I pulled the string, and the harsh light filled the closet. Where had I placed that case of jewels?

I took in the room with its covered furniture and paintings, skids of boxes and trunks filled with all sorts of Hollywood memorabilia and remembered that I'd left the gold-velvet box on the shelf, next to several old perfume bottles.

I froze, my heart nearly stopped, blood rushed to my temple. It was gone. Someone had been into the secret room and taken the jewels Collette had left Audrey. I scanned the room for anything else missing. But as far as I could tell, nothing else had been touched. Just the gold velvet box.

I noticed some other boxes in the room looked as if they'd changed position.

I dialed Den. "You won't believe this." My breath shallow.

"Try me."

I explained.

"Okay. That makes sense. They must have taken the jewels when we were all sidetracked with Gemma. Christ. I was right there and didn't even consider this."

"But Den, nobody there was aware of Justine's secret room. Why would you even consider that? C'mon."

"Well, someone there knew."

"You, me, and Kate."

"Did you tell Gemma?"

I paused, trying to remember the conversation I'd had with her about collectibles. "No. I told her I had a few things, but didn't tell her about the secret room. I didn't even know about it until Kate and I cleaned out Justine's' closet after she died."

"I'll get a fingerprint team over there immediately."

"Are you crazy? Word gets out about that room and shit's going to hit the fan."

Silence on the other end of the phone.

"Den?"

"I'll do it myself."

"You can lift fingerprints?" Something in my chest fluttered.

"Yeah, no problem. But if I find something, it's going to have to go official. You see what I'm saying?"

"We'll talk about that later." Justine's treasure chest going public was not a good idea. First, if I learned anything about collectors is that some of them were fine and interesting people, but there was an element that was nothing more than criminal. It seemed like trouble to me. I wanted to quietly get rid of the stuff in a way that had some kind of meaning and that might honor Justine, even though god knows how she'd gotten her hands on any of it.

"It makes sense that they tried to poison you. It wouldn't have killed you. They just wanted you out of the way so they could help themselves to your closet."

"And keep everybody else at the party distracted." Why haven't we considered that earlier? Why hadn't I thought of it at the cafe?

"These guys are master manipulators."

"Do you think that. . ." My voice quivered.

"Hold on. Let's talk about this later. I know you're upset. But you need to eat. How about I pick up some Chinese and be over about one?"

"Sounds good." I stood from the seat I'd been sitting on in the secret room. I drew in a deep breath, wanting to scream, cry, take a hot shower, and scrub away the negative energy. My limbs ached, a familiar raw ache. One I hated to recognize—the creeping flare of a Lyme flare. My jaws tightened.

I'd tell myself it was the strange bed I'd slept in and not a Lyme flare. Sometimes I didn't know what was worse—the fear of it coming over me or the episode itself. Though if true that stress brought on bouts of it, God knows the past few days had been off the stress meter.

Now this. Someone had been in the closet. Someone stole the jewels Collette bequeathed to Audrey. Even though I was alone, I shuddered, as if a thousand eyes bore into me. The secret space, exposed and violated.

I breathed in the dusty room, catching hints of old floral perfume, and Topaz, Justine's scent. Kate and I planned to sort through everything. We'd both been so busy. But we needed to make time for this.

Den showed up thirty minutes later with flowers, food, and a fingerprinting kit. I watched him lift fingerprints from several surfaces and place his sample back into his kit. He was going out on a limb for me. Best to pretend I didn't know he could lose his job over it.

He lifted his chin and grinned. "There. We've got prints. Anything else I can do for you? He lifted an eyebrow.

"Not that I can think of." Coy.

He sat the bag down among the dusty boxes. "Oh, really?" He slipped his arms around me, molten heat rushed through me.

"Come to think of it . . . there may be one or two things. Or multiple things. . ."

CHAPTER 13

Eating Chinese food in bed with Den wasn't the worst thing to happen in my life.

Neither of us wanted to get dressed, but were both famished. I needed to wash the sheets, anyway, so we ate in the sack. My grandmother would be appalled. But she'd have been appalled by other things that had just happened as well.

"This is superb." Still high from our lovemaking, I wondered if it had affected the taste of the food. Could the spice really be that perfect?

"Yeah. This place has been around almost as long as Layla's."

Layla's. I hadn't been there for months. It was a teahouse, members-only and Justine had been a member. I had met her there the day she died. In fact, she died at Layla's. Her membership passed on to me, but I hadn't gone since she died. I still missed her, and probably always would. The fresh memory of losing her sat beneath my skin.

"A lot of the guys go there. It's open all night."

"There's a lot of excellent food in this city, but dang."

"Yeah."

"Thanks for bringing it." I set aside my container of Szechuan chicken.

"I wish I could stay and bask in the glow, but the case took a bit of a twist." He extricated himself from the blankets. His muscles moved beneath his skin and a sinking tug came over me. I turned my face. Too soon. I swallowed the bitter-sweet tug. We'd been dating about six months and for me it was a long time—maybe not for him. Den liked relationships. He was a one-woman man, and I liked that about him.

But the last time I was this involved with someone it didn't end well, and I decided the pain wasn't worth the risk. The sleepless days and nights. The lack of appetite and concentration. The complete, raw despair.

"Sure, just love me and leave me." I sighed and batted my eyes. He laughed while buttoning his shirt.

"Don't you have a book to write?" He tucked his shirt into his pants.

I turned over on my stomach. He sat down on the bed next to me and stroked my back. "I do." If I was a cat, I'd be purring. Fully satiated. "But I may take a nap."

"You should," he said, still stroking my back, reaching down and kissing my bare shoulder, sending heated tingles through me. "You just, um, were very physical. You deserve a nap." He stood. "I better go before things get heated again. In fact, they kind of already are." He laughed, again.

"Do you need to go?" I didn't want to appear clingy, but I wanted him to consider the invitation open.

"Yeah, I have a briefing with the chief in an hour." He worked at his tie to make it perfect. "But if I can swing by tonight, would that be okay?" I caught the expression on his face—almost boyish.

"You don't have to ask."

"Yes, I do. I'd never presume." He grinned.

"Presume what?"

"That we are exclusive and I could drop in whenever."

"Stop it, Den. We are exclusive. We've been doing this awhile now."

How did the conversation take this note? From sexy to serious. "I'm not interested in anybody but you, just so you know." He bent down and kissed me. I held him there for a longer, deeper, heated kiss.

"I feel the same way, Detective," I whispered.

"See you tonight," he said.

AFTER HE LEFT, I slept for a while, later rose from the bed and probed the Collette jewel incident. I'd never understand these collectors—their abject desire to own a certain object. My grandmother was like that, but she took her obsession and opened a legit antique shop on Cloister Island. And the collectors who went after movie star jewels, paintings, or heck even underwear, were a different breed.

I clicked on the news items about the recovery. A complete fabrication. The article alleged that the jewels were discovered in the basement of an elderly collector who'd utterly forgotten she had them.

Stella Ross. Hmmm. Might be worth a little diversion. I googled her and found a thousand Stella Ross's. Okay. I narrowed it down to those that lived in New York City. Okay. There were twelve.

Three in Brooklyn. Voila. Two of them in their 30s and only one in her 70s. Must be her.

Now what?

I needed to remain on track with the Hepburn biography. But it was so tedious I wanted to scream. The woman was practically a saint. Nearly. But the flip part of that is her rigidity. Saintly. Rigid. She'd been through a tough life as a child during the war, and no wonder she was so uptight. But still.

I needed to interview Maude, the psychologist-consultant, more. I was having a hard time maintaining interest. What lies beneath that rigid, stately Audrey Hepburn personality?

Stella Ross's phone number blinked at me on the screen. I picked up my cell and dialed.

She probably wouldn't answer.

"Hello." Answered on the second ring.

I hadn't planned further than the phone call. What to say?

"Hi, my name is Charlotte Donovan. I'm writing a biography of Audrey Hepburn. I was wondering if I could chat with you."

"Of course." It was a little too easy. Someone calls you up out of the blue and asks to talk about Audrey Hepburn and you say yes without questioning?

"I saw the article about Collette's jewels."

She laughed. "They were very close. Collette, in essence, discovered her. And they stayed close through Collette's life."

I knew that. But that Collette handed her jewels down to her had been a rumour for years—no proof. Justine had them in her closet.

"How did you get the jewels?"

"They came down through my family. My great uncle was Maurice Goudeket, Collette's second husband. He was a jeweler, you know. He made the most exquisite pieces. Mostly with pearls. Which is what this set was. Audrey gave them back to his family after a few years. It touched her that Collette gave them to her, but she felt like his family should have them."

Pearls? No. This was a different set. The jewels stolen from Justine's closet were diamonds.

"Not diamonds?"

She paused. "No. He rarely worked with diamonds. Too expensive and showy for him. He was a Jew during the war, and even with her protection, he wouldn't have wanted any extra attention."

She sounded clipped, almost professional. Like her interest was more than personal.

"How do you know so much about it?"

"I told you Collette's husband was my great uncle. They both worked with the Resistance. As did Audrey. She is one of our heroes."

Okay, so Stella Ross had just climbed up to my A-list of interviewees.

"Ms. Ross, I'd like to buy you a cup of coffee. Are you free this afternoon?"

CHAPTER 14

So the Collette-Audrey connection deepened. Also, Collette had more jewels than merely my missing jewels. Was it a coincidence that Stella's jewels showed up the same time Justine's disappeared? (Coincidence? Just another plot twist, if you ask me. Something that Justine always said.)

When Stella found out about my membership at Layla's Tea House, she insisted we meet there. I protested as it was a long journey for her, at her age. "Nonsense. I'm a New Yorker. We keep moving until we die."

Okay, then. Some of us were just happy to be able to walk —when our bodies allowed it.

I strolled across Central Park. Layla's, an Upper West Side establishment, was one of the oldest in the city. The day was brisk and autumnal, and I basked in the blue sky and chilly air. Central Park was one of my favorite places on the planet. Since the experience with Justine's murder, I'd become a bit paranoid about people following me. So I tried to shake off the feeling that a man in a plaid jacket was following me.

By the time I'd arrived on Lyla's block, it was clear that he was following me. I picked up the pace. My joints screamed with pain. I'd have to cab it back to the apartment—and take another dose of my medicine.

When I walked into Layla's, he fell in behind me. I was no longer so paranoid that I imagined people following me—although sometimes my paranoia had been justified—but it seemed odd that the man who'd been behind me for most of my Central Park walk, slipped in right behind me. Few people were familiar with Layla's and even fewer were actual members.

The greeter approached me. "Ms. Donovan. How lovely to see you."

"Thank you. I'm meeting Ms. Ross today."

"Yes, I'm aware."

I scanned the place for any of Justine's favorite servers and my stomach churned. Perhaps this wasn't a good idea.

A staff member stopped the man who'd been tailing me. Were they asking about his membership? Maybe he'd just wandered off the street thinking he'd get a pot of tea. He could think again. Layla's had written the book on exclusivity.

"Please follow me to Ms. Ross's table."

She was waiting for me at an elegant table near the window. It would be a first for me, as Justine had regularly stayed in the back in the deep-seated curtained booths. The place was a peculiar mix Moroccan tea room and quaint British, but mostly Moroccan.

Ms. Ross stood, more patient than me, and tiny like a bird. Dressed in a casual array of blue and purple with a scarf tied around a long ponytail, giving her the air of youth, she held out her hand to me. "Nice to meet you, Charlotte." She pointed to the Jean Harlow biography on the table. "I hope you won't mind signing my copy of this. I ran out and bought it after I realized who you are."

"Thanks. I'm happy to sign your book." I vowed to never say no to anybody requesting my signature. I considered it an honor—Justine, on the other hand, thought it absurd. She'd shrug when asked. "What does my signature on a book have to do with anything?"

I paused to look behind me, but the man had vanished. I squashed the lump rising up in my throat and sat down. Odd. Had he been following me? Or did he have some other business here? *Calm down. You're getting paranoid. You've worked hard to not be paranoid.*

This place always smells of oranges, jasmine, and cinnamon. A pot of chai sat at our table. "Do you like chai?"

I nodded, finishing my signature. "Love it."

"Great. I'll pour."

She poured the steaming dark brown brew, and the scent curled its way to my nose. Spicy.

"So what can I do for you?" She took a sip from her turquoise and purple cup. She gazed at me with heavy-lidded eyes, lined in black.

"Tell me about Maurice Goudeket."

She sat her cup down and reached for a mini-scone, spooning crème fraiche onto it—white cloud of richness. "He was a talented jeweler and successful before the war. But, as he handcrafted all of his pieces, very few exist. Or at least that we can prove he made."

"So if someone had a piece of jewelry dating from that era and brought it to you, could you tell if he made it?" I brought the tea to my lips and blew, took a sip.

"Not me. But experts can. Provenance would be difficult to prove." She shoved the scone into her mouth. Her face softened with pleasure.

I reached for a scone. "So are there certain techniques he used?"

"I guess you could say that. But it was more his hand. Do

you know what I mean? Each artist or craftsman leaves a mark just because of how he handled it, how he fashioned it. You see?"

I plopped the creme fraiche onto my scone. "I guess."

"Come dear, you're a writer. Are there not certain writers you could read and know who they were, without knowing the byline?" One eyebrow lifted.

"Absolutely." I tried to bite delicately, but the cream dribbled on my chin. I wiped my chin. But I hardly cared. It was so delicious I wanted to swim in it—with my mouth wide open.

"So it's like that with artists and craftsmen."

I sized her up, she may open up to me now, after a bite or two of these scones. "I'm curious about something you mentioned during our last conversation."

"Yes?" She drank her tea.

"You mentioned that he rarely used diamonds."

"Ah yes. That." She placed her cup in its saucer and pursed her pink-colored lips.

My stomach sank. A darkness came over her. Had I already asked the wrong question?

"Yes. Family legend says two sets of diamonds existed. One was a gift to his second wife, the other to Audrey Hepburn, who tried to sell it to Tiffany, trying to forge a way for him to make a living. She met with Tiffany. Tried to get him a job as a jeweler. You see, by then Collette was long gone and Maurice was next to broke. Had no opportunities."

"And it didn't work out?"

"He took the jewels to examine them and Maurice never heard from him again."

"He took the diamonds? And didn't pay for them?" That didn't ring true. Why would the great Tiffany do that? Made no sense

She nodded. "Make of that what you will. But those diamonds are long gone."

Hard to say which one Justine acquired. But they were gone, too—unless we could find them. I wondered if Den had any luck. Now, I wanted those diamonds. Now, I felt a responsibility to give them back to what was left of his family.

Of course, Stella looked well off. She'd done okay. But that's beside the point.

"It's not the diamonds people want. Well, let me clarify. Collectors of jewelry would be quite interested in the diamonds. But collectors of Jewish resistance items even more so."

"Why? Because of Collette's husband?"

She opened her mouth as if to say something, then she thought the best of it. She gazed into her tea. "Yes. Exactly."

CHAPTER 15

I hadn't fallen off a turnip truck. Stella was lying, but I didn't want to push it. After all I wasn't sure how much related to my story. Besides, it took time for sources to open up about sensitive information. Or perhaps I was misreading. Treading lightly was called for. A measured approach.

"Let's talk about Audrey's resistance activities. You said she was a hero."

Stella nodded. "You're aware already, of course. But we now have documented it. She was one of the most active resistance workers as a child. Many other children carried notes to the resistance. But she more so than any. And they never caught her." She paused. "She was a talented actress even then."

"I read about the black curtain dances," I said. "Imagined Audrey Hepburn and her colleagues dancing to raise money for the Dutch resistance. Black curtains over the windows. No applause allowed."

"Ingenious, yes?" She cracked a smile, then finished her tea. "Listen, I've got to run. But please finish the tea and scones. I have another appointment. It's been great talking with you."

I stood as she left. "Let's get together again." The way she avoided eye contact. The way she couldn't wait to leave. She was hiding something. Something about Audrey and the resistance. My instincts crackled and popped.

"Sure. Call me."

And she was gone, leaving me thinking of Audrey, the Resistance, notes on the bottom of her shoes, and black-curtained performances.

I finished the scones and tea and looked around for familiar faces—Justine's pack of servers. I didn't spot any of them.

As I left the place and stepped into the open air, the luscious scent rudely left, replaced by something sour and rank. I stepped down on the sidewalk and missed it. I landed on the pavement with a hard, stone-cold thud. Several people rushed to me.

Heat rushed over me as I tried to lift myself, wishing nobody had seen me.

"Are you okay?" The greeter for Layla's sprinted to me.

I tried to stand with the aid of two men who ran up to me. A searing shot of pain vibrated in my ankle. "Damn. My ankle." I lifted my pant leg. Swollen already. Typical. I'd twisted my ankle.

"Can you help bring her inside?" The greeter said to the men.

"Sure."

The men helped me through the landmine of tables and bags and people, with very few paying any attention to us. Which was good.

They plunked me down on the same cot I'd been on once before. The day Justine died. I had an inkling it was a bad idea to come here. Back to the place I lost her. Tears pricked.

I sucked in air, trying to will them away. I couldn't cry here, the place she loved, the place she died, where her memory was still fresh and alive. I swallowed hard.

The greeter showed up with ice for my ankle. "Thanks."

"Will you be okay?" One man asked.

"She's fine. We'll take care of her," the greeter said. So the two men left me lying on the cot with my leg propped up, ice on my ankle.

I gazed at the ceiling, harboring the same stain from the last time I lay here. The place looked the same— a wall-hanging detailed the Heimlich maneuver, a poster on the correct method of hand washing, and a chart detailing tea varieties.

Soft footsteps came close. "Not you again," a man's voice said.

I lifted my head. "Sam!"

"What have you done this time?" Sam was there when Justine passed away and I passed out. At first, he was unconcerned and bored with me. But as our investigating into Justine's death wore on, he came around to liking me.

"Where's that handsome boyfriend of yours?"

Perhaps it wasn't me he liked?

"He's working a case. I twisted my ankle out front, stepping off the sidewalk." I lifted the ice pack. The swelling remained. My stomach waved. For a normal person, a twisted ankle wasn't a big deal. But for a Lyme sufferer, it could be. I had to get to a doctor.

"Do you mind calling me a cab, Sam? I'm a major pain in the ass. But I need to see a doctor."

His smile vanished as his all-business expression played over his face. "Sure. Let's get them to the back door, through the alley. I think it might be easier for you?"

. . .

As he helped me into the cab, my face heated. Slipping into a cab in the back alley, surrounded by misspelled graffiti and overflowing trash bins, wasn't high on my list of things I wanted to experience. Again.

"Let us know how you're doing," Sam said. "We've not heard from you in awhile." His eyes met mine, and we connected. Both there the day Justine died. The day my world turned upside down. "Keep in touch, Charlotte." He shut the door. Last time, he couldn't wait to be rid of me. I didn't blame him. Justine had died in the tea shop. It was a horrible incident. He just wanted to get on with business.

As did I. But I remained haunted by it. I still missed Justine. Sometimes, when I thought of her an almost unbearable ache erupted in my chest. And because of all that had happened since her death, I'm not sure I'd ever view the world the same. I didn't know if that was a bad or good thing.

As we drove off, the image of Stella Ross came to mind. I hoped to see her again. Perhaps this was a tangent I didn't have time for. My deadline loomed; pressed on me. But her image tugged at me. What secret was she keeping?

I'd been working so hard on the *Breakfast at Tiffany's* companion book, so focused on that aspect of Hepburn's life, that maybe I had overlooked something about her early years. Something important. It nagged at me all the way to Urgent Care.

X-rays taken and waiting on the results, I dialed Kate, who was just getting off work.

"I've got a bit of a problem. I fell, my ankle swelled, and the doctors here are insisting on admitting me to a hospital overnight."

"Holy shit, Charlotte. What do you need?"

"A new body?"

"Sorry, can't help you with that. How about your toothbrush?"

"That's a start." The doctor walked in with my X-rays in hand. "I should go. The doctor is here."

"See you soon. What about Den? Should I call him?"

My heart sank. He planned to stop by tonight. "No, I'll call. We had a date tonight."

The doctor glanced at his watch and folded his arms. "See you in a bit, Kate."

"Sorry," I said to the doctor. "What's the verdict?"

"You have a bad sprain," he said as he placed the film on the lighted board. "Have you been keeping up with your meds?"

"Yes, absolutely." Why was that always the first question? I was a functioning adult with Lyme. Why wouldn't I take my medicine?

"This joint doesn't look good. The sprain was just waiting to happen." He squinted his eyes. "We'll do a complete workup tonight as soon as a bed opens up at the hospital."

"Overkill, isn't it?" Ever hopeful.

"I'm afraid not. I've seen some Lyme sufferers cripple. I've seen some die from heart attacks." He stood back and let me see the X-ray. Hard to see the bones for all the swollen tissue. Bones. Tissue. Joints. Black and white and gray. I swallowed a scream of frustration. Cold crept over me. I'd been doing so well. Sometimes it just didn't matter. The body took over. I shivered.

"There's a new medication we've had great results with. It's a tedious regime. But I'm confident it can help."

He had my attention. "When do we start?" I asked.

CHAPTER 16

Doctor Paulo explained the Cowden Support program, intriguing, but tedious. Keeping track of all the dosages and different medicines would be a challenge for a normal person, let alone someone with the sometimes fuzzy Lyme brain.

"We have check sheets for you to use that will help you keep track of dosage. Most patients say it helps. But you have to use them." He handed me a paper.

I read over the list of medicines. "Parsley? Stevia? Sounds kind of new-age-y to me."

He moved his fingers over an iPad and looked at me over his glasses. "It's not. A highly respected cardiologist developed it. And if you look further into you'll see the stevia is just a part of a diet regime. Use that instead of sugar."

I groaned. No sugar? No dairy? How would I live?

"Look, you can continue on the same path you're on. It's up to you. Or you can make changes." He shrugged and snapped the iPad case shut.

Easy for him to say. I needed to be alone with my thoughts and chew on this. I'd do it. Or at least I'd try. But if I did it and I remained sick, I'd be pissed. Glancing over the protocol, it seemed like it'd take a lot of focus and time. And probably money.

Okay, so money wasn't the concern in my life that it was six months ago, but I still wasn't on what I'd call easy street, either. So much of Justine's money still just trickled down to me, and well, with publishing, you never knew when the check would come. So it was a concern.

I smoothed over my blanket. "How much is this going to cost?"

"About four hundred dollars a month."

"Do I still take my other meds?"

"Yes, but we'll taper you off of them. How does that sound?"

Kate appeared in the doorway, dressed in a red pantsuit, and draped in gold jewelry. "There you are."

The doctor looked up and cocked an eyebrow. Kate was an eyeful.

She didn't pay any attention to him, "I brought a bag for you."

"Thanks. Dr. Paulo, this is my friend Kate."

He shook her hand. "Nice to meet you."

"He was just telling me about new medicine."

"That's cool. How's your ankle?" She lifted the sheet and looked. "Ow."

"I feel nothing right now."

"Good pain meds, huh?"

"The best," Dr. Paulo said. "I'll check in on you later."

"Don't leave on my account," Kate said.

But he kept walking.

Kate pulled up a hospital chair. "What happened?"

I explained.

"What were you doing at Layla's?"

"I want to meet a woman I read about. A collector. She's

related somehow to Collette's jeweler husband. She also collects Jewish resistance stuff. A fascinating woman." I recounted what she told me.

"So what do you think she's lying about?'

"I don't know, and I can't get too sucked into that. But I think the Collette-jewelry connection is interesting and it may bring up a vein of information that has nothing to do with the story. I've already gotten several chapters written about Audrey's youth and her efforts in the resistance. I'm not sure there's more there."

"Why would Tiffany's take his jewels and not pay him?" Kate asked after a few moments of silence.

"I have no idea. Maybe there was some kind of mix-up." My head throbbed. I sunk back into the pillow, fighting sleep. "I planned to call Den. But do you mind? I'm getting so sleepy."

Kate stood. "I already called him. He should be here soon." She looked down and grimaced. "You ain't looking so good. You want some lipstick or something?"

I tried to laugh, but it took too much energy. Instead, I closed my eyes.

"What the hell happened?" A voice. A male voice. A Brooklyn accent that grabbed me in the guts.

"Calm down. She's sleeping," Kate said. "She sprained her ankle"

"Where? How?" He lowered his voice.

I heard the words, but couldn't lift my eyes. But then they stepped into the hallway and I couldn't hear them at all. Which was just as well. I didn't need to hear the story. I'd lived it. Repeatedly.

It would be a lifelong battle. There was no getting over it completely. It was just something I had learned to live with. I fashioned my life around it. Paying attention to the joint flares, alerted when I was too tired or cranky and couldn't think, and sometimes it was just too much to think about.

I couldn't imagine working a nine-to-five with this disease. A boss would have to be more than "understanding." I was so grateful for Justine when she said she didn't care about my Lyme, that she'd work around it. Now, I was grateful for the work she'd left me.

I drifted off and dreamed of a big-eyed, thin little girl named Audrey. Hungry. Ragged. Waif-like. Notes on the bottoms of her shoes.

CHAPTER 17

When I awakened, the scent of Topaz hung in the air, in another hospital room. I batted my eyes against the sunny room until they adjusted.

A nurse stood at the foot on my bed, entering information in a laptop. She must have taken a bath in Topaz—Justine's favorite perfume, still in the cracks and crevices of the apartment.

"When can I leave?"

She barely looked up from the screen. "When the doctor tells you."

Nice.

I tried to move my foot—and it moved, clumsily. But still. Movement was good.

The door swung open, and Den came through it. "Hey, you're awake."

He leaned down to kiss my cheek. His lips felt cool on my skin. "How are you?"

"I'd feel better without the perfume. I think it's giving me a headache."

"What perfume?"

"The nurse—"

"Nurses don't wear perfume," she said and left the room.

Den smiled that crooked grin of his. "You must have been dreaming."

The scent vanished. What was it about Topaz? I smelled it often. In Justine's home. Around the city. Was it lodged in my memory or was I really smelling it. "She's kind of grouchy."

He chuckled. "Yeah, I noticed."

"Have they said anything to you about when I can leave? I mean, I have a sprained ankle. This seems to be overkill."

"C'mon Charlotte. You realize with Lyme it's more complicated. And they won't tell me shit. I'm just the boyfriend. Not a husband." His eyes found mine and glanced away.

"You're better than any husband I ever knew." I hadn't known many.

He smirked, caressed my cheek. "You're still warm. You have an infection."

The cold lips now made sense.

"Well, if I have to have one, I'm in the best place for it, right?" I tried to sound chipper, but it was the worst place for me, with my immune system. I needed to go home. "Hey, how's the case?"

"Which one? The murder case? Or the jewel theft case?"

"Either."

"First, the Joliet case, well we estimate it was a hit, but there's no proof. Tight as a drum. Second, we've honed in on two of his employees as persons of interest. Maybe the DeSantis family was right. Maybe Gemma's poisoning came through the caterers. Makes sense. Two of their guys have records. Serious records."

My mind struggled to focus. Cotton brain. "Didn't you say it was meant to detract from the heist?"

"That's my theory. If it had gone right, you'd have been the one who dropped, and while everybody gathered around you, the thief would get the jewels."

"We need to figure out who knows about the secret room." My head swarmed, eyes felt as if hot warm liquid pooled on them.

"And another part worrying me is why would someone just grab that gold velvet box and leave behind everything else?" Den's eyes slanted and his chin tilted to the left, the way it always did when he was thinking. He lowered his voice. "I mean, you've got millions of dollars' worth of stuff in there."

"Priceless."

He crossed his arms. "I advise you to take inventory and get an insurance person."

"I've thought about it, but I'm aware most of that stuff is illegal for me to have."

"You inherited it. You're not responsible for how she got the stuff."

But that's not what tormented me the most. What bothered me was Justine's memory. I turned my face away from Den. I couldn't believe she'd take part in underground activities, like theft of priceless Hollywood memorabilia. It would ruin her reputation—and might ruin mine.

"You need to get over your adoration of Justine." His voice held a fatherly note. "It's causing problems in your life. And I can't have it."

The hair on the back of my neck stood alert. I'm sure he meant it as a show of concern, but my impulse was to tell him to back off. I'm a big girl. But this was Den. Den. I was speechless.

He grinned. "You know what I mean. I care about you. We'll figure it out together, okay?"

I nodded, too fatigued to talk. I soaked in my man, professing how much he cared for me. I sometimes counted the many ways this could go wrong. I suppose that was normal. Normal fears at the start of a relationship that was deepening. While I didn't want Den to pay for the sins of my previous relationships, I wasn't sure how to avoid it. My lack of trust was well-earned—straight from my father to several boyfriends and one fiancé. Which is why I decided on no relationships. Just sex. But it wasn't working with Den.

As hard as I tried to make it otherwise, there was Den, standing by my bed, bringing me Chinese food, helping me solve Justine's murder, aiding me in keeping my closet secret, a man who was always where he said he'd be, a man who always called to check on me, a man unafraid of caring for a woman with Lyme disease, or what that could mean for him. Like the man I almost married. Back when I was first diagnosed. What a shit.

Den. My heart cracked open.

He glanced at the bottles and jars on my nightstand. "I want you to take care of yourself. The new medicine looks complicated."

I barely nodded, swimming in a sea of medication, memories, thoughts plucking at me.

HE STROKED MY FOREHEAD, leaned over to kiss me.

"I'm not sure how you're going to do it. Get better. Write a book. Catch a jewel thief." He paused. "Leave that last part to me, okay?"

I nodded, now thinking about my book and about Gemma Hollins, Stella Ross, and Audrey Hepburn. Three very different women, all with their own stories braided together somehow. I'd developed a sense about this after years of doing research for Justine. Half of the time she ignored it. ("We don't have time for deep meaningful stories. Give me the juicy stuff.")

Threads of narrative plucked me. Stories to be told. People's lives were more nuanced and rich than the pop biographer's craft elicited.

CHAPTER 18

Three days later, I was home, with my new regime and my computer, picking up Audrey Hepburn's story.

I couldn't help but compare her to Jean Harlow, since she was my last subject.

"In some circles, Harlow's reputation was what her screen persona was, however, she was not that woman at all. Not that she was an angel. But, for instance, she never dated a married man and Audrey Hepburn did. When she dated William Holden, he was married and even brought her home to meet the wife. Mel Ferrer, Audrey's first husband, was also married when they first dated. In fact, he was still lawfully married when the two of them moved in together in a snug Greenwich Village apartment. Still, Hepburn's reputation was as classy and pure. "

I rubbed my eyes, burning from looking at the computer screen for hours. I took a break, hobbled into the kitchen and made a sandwich on gluten-free bread. Thank god I could still eat peanut butter. As I ate, my cell phone rang. "Hello."

"Susan Strohmeyer here," she said. "Your friendly lawyer."

"Ah, she lives."

"Calling to check in with you. Our monthly chat. Nothing has changed. Judith is still seeking to intercept your money."

"How much longer can she do this?" It was a lot of money. But I needed it to keep the apartment.

"Not much longer. She's using delay tactics. She cannot get her hands on Justine's money and certainly not her home."

Her comments did little to soothe my mind. "Why is she trying to delay it? Is there something I don't know? Some stroke of midnight thing?"

Susan laughed. "If I knew about that we'd have already dealt with it. But no. The will is solid from a legal standpoint."

I mulled over the whole thing. "Perhaps she figures I'll just give up, that she'll just wear me out."

"That theory is more likely."

My nerves were fraying around the edges, like a hint of unraveling at the edge of a sturdy cloth. The money situation was on my mind, along with Gemma dying in my apartment.

I walked to the kitchen to get a sandwich and stopped at the spot where Gemma died. Every time I passed the spot where she fell to her ultimate death, I shivered. Face your fears, head on, a voice inside my head said. It might have been my mom. Or Justine.

I sat down where Gemma died and observed. I wanted to see her view the last minutes of her life. It was on odd exercise. I also planned to figure out who was where. Who could have slipped out to my closet?

I studied the ceiling. Beautiful art deco patterns donned the high ceilings. Dust balls formed in the corners. I made a mental note to call the cleaning service. I loved the patterns —hell, I loved most patterns, found them soothing. My eyes scanned over the ceiling and something odd gave me pause. It wasn't a dust ball. But it was gray, standing out against the antique white ceiling.

I stood and squinted in its direction. What the hell? Some kind of little contraption was stuck on my ceiling.

My pulse sped. It looked like a small device of some sort. I shivered.

I pulled a chair over and started to climb, but dizzied. Okay, not a good idea.

Den.

I dialed Den.

"Yeah," he said.

My heart thud against my ribcage, and my mouth went dry, as I stared at the thing.

"Charlotte? You okay?"

"There's something odd on my ceiling." My voice quivered as I sat.

He spoke over the noise of paper rustling in the background. "What do you mean?"

"I laid down on the floor to see what Gemma saw when she was dying—"

"For chrissake, you did what? Never mind. Tell me about what's on the ceiling." The background noise faded.

"It's small, round, and gray. I can't see it that well. I tried to get up on the chair."

"What the hell, Charlotte?" His voice raised.

"Calm down. I didn't do it. But there's a thing on my ceiling." Den wasn't getting it.

"A thing?"

Okay maybe it wasn't Den. Maybe it was me. I'm a writer, dammit. Find the right word. "A suspicious device, Den. Nothing belongs there. What is it? What's it doing there?"

"Okay, calm down. Can you snap a picture?"

A picture! Yes, I snapped a photo and sent it to him.

"What is it?" I asked.

"I'm coming over with a crew. I can't be sure, but I think it's a camera."

With that, the line died.

A camera? A camera on my ceiling! What the hell?

I sifted through any memory of this ceiling—not that I had studied it keenly, but I tend to notice them.

My phone buzzed. I answered without checking the caller.

"Charlotte, it's your mother."

Just what I needed right now. She pressured me to go home to Cloister so she could take care of me with my bad ankle and my new regime. But it seemed too far away. It seemed better to stay in Manhattan with my doctors close.

"Hey mom." I tried to sound light and airy because god knows what she'd do if she was aware of the camera.

"You sound strange." Her voice held suspicion.

"I am strange. On new meds."

"Hmm. How's the ankle?"

"It's getting better." I lied. It was in a static state of swelling, which never seemed to go completely away.

"Your gram and I are in town," she said as if revealing a tragedy.

Now, my heart jumped. "What town?"

"Manhattan."

I couldn't remember the last time she was here. She favored her island.

She sighed. "We brought you some things from Cloister. Soup. Pie. The usual."

"What? Why? Where are you?" Mom and Gram wandering the streets of Manhattan with plastic grocery bags full of food struck me as a family emergency. Envisioning them here with Den and his crew made me dizzy, and trying to calm myself with deep breaths.

"We're in a cab, about three blocks from your place."

CHAPTER 19

My mind reeled with the convergence of mom and gram and Den and his crew. I wanted to tell her to turn around and not come, but I appreciated what it took for her to get here. I still didn't quite understand and wondered if it was part of her therapy. Mom was an alcoholic and had just gone through an intense program. She was going to need to draw on whatever she learned when the cops were crawling over my place.

When the buzzer went off, I didn't know who it was mom or Den. "I'm her mother," came over the speaker. Okay, then.

"Says she's your mom, should I let her in?"

Amusing man.

"Of course."

Within moments I heard the elevator, their voices and paper bags crinkling. I opened the door before they rang the bell.

Mom dropped her bags. "Oh my God, look at you! Let's get you off your foot!"

Gram stood by nodding her head, grimacing. Her eyes scanned the apartment. "Nice."

Mom slipped her arm around me. "Please. Let's go sit down. You look awful."

I positioned myself on the couch, and the two of them went back to their food.

"Where's the kitchen?"

"Through there.

"Nice kitchen," Mom said. I imagined my grandmother crossing herself to see her granddaughter's beautiful kitchen. It made me grin, even though my ankle pinged with pain.

In the meantime, Den would be here any minute. They hadn't met yet. Mom and Gram had both heard about him. Den wouldn't go across the water to Cloister Island. He had a fear of water. And mom hated Manhattan.

My heart raced. Once she found out why Den was here—the camera on the ceiling, she might never leave.

They entered the room where I was lying, Gram at mom's side, both of them still wearing their LL Bean coats from fifteen years ago. I remembered when they purchased them. It was a good year, and purchasing LL Bean coats was a big deal. Gram said, "If we take care of these, we'll have them our whole lives."

And there they stood, still wearing them. Mom in her blue and Gram in her gray. "Why don't you take your coats off?"

"We're not staying," Mom said, twitchy.

"Need to catch the next boat," Gram said, shifting her weight.

I was torn between wanting them to leave because Den was on his way and wanting them to stay because I hadn't seen them in months. My throat ached from swallowing unexpected longing for home. "Do you have to go so soon?"

Mom waved me off. "Don't fret about us. Now, you've got enough to eat. That fancy fridge of yours was empty." She sat on the edge of a chair. "You're not taking care of yourself."

"I am. I just order food. I don't cook."

Mom and Gram shot each other looks of concern.

"You need proper food, Charlotte," Gram said.

I smiled. "You know what? You're right. Thank you." I decided not to reveal my new dietary restrictions, yet.

I tilted my head toward my medicine. "My new regimen."

Gram stood over the table with bottles and measuring spoons and cups, picking the medicine up and studying the bottles. "Is it helping?"

"Too early to tell."

"Are you hungry? I'll get you something before we go. There're soups, lasagna, tuna casserole," Mom started, then my buzzer rang.

I got up from the couch.

"Yes," I said into the buzzer, an unfriendly contraption.

"Officer Den Brophy and friends." My stomach tightened.

"Send them up." I turned toward Mom and Gram, now both sitting on the couch, eyebrows lifted, Mona-Lisa-like smiles.

"Den? Your boyfriend who we haven't met yet?" Mom sat forward.

I nodded and opened the door, hobbled back to the couch.

"How about that? Come to Manhattan and look at what happens. I told you we should come more often." Gram elbowed Mom.

Mom shook her head, frowned, and waved. "It stinks. I can't stand the air in the city, Ma. I'm a Cloister Island girl."

Den rapped slightly at the door and walked in. "Charlotte?"

"We're in the living room."

He walked in, flanked by two uniformed officers.

"Oh, you have company," he said. "We'll get right to work and not bother you."

"Den, this is my mom, Mary Katherine, and Gram, Birdie. They came by for a surprise visit." I emphasized surprise.

His face fell, then gathered back into a smile. He approached them with his hand extended. Mom and Gram stood.

Mom shoved away his hand and opened her arms, hugging him. She stood back and took him in. "Nice to meet you, Den Brophy."

He turned to Gram and hugged her. He dwarfed my tiny gram.

"I've heard a lot about you both." He turned to the officer entering the room.

"Detective—"

"Oh yes. So distracted by these lovely ladies. Charlotte, where's the device?"

"Device?" Mom said, voice lifting.

I nodded. "I called Den because I spotted something peculiar on the ceiling."

"What?"

I shrugged. I couldn't hide, even if I wanted to. "That's why Den is here."

I pointed to it. "Right there."

Den turned to a uniformed man. "Can you please call apartment maintenance and tell them we need a ladder?" He turned back to us. "We're going to have to sweep your place, We've discovered that when we find one, there's usually more."

"Who would plant devices in her apartment?" Gram suddenly stood at Den's side.

"It may have to do with Gemma's death," I didn't want them to suspect it had anything to do with me. "But it disturbs me that someone was in here and planted that on my ceiling. It couldn't have been simple." My heat beat against my breastbone.

"Must be someone in your maintenance crew." Mom focused on Den.

"Mom, please, let the man do his job." That's all he needed —an armchair detective.

"She's right, Charlotte. If it wasn't a maintenance guy, it might be someone they know. Have you had any workers in and out of here?"

Mom beamed with an I-told-you-so look.

I ignored her and focused on Den. "Yes, to get ready for the party."

"I need a list." Den pulled out his phone.

A list. Okay. Either my brain was still in the strange cottony state of Lyme, or it was reeling from the weirdness of the moment. Writing a list seemed insurmountable. I had tried to keep my love life out of my family life and had succeeded until this moment. Even though it seemed to go okay, I wondered how much longer it could last. A cop boyfriend just trying to do his job. A Gram who spoke her mind and was not easily impressed. And an alcoholic mom, deep in therapy. Could be a recipe for disaster.

CHAPTER 20

Mom and Gram took off their coats and explored, mostly at Den's heels. Two of our little beach cottages would fit inside this place—maybe more.

Finally, Gram stopped following him. "How many more rooms are there for him to investigate?"

"There are four bedrooms, two with their own bathrooms. A study. A dining room. The balcony. I've told you there's enough room for you to move in here."

She waved me off. "As if."

Den came back into the room in a huff. "You got bugs in every room."

"Should you say that out loud?" Mom's voice was hushed, but she swung her arms wide, as if to shush us.

"If someone is still following the place, we alerted them the moment Charlotte called me. My guess is they're long gone. My guess is this all had to do with the party. But we'll find out. Might be paparazzi."

My heart galloped. Someone had been spying on me. I glanced at Den. Spying on us. My face heated. Our most intimate moments witnessed by a stranger. If I wasn't already sitting down with my leg propped up, I would have dropped. I sank further into the couch, curled into myself, and tried to vanish. My whole body vibrated, skin tingling.

I bit the pillow hard as thoughts reeled through my mind like an unedited film. Gemma dying in my home as someone watched from the camera. Joliet dying in the public cafe. Now, this. I pulled a pillow into me and embraced it. If I could only disappear. If only I could wake up from this and find out it was a dream. I pulled my pillow in tighter and planted my face in it, holding back a scream.

"Are you okay, Charlotte?" Mom sat next to me on the couch as Den stood over us.

I nodded. Breathing. Just like my therapist taught me. In, one, two, three, Out, one, two, three. And again. Mom rubbed my shoulder. I opened my eyes to her face, brow crinkled, crow's feet pronounced. We'd been here before. Her at my side. Or me at hers, usually after a drunken bender.

Den leaned over her. "We can trace this. We'll figure it out."

"Of course you will," Gram said.

I uncurled myself, took in air, and concentrated on the list of names of people who had marched through my place to prepare for the party. Caterer. Cleaners. Florists. Musicians.

The musicians were on the makeshift stage, curtains behind them. The florist placed flowers on the tables before the party. The dining room table, two tables in the main room, and on either side of the "stage." I remember them leaving right before the party started. They had no ladders. Neither did the caterers, who were everywhere in the place. Even the cleaners had no ladders—or at least that's what I could remember.

"Here's your list, Den. I think that's everybody, but I don't quite have a clear brain these days. With the Lyme episode."

"Thanks." He took the paper from my hand.

"How are you feeling?" Den's weight shifted from right to left. My mom and gram watched his every move.

"About the same."

"Detective, we're done," said one of the uniformed officers.

"Be right there." He turned back to me. "We'll see you later." He leaned in for a kiss but caught himself. Gram and Mom's presence loomed, making a kiss seem a bit uncomfortable.

I nodded.

He left me with them. Mom turned to me with an enormous smile on her face. "Nice looking man."

"Eh," Gram said, waving her hand.

LATER, everybody gone—Den back to work, Mom and Gram back to Cloister—I sat with my laptop propped on my legs and wrote. It was not the best way to position myself when writing, but I had no choice. Thoughts formed and I needed to get them down on paper. Besides, I had a deadline, though the publisher wasn't breathing down my back like it was with the Harlow book.

I struggled against this paranoid feeling. This feeling that someone was watching me. But I was alone in the apartment, just me and my computer, and words, ideas, sentences forming on the screen. I focused the way I'd always done. I wrangled the emotional upheaval into nervous energy and focused on my work.

A week later, Den had worked his way through my list of people who'd been in and out of the place to prepare for the party. So far, everybody checked out.

My phone alerted me to a text message from Den. I

walked across the room to pick up the phone—without a limp.

"We found the manufacturer of the device."

"What about where they were purchased?" I texted back

"Nothing yet. Brace yourself for this. I wanted you to know about it before you see it on the news." He sent a link.

I clicked on the video attached.

The room looked familiar. The people familiar. My place! There was Gemma on the floor, dying. Then it fizzled out.

Someone had gotten a hold of the video of her death. My heart sank.

"What the hell?" I texted Den back.

"Go to Hollywood Underground. Website with film clips."

I clicked on the site, which offered clips of dead celebrities' funerals, along with other "personal" moments. but Gemma's clip was featured, with over a thousand comments.

People and their obsessions! Why would people want to see this? And judging from the comments, some were viewing it repeatedly.

My chest burned with rage. Gemma was an up-and-coming movie star—not even ever featured in anything, just bit parts here and there. Sure, she gained popularity because of the reality TV show, but this was absurd. Empty, shallow people getting off on the death of an almost star.

"Charlotte?" A text came zooming onto my screen.

"Yep."

"Guess who runs this site."

"Not in the mood for games."

"Dream Girl Agency."

The same agency that ran the impersonator and drag queen club. Finding out they were involved fit into the puzzle. They thrived on the cult of celebrity. "How did they get the film clip?"

"We're sending a team to find that out."

"A team? Why not just one person? Me?" I became fond of the young person who played Madonna. She'd helped us out with Justine's case. She still worked there.

"No reason for you to go down there," he said. "Besides, you're not up to it."

Pangs of acknowledgement tore through me, while tamping down the frustration. Years of therapy, and it still sometimes felt like my body was letting me down. Like I should be able to overcome this. It stung. "Hey, I walked to the cafe yesterday. No problem."

"Ain't the same thing. Don't make me sorry I told you about this."

"When they find something out, can you please let me know? I mean, they had cameras in my home. I want to know who did it and why I was being watched. Or if the cameras were just there for the party."

"Could be nothing more than paparazzi."

The word sounded odd coming from Den. Brooklyn cop. Down-to-earth sort. *Paparazzi.*

"Don't forget someone poisoned Gemma. And stole jewelry from me. I don't think it's that simple."

"No word on the jewels?"

I had just checked the chat rooms that morning. "Nothing yet. Quite a heist for someone. They've got to flash those pieces around somewhere."

"Well, please monitor the chat rooms and I'll let you know what we come up with here." He paused. "You up for a little Chinese tonight?"

The memory of our last Chinese food date made heat pool in my belly. "Sounds good."

I turned back to my work. My computer was still wonky. I jiggled the mouse repeatedly. The lag time was getting to me. I needed to call my guy again—only I didn't think he'd fixed it right the first time. And I still felt creeped out by him.

Memory unearthed from my Lyme-brain. I didn't recall if I'd placed Matthew's name on the list of people in the apartment before the party. I made a note to tell Den about him, then I dialed his number, not sure what I was hoping for. Validation, maybe.

Disconnected.

Odd.

My thoughts clicked together. It was him. It was my computer nerd, the man who fixed my computer. I remembered the day. Flitting in and out of the room, and distracted by the caterers, I paid him no attention.

Also, at one point, I'd found him wandering the hall, looking for the restroom.

Stupid. How could I not have remembered him? I couldn't tell Den about this yet. Why didn't I remember this earlier? If Den wasn't already leery of a Lyme girlfriend, this might do it. Heat spread across my face. I wouldn't tell him until I was certain, and I needed to talk to the guy.

I reached for my coat and laptop case. Matthews may have gotten a new phone, or maybe it was broken. I'd catch up with him in person. Face to face.

I hailed a cab, not wanting to risk overdoing it just a week after my ankle situation healed and pushed forward.

Damn. Please. Don't let him be the guy. Justine trusted him. The cab weaved in between the traffic. My stomach waved. We passed the other cars. Honking horns. Pedestrians gathered on street corners in clusters, waiting to cross. My fingers pulled at my silky shirt, leaving sweat stains.

The cab pulled up to the building; Manhattan IT Services was still there. A receptionist greeted me.

"I'm here to see Ron Matthews," I said, pulling my laptop case back up on my shoulder as it kept sliding down.

Her eyelids fluttered. "I'm sorry. He's no longer with the company."

My stomach clenched. "Do you know where he went?"

"No, I'm sorry. He just left. No notice or anything. Didn't even bother to pick up his paycheck."

I struggled to keep my cool. "I'm sorry to hear that. He fixed my computer, and I wanted to ask a few questions. He said he'd be around."

She shrugged. "I don't know what happened. He's been gone for days. We have an entire team of people who can help you."

"I really needed to see him."

She leaned forward; penciled eyebrows lifted. "Do tell."

I slipped a one-hundred-dollar bill toward her.

"Say no more," she said, reaching for the money. "Let me get his address for you."

CHAPTER 21

Back in the cab, chuffed. Holly Golightly would be proud of the way I handled that. Here I am again considering my subjects as people I know. They often developed into a part of my subconscious. But never a character they played. Holly Golightly was iconic, though.

I took in the neighborhood as we drove down the street—East 71st, the home of Holly Golightly's brownstone, only used it for outside shots. I never understood why this brownstone. It resembled many of the others. We drove by it, and it surprised me not to find any fans snapping photos. There wasn't even a number on it, let alone a plaque, perhaps in deference to the people who lived in it.

Holly lived there alone. Women in the early 1960s didn't, as a general rule, live alone. If they moved from home before marriage, it was to attend school or to live with a relative or friend. Not alone. Holly became a role model, an usher of the modern woman.

The fact the Holly was a prostitute of sorts escaped many. My mom saw the film and never even realized it. It was clear in the book.

The production would never have flown with the studios if Marilyn Monroe had played the part. The only reason it got by the code folks was that pure Audrey Hepburn played the role.

And she admitted it was one of the most challenging roles for her. When she indicated she was having a hard time playing a hooker, the director told her, "You're not playing a hooker, you're playing a kook." That did it. The word kook was her way into the role. Words make a difference.

"Are you sure this is the right address?" The cabby asked.

"Yes." He pulled up to what looked like a bodega. A "Donuts: 2 for $1." sign hung in the window. "He must live upstairs." I exited the cab and paid him.

I walked around the corner store and saw no telltale door that would lead to an apartment upstairs. Yet, there were two more floors above the store.

I entered the store, jammed packed with food and drink. The man behind the counter looked up at me. "Can I help you?"

"Yes, I'm looking for someone who lives upstairs. I guess. Name is Ron Matthews."

He slanted his eyes. "Do you know Ron?"

"He fixed my computer and I have a few questions for him. I stopped by the office and they said he doesn't work there anymore."

A woman within earshot sauntered up to the counter, eyeballing me. She perched her cans of Campbell's Soup on the counter.

"Sorry," I said and stepped off to the side.

The man rang her up and turned back to me. "He no longer lives here."

My heart sank.

"He left no forwarding address. He just disappeared one day. Left half of his shit here, too. Is he in trouble?"

"If I'm right, he's in the worst kind of trouble, which he deserves."

He looked me up and down, cocked an eyebrow, and said, "You don't seem like his type."

"What do you mean?"

"He likes blonde and busty." He smirked.

"Ah, I told you, I'm interested in his computer skills. Nothing like that. Sorry."

He laughed.

"You said he left half his stuff here?"

"Yeah, my wife is champing at the bit to pitch it so we can rent the place. But she's been sick and I'm running the store, so it's not gotten done. I've not even inspected the place yet."

"Can I see it?"

He hesitated.

I pulled out my phone. "Never mind. I'm sorry. I'm calling the police. It's better if they go in and lift prints before anybody else goes there."

"Why?"

"If I'm correct, he had a part in a murder." Den's phone rang.

"What? A killer?"

"No, he just had a part in it."

"Yeah," Den's voice focused my attention on the phone.

"I remembered something important. There was a guy in and out of my apartment working on my computer."

"Yeah?"

"So I've been trying to reach him."

"Why? Why not let us deal with it? What the hell are you doing?" Exasperation poured through the phone.

I ignored it. "He quit his job and left his apartment. No notice. Half his stuff is still in the place. Do you want the address?"

He breathed into the phone. "Yes, but you've got some explaining to do."

"I just told you everything."

"What's the address?" All business. My guy.

"Can I get half a pound of pastrami?" A customer said to the guy behind the counter.

"Sure thing." He sliced meat, and the man stood and watched.

The deli case was chock-full of meat and cheese, and my stomach growled. I wasn't allowed dairy, as part of my new diet. I may have missed cheese the most. Or maybe it was donuts.

I'd been so stupid. Of course he planted the bugs. And I didn't even consider him at all. So nondescript. So friendly. He disappeared without too much effort. Took his time because we weren't onto him at all. But now he was gone.

As I stood waiting for Den, I wracked my brain. Was there someone else? Was I forgetting another important detail?

I wanted Gemma's killer brought to justice. I didn't care if it was a mistake of a murder. I didn't care about the jewelry. I cared about her. And I wanted to untangle it all.

Okay. A thief provides a diversion with making someone sick—or killing them by mistake. I get that. But what I didn't get was why they only swiped the gold velvet box and nothing else from my secret room filled with priceless Hollywood memorabilia.

I shivered.

Thieves were thieves. They helped themselves to things. So why didn't they take more? Why that box of diamonds? So specific?

They must have had a buyer. A collector who wanted it. A *Breakfast at Tiffany's* collector? An Audrey Hepburn collector?

To not nab anything else in the secret room, must have taken some measure of control. Cold. Calculating. Thief. Also, a killer.

CHAPTER 22

I followed Den up the stairs to the apartment. The stairs and hallway stank of mildew. When the landlord opened the door, Den stood back and lifted his eyebrows. "Jesus Christ."

I peeked in. A Nazi flag hung on the wall. A chill shot through me. "What the—"

"Man, I knew that guy was weird," the landlord said. "But I didn't know he was an asshole like this." He gestured to the flag. "What the hell, right?"

We all stepped inside, there were scattered clothes and dirty dishes piled everywhere.

"That's perfect," Den said as two guys followed behind with equipment. The flag. The dirty dishes. The stink. Mildew and old food. I dizzied. "I need to sit down." Den moved a magazine off of a chair. And when he picked it up, I saw my name. On the cover—this was the *Rolling Stone* article about me. I pointed to my name.

"Shit," Den said, helping me sit down.

He opened the magazine to the article, pieces of the text

highlighted in yellow. The photo of me sitting behind my desk had a red x drawn over it.

If we had any doubts before, now it was clear. I was the target. Gemma was killed because of me. Because of some crazy neo-Nazi fascination with me. But why? I'm not Jewish. I'm Irish-American. Since when did neo-Nazis target us? It made little sense.

My chest burned as my blood rushed, and my heart thudded. Gemma died because of me. The poison was meant for me.

"Charlotte? Listen, I know what you're thinking. Let's not jump to any conclusions. Yeah?" Den said. His voice soothing. His tone reminded me of the day I met him. The day Justine died.

"Don't patronize me!"

He lurched back.

"I was the target! Look, it can't be any clearer!"

"It's just a drawing. We have no idea what it means. Not yet. Hell, maybe he has a crush on you. Maybe he's trying to distract us once again. Believe me, things are never as simple as they look. So, don't panic."

I gazed into Den's calming blue eyes, let that voice of his reach out and soothe me and calmed a bit. But still. A Nazi flag? The *Rolling Stone* article? I shivered, but I nodded, pretending, so that Den could focus on the work at hand.

The landlord stood with his hands in his pockets.

Den focused his attention on him. "Anything you can tell me about him?"

"Well, ah, he was odd. Like I dunno, very quiet. But always had good-looking women up here." He glanced at me. "I mean blonde bombshell types. I didn't get it. But who knows what women see in any of us?"

When he said blonde bombshell, my mind flew immediately to Jean Harlow, of course. Then briefly to Marilyn

Monroe. Madonna. But I'm certain none of his women were real blonde bombshells.

"Was it the same woman? Or different women?

"I can't say for sure. Might be the same one a few times."

The men Den brought with him were moving through the apartment with meticulous prowess.

Den turned back to me, "We need to get you home. Call you a cab?"

I wanted to stay. I didn't reply.

One officer came back into the living room. "Didn't leave much behind in the bathroom, but I did get some great prints. Perfect."

If the guy was already in the system, they should be able to find him soon. I was no detective, though, just a biographer trying to work on the Audrey Hepburn story. Someone didn't like it. I didn't care what Den said. I felt it in my bones I was the target. It wasn't Gemma, this guy wanted to kill me, not just provide a diversion.

He'd been in my house, left devices behind, had been observing me. And he'd worked on my computer.

I sat straighter. "I need to have my computer looked at."

"What? Why?"

"He worked on it. Could he have access to my files? Like could he have planted something in my computer, as well?"

Den looked confused. "I have no idea. But I'll take your computer into the cybersecurity guys for review."

I shivered. My life was on my computer—my writing, thoughts, files, credit card information, accounts with research libraries, and all of my access to the underground chat rooms I used. Shit.

"What's wrong?"

"If he's been inside my computer, he has access to everything. Everything."

Den frowned. "Let's hope he didn't go there. Let's hope he

just planted devices around your apartment. I'm calling you a cab. And I'm calling Kate."

"What? Why?"

He ignored me and made his calls. He stood and ushered me out of the apartment, walked me down to the curb. "Hate to send you away, but I got a job to do, yeah? And you are more than a bit of distraction." He lifted his eyebrow and grinned.

I wrapped my arms around him. "I'm sorry that I took off like that on my own. I wasn't thinking clearly."

"Okay. But you saved yourself by calling me. Otherwise, I'd have been pissed." His hands brought my face closer to his and he put his lips on mine, sending ripples of warmth through me. Up for a breath. "Next time call me from home, okay? Don't take off on your own."

The kiss left me breathless, and I couldn't have spoken if I wanted to. So I nodded. I didn't want to play detective. Last time it went wrong in every way—except that we caught the guy who killed Justine. I don't know if they would have without my research skills. Research was my jam. Not chasing criminals.

I slipped my bag from my shoulder as the cab approached and handed it to Den. "Please don't keep it long. I have a book to write."

"We'll get right on it. I promise. Behave yourself."

I slipped into the cab. "I promise."

He pointed his finger at me. "I mean it." He leaned in and stole a quick kiss and shut the door.

My thoughts spun as the cab weaved in between cars and bikes and pedicabs. What was this man after? If he'd planted something in my computer, there was nothing I could do about it now. I'd have to change all my passwords and change backup systems. Call my credit card companies. Well, everything. Life just got a wee bit more complicated for me.

A sliver of hope existed that he didn't hack my computer. Maybe he just planted the devices around my house. Perhaps he wasn't also a computer hack. Maybe he just fixed them. But it had been acting too weird for months. Ever since I started working on the Golightly show.

And Matthews had been very persistent. I still had several messages on my phone from him I hadn't answered. But he was like that before the party, too. He wanted to upgrade Justine's computer, which I still used. And he looked at mine, too. Justine had purchased a service plan, and he was supposed to check on our computers twice a month. He'd been working for Justine for four years.

He had the *Rolling Stone* article about Holly Golightly and *Breakfast at Tiffany's*. What could some sicko have against my work with the series?

My thoughts rolled even further along the closer we got to the Upper East Side. With the image of the Nazi flag emblazoned on my brain, I couldn't help but wonder why a neo-Nazi would care about any of this. And then I recalled Stella Ross and her museum-like knowledge. I dialed her and the phone rang and rang, never going into voicemail.

CHAPTER 23

By the time I arrived back at my place, Kate was waiting in the lobby.

"Woman, what have you done? You aren't supposed to wander far."

"I'm fine," I said. Even though I was exhausted, frightened, and pissed. But mostly exhausted.

"Let's go upstairs and get you settled in. I don't know what's wrong with you sometimes."

As we rode in the elevator, I recapped what happened. By the time we entered my apartment, Kate was as frightened as I was.

"What the ever-loving hell? A Nazi flag?"

I plopped down on my couch. "I don't get it. What could a neo-Nazi have against me? Or *Breakfast at Tiffany's?*"

Kate shrugged. "I mean, I know some people think the movie is racist, you know, that awful portrayal of that Chinese character by Mickey Rooney. That was terrible."

"Some people just think the movie is sad, like my mom. She hates it. Always has."

"I know. How strange, right?" Kate said. "Let me get you some water. Have you been keeping up with all of your medicine."

"Yes and it's helping. I'm feeling okay." But my ankle still hurt and was still slightly swollen. Going out on it was not wise. It was as if something compelled me to go against my good sense. But then again, I remembered that when I'm dealing with Lyme, I sometimes don't think clearly.

Kate came back into the room and handed me a glass of water. "What were you thinking?"

"I wasn't thinking."

She placed her hands on her hips. "Do you need a babysitter?"

"Come on, Kate."

"Don't come on Kate me. This is serious. New medicine. You need to be careful."

She sat down on a chair; her aquamarine skirt splayed out in soft folds.

"And now that we know some creep is after you, you'd just better hunker down here."

Tendrils of fear raced through me. "But he was here. That's what creeps me out the most. He was here in my home, fixing my computer."

She grunted. "Do you think he took the jewels?"

"I have no idea. We have missing jewels, two deaths, and now find out my place was bugged. Add a little neo-Nazi bullshit into the mix and I'm more confused than ever."

She took a long drink of water. "So good. I hadn't realized how thirsty I was. Look, first you need to get healthy. One hundred percent. Before you do anything, right?"

"If some neo-Nazi creep killed Gemma, I want justice for her."

"We all do. But it's best left up to the cops, right? Den's working on this case. He's a good cop."

"But his working theory was blown to bits this afternoon. We now are one-hundred percent certain the target was me, not Gemma. They evidently wanted me out of the picture so they could ransack the closet."

Kate sighed. "Let's make a date to inventory what you've got in there."

The sooner the better. I needed to know. And I needed to figure out where the stuff came from, why Justine had it, and what the hell I was going to do with it.

"I wonder if I should talk with Susan about the secret room."

Kate grimaced. "The lawyer? Nah."

"She may already know about it."

She ignored that and went on. "We need to find out if Judith knows about it."

Judith.

I was reminded that Den hadn't found her yet. Where could she be?

"If Judith knows about it, there's your killer. Or your person who hired the killer."

"I don't think Den has been able to find her yet." I drank my water, leaned back into the pillows.

"How hard could it be to find an old woman?"

I shrugged. "If you're wealthy and don't want to be found, it's pretty easy to hide. Look at Justine and her club."

Club Circe was an elegant all-women's social club in the city. Justine often went there to stay off the radar of people. I didn't even know about it until she passed away and I found her key and membership documents in the secret room behind her closet.

"I wonder if Judith is a member?"

"Well, she lives in Florida, so I don't know why she'd be a member of a New York club. But it's worth a shot." I reached for the notebook I kept beside the couch and jotted Club

Circe down to make a follow-up call. The women knew me now, though I wasn't sure they'd tell me if Judith was a member.

"She and Justine didn't get along?"

"No, Kate, Justine was shunned by her family. She was a lesbian at a time that people were unforgiving. Even families. She cut all ties to them. Judith was the only person left in the family at one point and she tried to reach out to Justine. And Justine found her obnoxious."

Her famous lesbian cousin trinket to show off to her PC friends. What bullshit.

Kate sat her empty glass on the table. "If they weren't close, Judith probably doesn't know anything about the secret room."

"Yeah. She's probably not involved in this at all."

But the woman was vicious. She grabbed my arm so hard at one point that she left a bruise.

"We need to find out who knew about the room and what's inside it."

"How about the maid?" Kate asked.

"Justine has had several maids over the years. I'll make a list and start making inquiries."

"What about the one you've been using?"

"It's the same one Justine used at the end. Hilda. She rocks. I can't imagine her being involved in anything like this."

Kate cocked an eyebrow.

"The police have already talked with her and looked into her background."

Kate pursed her lips. "Did they ask about a secret room that they don't even know about?"

Suddenly, a moment of clarity came over me. "He didn't need to know about the secret room. All he needed to know was that the jewels were here somewhere and needed a way in to see where they might be. He may have been here looking for a safe and what he found was a room."

CHAPTER 24

Kate stayed with me until I fell into a hazy, light, sleep and I was awakened by my cell phone. I batted my eyes to see the screen more clearly. It was Natalie.

"Yes?" I answered the phone.

"Have you read the news?" she sounded breathless. Whatever it was, was a big deal. At least in her head.

"No. I don't even have my laptop right now." I tried not to sound as if I'd just woken up. You know, maintain some sort of integrity.

"Why not?"

"It's a long story. I'll fill you after you tell me the big news."

"They've cast Zoe Noss as Holly Golightly,"

My heart felt as if it slipped into my stomach. The part that should have been Gemma's. Time marches on in an uncanny march.

"Are you still there?"

"Yes. I'm here."

"Were you hoping for Jazz?"

Hoping? No. I was wishing the whole thing would go away. My head started to hurt.

"Not really."

She paused. "Well, the production starts in a few weeks. They'd like you on set for the whole first week."

"Me? Why?"

"In your consultant role. Then maybe once or twice a week." She breathed into the phone. "Will you be able to manage?"

Was she referring to my Lyme? "I hope so. I'm feeling better, but still not quite myself."

"I understand. I'll be in touch with the schedule. If you can't manage, we'll work it out. No worries."

"Thanks."

"So what happened to your computer? Is it at the shop again? We'll get you a new computer."

"Nah, that's not it." I filled her in on what was happening.

"What a mess." She breathed into the phone. "When will you get your computer back?"

"I hope tomorrow, but I can't say for sure."

"How is the book going?"

I knew that question was coming. "Very well." It was true, the writing was zooming by with little effort. Audrey Hepburn's story had been told so many times by so many people, it was just a matter of finessing the language and the story. Even though I didn't really want to write about her, I had to admit, it was refreshing after writing about Jean Harlow. Harlow's story, a tale of a rise to stardom, unhappiness, and early death, depressed me for weeks. Hepburn and her story was certainly more uplifting. Except for her early years during the war where she witnessed atrocities and almost starved to death, Hepburn's life was inspiring and uplifting. Not to say the woman didn't have heartache and other problems.

Her miscarriages. Her failed relationships. Her affairs. Her relationship with her parents. Her father taking off when she was young. Any number of those life events would have sent a lesser individual on a downward spiral. Not Hepburn. She worked her way through each setback—some more easily than others.

Hepburn often remarked on how lucky she was. Maybe the luckiest part of her life was that she actually had a long one, which gave her time to heal and reflect on her personal setbacks. Harlow didn't have such luxury, cut down at the age of 26.

After our conversation, I dozed off again for a bit. Then later, I woke up, clear-headed, alert. I made my way to my desk and pulled out my Hepburn timeline. When Justine and I settled on a biography subject, my first task was to build a timeline of the subject's life on one side and on the other side historical events, popular songs, movies, and so on. I looked the Hepburn timeline over. Something had been nagging at me.

Breakfast at Tiffany's was made in 1961. Collette died in 1954. If she willed her jewels to Audrey, she must have had them all that time. Her husband died in 1977, having been much younger than her. When they married, she was 52 and he was 37.

So, I needed a bit more clarification here from Stella Ross. Why would Hepburn be trying to get Collette's husband work in the 1960s? Collette had been dead for years. And he was married to another woman by this point and had several children.

Perhaps they had kept in touch. If Stella's story was true, they must have. But by this point, Audrey was a huge star with an incredibly busy schedule and hectic family life. It would have been difficult for ordinary people to reach her.

Yes, I needed some clarification about this. About the stolen diamonds —and about Stella Ross's jewels.

It struck me that this might indeed add an extra narrative thread that other biographers of Hepburn hadn't explored. If she kept a connection with Collette's husband through the years and helped him out occasionally, an exploration of that would be advantageous.

My head swam with thoughts as I scanned the Hepburn timeline.

Of course, Stella Ross could be handing me a line of bullshit. I needed to find another source on this. My rule was three sources before I'd report on anything like this.

I jotted down his name, with the words "follow-up" beside it. I also wanted to research Ron Matthews who'd been in my home, working on my computer, who bugged my place. I couldn't do it without my computer. And Den wouldn't be happy about it. But I felt a compulsion to know more about him.

I wanted to understand what role he had in the heist and the murder. I wanted to understand his motivation for everything, including the Nazi flag left behind in his apartment. But mostly, I wanted justice for Gemma.

It was me they were after, and Gemma was an innocent bystander, caught. So it was me who should find the killer. Or at least try to.

CHAPTER 25

I had to be careful. I knew Den wouldn't appreciate me poking my nose into this case. But I was a kick-ass researcher and figured there might be a few workarounds him actually finding out. Once I got my computer back, there were several threads of query I could start with. First, who was this Matthews? Was that even his real name? Who were his associates? And was there a branch of some kind of neo-Nazi organization in the city?

I shuddered. Of course there was. This was New York City. Everything was here. Or at least a connection to everything was here. *If it's not in New York, it doesn't matter.*

When I thought of New York City, even though I grew up nearby, I fell into the same media trap as everybody, I suppose, in thinking we were mostly liberal. But I also caught myself, from time to time, realizing that was not the case. It was as diverse as any place in the United States—even more so—with ethnicities, genders, and even politics. When I thought about where I grew up, it was very conservative, and it's not far from the city.

So, I tried to be careful about making assumptions, especially when it came to research. God only knew how many neo-Nazis were here. I thought about Southern cities as haven for them—but I knew that was a wrong assumption. Look what happened in southern Charlottesville, Virginia. That was a community that definitely did not welcome racists or neo-Nazis.

What would I do if I found out which group Matthews belonged to? Well, I'd cross that bridge when I got to it, I suppose. Maybe I'd turn it over to Den.

My phone alarm beeped. It was time for another dose of medicine. After I took it, swallowing back the bitter taste, I made my way into my bedroom and fell asleep amidst thoughts of neo-Nazis and Matthews traipsing through my house.

"You need to smudge this place thoroughly," Justine's voice said. "He didn't just leave bugs here in my home. But he left trails of his evil everywhere."

"Justine?" I said, sitting up.

But my room was empty. There was the chair. There was the mirror, The closet. But something else was in this room.

I turned on the light and pulled the covers over me. Justine's voice echoed in my mind. As plain as the chenille bedspread I was underneath.

The room felt cold, still, and oddly electric.

Get a grip. It was a dream. You are wide awake now.

I flung the blankets off and made my way to the kitchen. I'd slept longer than I figured. The marble felt cool on my feet as my stomach growled loudly.

What had Justine's voice said? It was fading from my mind. Something about smudging and trails of evil. Okay, so I kind of knew what smudging was, but it certainly wasn't something I thought about as anything other than some kind of strange New Age mumbo-jumbo. Why would I have dreamed such a thing? The medicine was really messing with my brain.

I reached for the peanut butter and a slice of gluten-ree bread and made a sandwich. I sat down and pondered the dream. I didn't see anything in my dream. Only heard Justine's voice. Sometimes it was hard to shake dreams off, even naptime dreams. I glanced at my medicine set up, realizing it looked like a mini-lab, and recalled the doctor saying the meds could make me dream vividly. Is that what was happening?

Or was my subconscious advising me in the guise of Justine? Should I smudge this place? I'd have no idea how to do such a thing. I'm certain I'd feel quite silly. But at the same time, there may be something to evil leaving little psychic trails wherever it went.

I dialed the one person I could think of who knew anything about smudging and psychic trails, evil or not.

I sat my sandwich down. "Hi Maude, it's Charlotte."

"What can I help you with, Doll?"

I explained my dream. "The clarity of Justine's voice." My own trailed off. "I don't know what to say."

"Well, your assessment that it may be your subconscious speaking through her voice is probably spot on."

Something in my stomach settled. I hadn't even realized it was unsettled before.

"Good."

"But then again."

Oh no. "There's more?"

She laughed. "There's always more." she paused. "There's a lot to the universe we simply don't understand. It serves us to keep an open mind, not to disregard matters that don't make sense to our intellect. Do you follow?"

"Sort of." Though I didn't get it, if it didn't make sense to your intellect, how else would it make sense?

"It makes sense on a gut level. No explanation needed. Now, when was the last time you heard the word smudge?"

I tried to recollect. "I can't even remember. It's not a term I use."

"Justine did."

"She did? I don't think she did around me."

"Probably not. I'm going to tell you something about Justine that you might find hard to believe."

I doubted that, given the closet full of millions of dollars' worth of illegal movie memorabilia. I kept my mouth shut. "She thought her place was haunted. To tell you the truth, she had me convinced, too."

"Seriously? Like, haunted? I don't buy it. Utter nonsense."

She laughed again. "Okay, Doll. But you called me for a reason. If you want my advice, I'd say get the place smudged. I know someone who can do it. Someone who is very familiar with Justine's place. She's been there before."

"It seems a waste of time. I need to think about this."

"What there's to think about? It's not going to hurt to get it done. She just goes around with a smoking wand of sage and cleanses the place. You don't even have to be there. Justine trusted her implicitly."

She sounded serious. I couldn't imagine allowing anymore strangers to come traipsing through the place after everything going on, but I thought I'd placate her. "What's her name?"

"Hmm. Let's see. I have her in my rolodex." Papers shuffled, then she breathed into the phone. "Okay. Here we have it. It's Stella Ross."

My heart stopped cold.

CHAPTER 26

Den wasn't answering his phone. I'd left three messages.

Stella Ross knew Justine. Stella Ross had been in this apartment. And Stella Ross was a collector.

Not only was she a collector, but she was a manipulator. I mulled over the scene at Layla's, with her asking for my autograph. She knew Justine and never mentioned it. As far as I could figure, there was only one reason for not mentioning it. She had somehow managed to steal those jewels.

Now, I trusted nothing she said. She may not even be a great niece of Maurice. Damn, how stupid and gullible could I be?

Wait. I did know she was lying. I just didn't know that she was lying about everything.

She and Matthews had both pulled the wool over my eyes. But I knew they couldn't be working together—that's what made little sense. He was a neo-Nazi and she had built her life around collecting Jewish heirlooms. Cherishing them. So were they both after these jewels? If they were, which one had them?

I dialed Den again and this time didn't bother leaving a message. I paced back and forth in the office. My ankle pulsed with pain with each step. Finally I sat down. I wasn't even up to pacing suddenly. I had been feeling better. I'd been keeping up with the medicine and doing very well.

But I'd had two people in my home who should not have been. Which reiterated that I should follow my natural tendencies to never let visitors in. Den. Kate. My mom and Gram.

I knew the party was a bad idea. And it was. But Justine's will stipulated that before I received money from the will, I had to have a party. And it satisfied Natalie's desire to have a Hollywood party in the Upper East Side.

I drew in air, trying to calm my racing heart and thoughts. *This is what happened. Nothing you can do about it now.*

The door buzzed and I jumped. Who could it be? I had just vowed not to let anybody else in this place unless I knew them. Knew them very well. I was beginning to not trust anybody.

"Yes?" I press the intercom.

"Den Brophy."

Thank goddess.

"Yes, please. Send him up."

When Den walked in with my laptop, I tackled him

"Whoa! What's going on?" He handed me the laptop, kissed me, and headed to the kitchen.

I followed him and sat my computer on the island, turned it on, as he reached in the fridge for a bottle of water. I sat down. "You won't believe this shit, Den. Just won't believe it."

"Three messages?" He grinned and tucked his phone back

into his pocket. "Sorry, I was already on my way. Wanted to surprise you. So what's going on?"

My scene flicked on quickly and the web came up in a flash. There was no more slowness. "My computer?"

"Spyware."

"Holy shit."

"It's clean, now. But you should change all your passwords." He took a pull of his water. "You need to tell me what's going on."

My mind reeled around the knowledge that the computer had been bugged, too. Why? What could a jewel thief want with me and my information? "Okay, Den. You're going to need to sit down for this."

"That bad, huh?"

As I revealed what I had found out, his blue eyes widened.

"Stella Ross." He repeated her name as he texted it into his phone. I didn't know if he was making a note to himself or sending it to someone. His eyebrow lifted. "She's a collector. Here we go with the crazy collectors again."

"Justine has kind of set me up for this craziness."

"Obviously, she told this Stella about her collection."

"Not necessarily." I paused. "If she was here smudging the place, and Justine wasn't here, she possibly found it on her own."

He took a drink of water and we sat in silence with our thoughts.

"We have two names, two people who are of interest. Any movement finding Matthews?"

"Not yet. It was a fake name. Par for the course. My guys are on it. Special team."

"Special?"

"Yeah, it's a group working with Homeland Security. Hate groups are risky to everybody. They skirt along what's legal. Take advantage of having the right to their opinion but are dangerous about how they behave. I'm grateful for the help from the guys. They know what they are doing. I'm sure they'll find him soon."

"Now, we also have to find Stella Ross."

"She's going to be a bit easier, I think. You said she lives in Brooklyn? I've already texted my guys to apprehend her for questioning."

I keyed in "Stella Ross, collecting." A string of information came on to my screen.

Den read along with me.

Everything we read assured us she was legit. But I knew that collectors on this scale often skirted around the law. And the internet was sometimes nothing more than smoke and mirrors when it came to these folks. Hell, when it came to a lot of people. Look at Gemma.

The more I thought about her, the more I felt like a fool-- even thought I knew I wasn't alone in feeling that way. She fooled her fans, the people with the show, all of us.

It was harder and harder to fool people about identity. She had a lot of money and manpower to do that.

"I gotta wonder if they are in this together."

"But, Den, she's a collector of Jewish things. He's a neo-Nazi. No way."

"Stranger things have happened." He cocked an eyebrow and grinned.

"True. And we've both seen some of those things."

"Now about Justine and her ghosts. . ."

"Den, seriously?"

"Yeah, man. Don't rule it out. I've seen some shit. Shit I can't explain. I'm telling you."

"I've not seen anything that made me think there's ghosts here."

"But Justine did?"

I shrugged. "I guess."

We sat in silence for a few beats.

"She felt so strongly about it that she hired someone to come in and do some kind of cleansing. You've said she's a smart woman."

"Yeah, very smart."

"Why would she think there were ghosts here?

"I don't know. But I'm sorry. I don't believe in ghosts. If she thought there were ghosts, maybe someone was actually messing with her. Trying to scare her."

Den laughed. "You've watched too many episodes of *Scooby Doo*."

I laughed. "Every Saturday morning."

CHAPTER 27

Den was fast asleep. Our visit ended up where it usually did—in the sack. Deep in an after-sex haze, I drifted off as well. But I awakened with thoughts swirling through my brain. All of this talk of Justine and ghosts reminded me that I wanted to research her apartment, um, my apartment.

Still working on believing it was mine.

Apartments like this barely existed in New York anymore. Most of the grand old apartments had been cut up into smaller places and made into condos.

I wrote down: research apartment building on the notepad I kept next to my bed. Might give me some idea why Justine thought the place was haunted.

Then—Stella. Matthews.

Could there be two people involved in the heist, as well as the murder? We knew they couldn't be working together, but maybe they were competitors of some sort.

Den's phone buzzed somewhere in his pockets. I rummaged around and found it and handed it to Den who was partially awake by this point.

"Brophy."

I pulled on my jeans, felt him watching me, and turned to smile at him. His eyes held my gaze.

"Good work," he said. "I'll be right there."

He sat the phone down on the bedside table. "Damn, I have to go."

"What's going on?" I sat down on the bed and nestled into the curve of his body. Warm.

He paused. "We've picked up Stella Ross."

"Good. I want to talk to her."

"You'll get your chance," he said, fingers trailing along my side. "But we need to do this by the book. You've done your part by informing me. Let us take it from here."

"She played me, Den," I said, standing from the bed.

He sat up, swung his legs onto the floor. "I get that. I got no problem with you talking with her after we do. But this case is too important to mess it up on a technicality. We play by the book."

My heart sank. I wanted to get my hands on her. I'd ignore my impulse to strangle her just so she could satisfy my curiosity and maybe help to get justice for Gemma.

"So here's what we have so far. Matthews, who bugged my place and seems to be a neo-Nazi. Homeland Security is looking for him. And now we have Stella, who is a collector of Jewish antiques and recently found a valuable set of jewels in the basement. Oh, and by the way, she was in here smudging the place because Justine thought it was haunted."

"Yeah." Den buttoned his shirt. I took in the view.

"What about those people from the catering company? You said there were a few people of interest?"

"Still working on it. I've told you before. Good police work is tedious and takes time."

. . .

I THOUGHT about that statement as I boarded the subway train to Brooklyn. I elbowed my way to a seat and sat next to a woman smelling of peppermint and cracking her chewing gum.

I had Stella's address from the web—she wasn't very careful about that. I planned to sit and watch her as she came back from questioning. Just watch her. I was in no shape to do anything else at this point and I was simply wanting to gather information on her. I wanted to know if the police questioning her would make her nervous, if she'd call any partners in, and if they were waiting for her at her place.

In the meantime, I pulled out my laptop and worked on the Hepburn book. I had a good hour ahead of me on the train.

Audrey had been offered the role of Anne Frank. She immediately turned it down. There were too many similarities in their lives and Audrey knew herself well enough to know she didn't have the emotional fortitude to play a part such as Anne Frank. One of Audrey's statements that I've been thinking a lot about lately is, "Whatever you're heard about the Nazi's, in reality, it was worse."

The image of that Nazi flag emblazoned in my mind. The man who owned that flag had been in my apartment, in my computer, had been watching my every move. Why? Was it just to get his hands on the jewels Collette had given Audrey? Or was there some other reason?

And what did Stella have to do with it? As far as I knew, she'd not been in the apartment since Justine died.

Of course I didn't know her before I'd called her. She may have been at the party and I didn't know it. Was she? My mind strained to remember.

If she'd smudged the house when Justine wasn't there, who knows what she saw? She may have known about the secret closet room.

The train finally reached my destination. I exited the car and made my way to Stella's place. She lived in a brownstone that probably cost millions. A brownstone similar to the *Breakfast at Tiffany's* brownstone. Across the street, there was a park. Perfect.

I took up residence on a bench and took in my surroundings, keeping a watchful eye on the brownstone.

My cell phone buzzed, and I read that it was Natalie, so I answered.

"Yes?"

"You've been invited to the private memorial service for Gemma."

My heart leapt into my throat. "I don't think—"

"Think about it. I think you should go. It would look very bad if the hostess of the party where she died didn't show up for her service."

Damn. She had a point.

"Okay, I'll go."

"Where are you? It sounds like you're outside?"

"I'm sitting at a park." Watching the home of the woman who may have stolen priceless jewels out of a secret closet in my apartment. A woman who smudged Justine's house.

But it was getting late and she still hadn't showed. I'd have to leave soon, whether or not she showed up.

"You must be feeling better, then?"

"Yes." But I wasn't sure I did. On the one hand, my ankle wasn't swollen and hurting, but on the other my brain was still foggy. I blinked, but didn't take my eyes from Stella's front door.

I drew in the air. It didn't look like the collector was coming home anytime soon.

CHAPTER 28

I called Den as soon as I got home.

"What happened with Stella?'

"She lawyered up and has a rock-solid alibi. Apparently. It was almost as if she was prepared for us."

Why wasn't I surprised? If she lawyered up and was let go, where did she go? She still hadn't come home when I had to leave my park bench. She was lively, but I didn't think she was out partying. Also, I doubted there was a back door to her brownstone. But I might be wrong.

She must have stayed elsewhere. Maybe with a friend. Maybe the cops questioning her upset her and she needed to stay with a friend.

ONE THING that happens when you have a boyfriend who's a cop and you've been invited to the funeral of an almost movie star with strong ties to the mafia is that he insists on going with you. Taking a cop to a memorial service filled with probable criminals seemed ill-advised. But I had no choice.

Den in his black suit was inspiring un-mourning-like thoughts in me, even as I sat next to him in the tiny chapel in New Jersey. Surprisingly enough, the service was small. I was one of the few people invited from the show. Biz and Levi were also there and that was it. Three of us. I didn't even see her agent.

Gemma had three brothers, Salvatore, Ricardo, and Vincent. But Vincent was the only one not doing time. Maybe what he'd said was true. Maybe he wasn't in the family business. I had no way of knowing—crime families had long tentacles reaching beyond places I even wanted to know about.

The service was intimate and sad. Respectful. And the love the family felt for her was evident. Den squeezed my hand as Vincent spoke about his sister's decision to cut ties to the family.

"On the one hand, it was heartbreaking. On the other, we understood, wanted the best for her, and wished her well. Love is like that. We just wanted her to be happy. So we helped her erase her ties to us. At least the visible ones. Of course, she was still a part of the family."

Something about the way he said family made me shiver.

After the service, we gathered in the church hall for an Italian feast, the likes of which I'd never seen before. The scents of tomatoes sauce, garlic, and rosemary plucked at my nose, sending my stomach into spasms of hunger. I had to be careful with my no-dairy diet. I had to pass the lasagna and the manicotti. I made do with spaghetti and homemade bread.

Den tucked into the manicotti. "Christ, these folks know how to cook."

"You're not kidding. This is the best spaghetti I've ever had in my life."

I watched as the cheese spread out on Den's plate. I

wondered if it would be okay to just have one little bite. As I pondered the cheese, Vincent sidled up to our table.

"Thanks for coming." He pulled up a chair. "It would have meant a lot to her. She liked you."

"I liked her, too. Vincent, this is my boyfriend Den Brophy." The word boyfriend fell across my lips comfortably. It surprised me.

Den wiped his mouth and shook Vincent's hand.

"Detective Brophy, isn't it?"

Den nodded. If he was surprised, he didn't show it.

"Any word on Gemma's case?" He leaned forward.

"We're following several leads."

Vincent's head tilted. "So are we. I don't know if Charlotte told you, but we hired an investigator."

"Yeah, she mentioned it."

I thought Den would say something about how the police department had the case covered, that a private investigator wasn't necessary. But he didn't. He sat and didn't say another word on the matter.

"We hope it helps," Vincent said, his voice cracking a bit. Suddenly, I thought he was going to cry. But he didn't. "We want justice for her."

Den nodded with consideration.

"I can't believe who they picked to play the part," Vincent said to me.

"I was a bit surprised myself." I sat my fork down half on my plate. I glanced off to the right where Biz and Levi were sitting. I wondered if they were nervous being surrounded by members of a crime family. They seemed at ease. But they were Hollywood people and were used to seeming cool, no matter what.

"You know, she has issues."

I'd seen that crazed look in her eyes. "What exactly do you mean?"

"I mean, she has a past. Maybe the NYPD should look into it." His voice had a mocking edge, which made the hair on the back of my neck stand at attention.

Den didn't respond. He was so cool-headed. He wasn't going to allow himself to be goaded. He tucked into his manicotti.

Vincent cracked a smile. "Good food, huh?"

"Incredible food," I replied, grateful for a change in topic.

"Gemma's favorite restaurant catered her favorite food," he said, then gazed off into his own thoughts. We all sat quietly for several beats with the murmuring of the crowd around us.

"Do you have any leads?" I asked. Den shot me a glare. Vincent leaned forward. "It's just that Gemma died in my home. She was my friend. I want justice for her. The police, of course, work under certain constraints that you don't have. So, if you have some information, a lead, or two."

He leaned in even further. "I just gave you one."

A woman came up to Vince and whispered in his ear. He sat up. "Nice talking with you two."

As he walked off with the woman, my eyes went straight to Den's. I didn't know if he'd looked into the other actresses' backgrounds. My guess is that he did and did not share it with me.

"Why did you have to go there?"

"Why not? I want information. And you're not telling me much."

"Christ, Charlotte. You know how things are. I can't discuss ongoing cases in detail with you."

"Okay. I get that." I sipped my wine. "So I'll get my information in other ways." I winked at him.

He laughed, even though he tried not to. "You're too much."

"So you know I can research her on my own."

"Yeah, I know. And that's exactly what you'll have to do."

"Come on Den. I don't have time for research tangents. I have a book to write. Besides, I've given you several leads on this case."

"True." he put his arm around me. "But I'm not interested in you for your leads. "His voice lowered. He placed his other hand on my knee, sending tingles up and down my inner thigh. The message was clear.

"You've had a bit too much to drink."

"Maybe. But I noticed a really nice, kind of private park in the neighborhood earlier."

He had my attention.

CHAPTER 29

Den phoned his office on the way home. "We need a tail on Zoe Noss." Pause. 'I know she has security. Work with them." He sat the phone down on the car seat.

It hadn't occurred to me that she could be in danger. "Are you concerned the mafia will kill her?"

"Nah, not really. That would be stupid of them. Offing a nobody caterer is one thing, but a movie star is another thing. But I'd not be surprised if they're watching her. Maybe trying to get close to her, to investigate her. See if she killed Gemma."

I winced. Could it be that simple? Could another competing actress have hired someone to kill Gemma? But what would any of that have to do with the heist going down in the secret closet. My head was spinning.

"What if they think she killed Gemma. Then what?"

The car came to a stop at a red light. Den looked at me. "Then they will probably kill her. Movie star or not. But I think they're barking up the wrong tree."

My stomach clenched, I didn't like the woman, but I certainly didn't want to see her dead. Even if she killed

Gemma. I'd like to see her pay, of course, with a long prison term, where she'd suffer at the hands of her fellow prisoners. . .

We rode in silence for a few minutes.

"Hey, how's the book going?" Den was trying to get my mind off the murder. Off Gemma. And Zoe.

"It's going well."

Actually, it had come to a standstill because I'd been trying to track down Stella and investigate her. Fascinating woman. She'd been a Harvard-educated medical doctor who started collecting Jewish War items in the 1970s. She retired in her forties and, from what I'd read, it seems as if she did nothing but collect and consult on Jewish ephemera, along with psychic-type things, like smudging apartments of wealthy people who believe in ghosts and demons. I found it hard to believe that Justine fell for that.

I'm full of surprises, aren't I?

But I wondered why Stella gave up her obviously successful medical practice so early. I had begun to research to see if there was a malpractice suit or something that prompted it, but I'd gotten pulled away.

But if Den was trying to gently tell me to focus on the book, not on the murder, point taken. He was right. I need to get some writing in. but I didn't think I could completely drop my own side investigation. It had all happened in my apartment. The murder. The heist. The devices strewn about my place. It was hard not to take it personally. And that meant I needed to find answers. It was my form of revenge.

I'd gone over my conversation with Stella in my head countless times. And I went over the fact that she conveniently found the other jewels in her basement at the same time the diamonds disappeared. Was it a strategy to keep the attention of collectors and buyers away from the diamonds and on the pearls?

So far, we'd been able to keep a lid on the fact that the diamonds were gone. Nobody knew I had them, let alone that they were missing. Which was, I imagine, the perfect set-up for a thief. A collector of all things relating to the Jewish war resistance. Stella must be at the bottom of the heist. But how is it connected to the murder of Gemma Hollins? Or, to a planned murder of me? Why kill anybody over jewels? Especially when you successfully nabbed them? It didn't make sense.

"Jewel thieves aren't murderers."

"What?" Den pulled the car up to the apartment building.

"Didn't you tell me that jewel thieves aren't murderers?"

He tilted his head. "Sounds like something I'd say. And, to tell you the truth, it's a pretty accurate statement."

"I'm not convinced that one incident has to do with the other."

"I don't know about the statistical probability of that. Two separate crimes on the same night in the same apartment? Both related to *Breakfast at Tiffany's?*"

I mulled that over. Maybe he was right. My head swam with probability and statistics and weariness. It was time for sleep. Den exited the car and opened my door. I exited. "Do you have to work tonight?"

He nodded and wrapped his arms around me. "Good night, Charlotte. Try to get some sleep."

He knew me too well. My mind was on fire. Sometimes I'd get on a research or writing jab and not sleep. But that would not be the case tonight. My new medicine made me sleepy—true it also gave me weird dreams. But at least I was sleeping.

CHAPTER 30

I loved to look at Audrey Hepburn. Who didn't, right? But looking at Zoe Noss dressed in a little black dress amid the whole *Breakfast at Tiffany's* ensemble was earth shattering. As we stood in the dressing room while the pros were fussing with pins and bobbles to make the dress fit right, I realized I hadn't noticed how stunning Zoe is. I had been transfixed by Gemma. Maybe we all had been. All others fell away in her presence.

Zoe was long and lean like Audrey. Had beautiful lines and one of those necks that went on forever. But her face bore no resemblance. I'm certain the make-up magic of Hollywood could help with that.

But her acting ability is supposedly what got her the part.

"It's a little too loose here," she said, pulling on the dress near the bosom.

"Yes, we'll fix that." The seamstress grabbed it and started pinning. 'You're losing weight."

Zoe's eyes caught mine and she shrugged. "I'm a bit like Audrey in the lack of a heaving bosom." She laughed, but seemed a little winsome, a little like she wanted to have big breasts.

"Nobody is ever happy with the way they look," I said. Some of the women turned around and looked at me. "Audrey herself wanted to look like Elizabeth Taylor."

"Don't we all?" One of the girls primping on Zoe stood. Several of them laughed.

For the first time since meeting Zoe, I saw her as a bit vulnerable and a lot human as she looked in the mirror, obviously unhappy. "She could have gotten breast surgery; she could have worn falsies—and she did from time to time. But mostly she dressed to accentuate her good features." I paused. "And she dressed to please herself, not men. And for the women of the 1950s, that was a revelation. Most women dressed to please her man."

The women in the dressing room went silent. One man turned and focused on me. "I don't know why women bother with men."

"Well if you don't, honey, let me tell you why!" One of the women quipped. Laughter erupted in the tiny room full of people, fabric, and sewing machines.

Biz walked in the room and pulled me by the elbow out into the hallway. I still didn't know why I had been summoned to be a part of this. But since they were paying me, I thought it best to go along with it.

"That was valuable information you just gave her. I don't know what I'm going to do with her. She's barely done any research all, refuses to work with a voice coach, and her Audrey Hepburn accent is terrible. She seems to like you."

"I wouldn't say that." That withering mad-Alice look at my party fresh on my mind.

"I would. So I'm going to ask to keep dropping your wisdom on her. Hang around her and when you see an opportunity. . ."

"You want me to coach her?" I was kind of appalled. She was a grown woman and a professional actress. She needed to bring her professionalism to the part.

He nodded. "Yes."

"Well, I'll do what I can to help, of course."

"How is Gemma's case going?" he asked after a long pause.

"I think the police have several leads. Did you say you were hiring an investigator?" That would make two private investigators—the DeSantis family had hired one, as well.

"Yes, but I fired him. He was getting nowhere fast. No leads. I've been meaning to find another one."

"Between the police and the DeSantis family, I'm sure something will happen." I didn't want to tell him the mess of leads I knew about. Not yet. Not until I made some kind of sense with them.

"The DeSantis's hired an investigator?" His black eyebrows arched over his eyes. "Oh, I'm sure they will find our killer. They have their ways."

I laughed a little. "I think that's more Hollywood than reality."

"Honey, there's nothing more real than Hollywood," Levi said as he came up beside us. "You're needed on the set for blocking questions." He said to Biz.

I followed them to the set and as I stepped into the room, beyond the camera, I reveled in the feeling that I was in Holly Golightly brownstone apartment. The little white kitchenette. The groovy black and white wallpaper. A little white tattered suitcase on the floor. The clawfoot bathtub sofa.

For a person like me who had studied *Breakfast at Tiffany's* and written about it, the experience was surreal, it was like walking into my own imagination. Chills ran up and down my spine. The moment was over in a rush as people swarmed in and around the set. I found a seat and tried to stay out of the way, watching the organized chaos.

When Zoe walked on to the set to rehearse, I barely recognized her. Makeup had done an extraordinary job—she resembled Audrey much, much more, and she carried herself just like the posed, ballet-trained Audrey Hepburn. She hadn't said a word. Yet, she was definitely channeling Holly Golightly, or maybe Audrey Hepburn herself. Whatever magic she was working worked on me.

"We need more eyeliner for the actual shoot," a voice came over the crowd. "It's not quite right."

"Darling," Zoe said, to my ear sounding exactly like Hepburn. "Fuck you and your eyeliner."

Suddenly, I like Zoe a whole lot more—crazy or not.

CHAPTER 31

Deep in the world of Holly Golightly, I needed to move on with the book, even though I needed to focus on Golightly for the TV show. I skipped over *Sabrina* and all of her other films to write about *Breakfast at Tiffany's* for the coffee table book. I recycled that info for my actual biography of her. Then I worked my way up from *Roman Holiday* and *Gigi*. The more I read about Sabrina and watched *Sabrina*, the more I saw Holly Golightly.

Was I crazy?

Sabrina was made in 1954. It was her second Hollywood film. It was the first film where she paired with Givenchy–a relationship that took hold for them, and for the rest of the world. Audrey has often said he was her great love. Thinking about it, *Sabrina* was the first of the Audrey Hepburn "Makeover" films. She starts out as a normal girl and is changed into a sexy, sophisticated woman—without losing her independent spirit.

Yes, I think I am right without *Sabrina*, there would be no Holly Golighlty.

It's hard to express how much Audrey Hepburn's style

influenced the women of the 1950s. She was a totally different type from the Hollywood bombshell.

My fingers clicked at the keyboard and I was deep in thought when an odd noise interrupted my revelry. A low, soft moaning noise seemed to be coming from inside Justine's room. What could it be?

When I entered the room, the noise stopped, yet the air bristled with something like anticipation. I walked around, checking behind the curtains and even under the bed. But whatever the noise was, there was no evidence of it now. I shivered.

Perhaps it was in the closet--the closet behind the closet. I approached it with trepidation, shoved aside the few clothes hanging there, and opened the small door into the secret little room, or big closet. However you wanted to think about it.

I pulled the string and the light flicked on. I glanced around the room and saw nothing out of the ordinary. Just boxes of shoes, perfume bottles, clothing, and so on, all belonging to famous people.

I hated the closet. Hated what it had become to me—a measure of Justine's dishonesty. She had to have known that if something happened to her, I'd find this. After all, she had left the apartment to me. What did she expect me to do with all of this?

"Goddamn it Justine."

I flicked off the light and left the closet and the room. There was nothing making any noise anywhere now. It was quiet.

As I walked along the corridors, I swore I heard a creak. Marble didn't creak, I told myself and continued into the office-library, the room I still felt the most comfortable hanging out in. Getting used to living here was easier than I expected in most ways, but in other ways? I'm not sure I'd ever get used to it. I suppose most people had a starter apartment when they got out of school or something. But I had moved directly from home, after living there far too long, to this luxurious apartment.

Another creak interrupted my thoughts. Maybe someone is doing work in a nearby apartment. I probably wouldn't have even noticed it if there wasn't all this talk about ghosts and smudging. When I thought about Justine believing in ghosts, it didn't make any sense. But then again, I had a closet full of things that didn't make sense. I thought I knew her.

But how well did any of us know any of our acquaintances? We all had our secrets. I sat down at my laptop. What was Audrey Hepburn's secret?

Okay, so she slept with married men, broke up a few marriages, maybe, and maybe in those days it was a big deal. More likely it was a big deal for a woman with a pristine Hollywood reputation. I was in no position to judge any woman on their choice of lovers—I'd lost count of my one-nighters a long time ago.

Audrey suffered from survivor's guilt, for sure, and a kind of a shame from her parent's political views and the fact they actually painted with Hitler before the war. But we all know that children have no choice on these matters.

Maybe Audrey had no secrets? Maybe her life really was the open book she claimed it was. Nobody had ever had a bad word to say about her. Well, except for three people—one of whom was hurt by Audrey, unknowingly. Humphrey Bogart, who co-starred with her in *Sabrina*, didn't so much as dislike her, as distrust her and the situation of the movie.

Billy Wilder, the director, favored Audrey and William Holden during the whole movie. And Bogart was no dummy. Audrey and William were sleeping together at the time and it made Bogart uncomfortable on the set.

The other person she'd hurt was Edith Head, her costume

designer, who was given the short shrift later. Edith and Audrey had become friends, and Edith took it personally when Audrey no longer used her. When Audrey found out about it later, she set it right. Well, as much as she could.

Of course, Audrey left a string of broken-hearted men—but that was not her fault, for the most part.

I continued clicking away at my keyboard until a phone call interrupted me.

"Hey Kate."

"I'm in the neighborhood. Want to grab a bite?"

My stomach growled in response. I hadn't realized how hungry I was.

"Does that mean I have to get in the shower and get dressed?" I whined.

"You know I won't be seen with you in your sweat pants and Steelers T-shirt."

I glanced down at what I was wearing—she knew me too well. "I'll have you know it's a Billy Joel T-shirt today."

CHAPTER 32

As I walked down Fifth Ave, navigating through the crowds as well as I could, I took in everything and everyone. It was a habit I picked up from when I was finishing the Harlow book. A woman passed by me carrying a briefcase and a tiny fluffy dog. Another woman was in my group of pediatricians, in her own little world listening to something on her ear buds, wearing sneakers with her floral dress. I noted a tall skinny man in the group wearing a blue suit. Suits were getting rare, even in this part of the city. Another man wore jeans and a thick flannel shirt. He wore sunglasses and I couldn't see where his eyes were glancing, but it felt like he was looking at me, watching me. And there was something vaguely familiar about him, The plaid took me back to the day I met Stella. I had thought someone was following me then, too. He was gone by the time I left and took my fall in front of Layla's.

I was almost one hundred percent certain this was the same guy. I ducked into a tiny clothing store. One I'd never heard of. But then again, I didn't pay much attention to fashion. I glanced out the window to see if the man was still there or if he'd moved along.

I spotted him, through the crowd. He'd crossed the street and stood near a trash can. He pulled something out of his pocket.

"Can I help you?"

I nearly jumped out of my skin. "Oh, sorry. No, I'm just looking." I turned back to the window.

"If you need anything, just let me know."

Just go away, please.

He stood there with his ear pressed against a cell phone, which must be what he was pulling out of his jacket. He walked along the edge of the curb. The red light turned and cars skewed my view as they moved along the street.

What was he doing there? Had he been following me? Or was it just my paranoia? One way to find out. I exited the store and tried to disappear in the crowd. As I was standing at the corner waiting for the light, I saw him again. Out of the corner of my eye. That plaid jacket. He was still on the other side of the street.

But he was moving in the same direction as me. Great.

Why would someone be following me unless it had to do with the heist or Gemma's murder?

But why me? I was just the person who had the party. I was just the person who was ripped off, and nobody knew it, except Den, Kate, and me.

I moved along, trying to watch him out of the corner of my eye. Finally, I arrived at the restaurant where Kate wanted to meet. I stood in front and pulled out my phone. The man in the plaid, still across the street, kept walking.

Running a bit late. Get us a table, will you?

I stood in front of the place and took a good look around me. It seemed as if he were gone. Maybe he wasn't watching me. Maybe I was just being paranoid because of what had happened before, and because, let's face it, someone was killed in my living room—a murder that might have been meant for me. I decided I wasn't paranoid. I was careful.

Okay. I texted her back.

The scent of cumin and onions wafted by me as someone entered the new Indian restaurant. My stomach growled.

Should I order for you?

No. I'll be there soon.

Okay.

I turned to enter the restaurant. And there he was. He looked directly at me, sending my heart into palpitations. I rushed into the restaurant. Who was he? What could he possibly want from me?

"Good afternoon," the greeter said.

I nodded; my mouth dry. He was definitely following me. I wasn't just being paranoid.

"One?"

"No two, my friend will be her soon."

"She's behind you," came Kate's voice, startling me. I was so on edge.

A group of women came up behind her.

"Four?" The greeter said.

"Yes."

"Okay." She turned back to Kate and me. "Follow me."

She led us to our table, amidst a sea of scents, half of which I didn't recognize.

"They say this is the real deal," Kate said. "Real Indian food. Not Westernized." she sat down, slinging her bag on the back of her chair. She sat down across the table from me. The chair felt good. Like it was just what my wobbly legs needed. "Good God, what's wrong with you? You look like you've seen a ghost."

I drank from the fresh glass of water the server had set in front me. Brief flashes of Stella smudging Justine's apartment, the weird noises I'd been hearing, and all the talk of ghosts. "No ghosts. But I think I'm being followed."

Kate's back went straight. "What? Who?" she looked around. Her necklaces clanged against the table.

"Calm down. I left him outside." I told her what he looked like and what he was wearing.

"I'll go out and see if he's still there." she stood and took her leaves.

She was back before they even handed us menus. "Nobody is anywhere around wearing a flannel shirt like that. Whoever it was is gone."

The servers came along and handed us menus.

"Thank you," I said, then turned to Kate. "Why would someone be following me?"

"I'm guessing it has to do with Gemma or Stella. Could he be a reporter? You know, one of those seedy tabloid guys? This menu looked fab. It's going to be hard to make up my mind. Let's get different things and share. It's on me, okay?"

"Sure." I mulled over her tabloid reporter theory. It didn't sit right with me. Even those reporters would have some scruples, would have at least tried to talk to me before following me. I think.

"You need to let Den know about it."

"Yeah. I'm a bit freaked out by the fact that my computer was bugged. It's clean now. But still."

"Honey, your computer doesn't even have to be bugged these days. Some of the viruses out there allow anybody to look through your camera."

"What? That's the stuff of fiction."

"It's not. Don't you read the news? There was a guy in Ohio who was just busted for that. He created a virus and infected like 13,000 computers. He was able to watch and listen to any of those people at any given time."

"Holy shit."

"Yeah, he was like twenty-eight, living in his parent's basement, didn't have a job."

"So cliché."

The server came and Kate and I ordered, my mind spinning with what she'd just told me—and the fact that my IT guy had been in the apartment.

Kate took a sip of her water after the server left. "I bet the poor guy was disappointed."

"What do you mean?"

"I mean I think a lot of those guys think women are sitting around in their underwear or naked in front of their computers." She laughed.

I laughed too. And it felt good to laugh. "The typical guy fantasy, like we're all hanging out together in our undies having pillow fights."

Kate howled.

CHAPTER 33

Just going out with Kate for a meal wore me out. Even with my new meds, it was taking more time than I wanted to get my energy back up where I thought it should be. After taking my next round of meds, I went straight to bed and fell into a deep sleep.

A high-pitched scream awakened me. I sat up, heart racing. Was I dreaming? The house answered me with silence. My thoughts rolled around in my mind. No, I didn't think I was dreaming. There was a scream, or a high-pitched wailing. And I think it was coming from Justine's room.

What the hell?

I jumped out of bed and ran toward her room. Was there an animal in her room? Had some kind of alarm gone off? I opened the door to nothing but dust trails in the stream of sunlight. No skittering movement. No sound. Nothing.

I turned to the closet and opened the secret door, stepped inside and turned on the light. Once again, there was nothing or nobody in here. Where was that noise coming from? It sounded like a creature from another world.

My heart stopped cold. Had Justine heard these same

noises and thought this place was haunted? My eye took in the scattered boxed and sheet-covered furniture and paintings. Something was off about one of the hat boxes. I reached over to the shelf and picked it up, examined it carefully.

The seams were tattered. I held it up to the light. It looked as if the box was falling apart. Has this recently happened? Most of the stuff in here had been in pristine condition. I shrugged it off and placed it back on the shelf. Maybe whomever had been in here and taken the Hepburn jewels had knocked it over.

I was struck with a sudden longing for Justine as I stood there in the center of the secret closet room. I hated this space and what it had come to represent. Yet, for some reason, I felt close to her here. Whatever she'd been up to with collecting all this stuff and hiding it away here, it was part of who she was, whether I liked it or not. You didn't get to choose your friend's faults—even if they were illegal and worth millions.

I rubbed away the hot tears streaming down my face. Oh Justine, what the hell am I supposed to do with all of this?

I shut off the light and left the room, heard the ringing of my cell phone, and ran into my room to pick it up.

"Hi Charlotte. It's Zoe. I've some questions for you. Do you have a minute?"

I reached for a tissue and dabbed my nose. "Yes, sure." I sat down on the bed, which suddenly looked extremely welcoming. I slipped my legs back under the covers and propped myself up with pillows.

"How much of Audrey Hepburn was in this role of Holly Golightly? I mean, I'm totally having trouble separating the two."

I was surprised by that question. I was prepared to answer something like what shade of lipstick she wore. "Uh. Well."

"I mean, I know it sounds like an odd question, especially coming from an actress. I mean, I know we all put parts of ourselves in roles. It just seems to me that it's hard to separate Holly and Audrey."

"I know what you mean." I paused. I thought about that very thing from time to time. "Audrey's image and *Breakfast at Tiffany's* sort of became intertwined. I met a young woman who confessed to me that she had a poster of Holly Golightly on her wall, but she'd never seen the movie, hell, she'd never seen Audrey in a movie."

"Millennial?"

"No." I found myself smiling. Because Zoe was a millennial, wasn't she? "My point is that Audrey as Holly has become an icon that has maybe gone beyond the memory of Hepburn herself. Have you seen her other movies?"

"Some of them. *Roman Holiday*. *Funny Face*. *Sabrina*."

Sabrina. "I've been thinking about *Sabrina* a lot and thinking if there was no *Sabrina* there might not ever have been the Holly Golightly of *Breakfast at Tiffany's*."

"I think I can see what you mean," Zoe said. "It's just hard not to play this role as Audrey Hepburn playing Holly Golightly."

"But Zoe, I think that's exactly what you need to do. I think that's what people are expecting. Give them Audrey as Holly."

"Christ, Gemma could have done that so much better." I heard a strain of fear in her voice. Actresses were all the same insecure messes. Suddenly I felt for Zoe. Not only did she have to play this part, but she had to do it in the face of Audrey Hepburn's memory—along with Gemma Hollins's. It couldn't be easy.

"We will never know that. I think you're going to do great."

"Thank you." She paused. "Do you know anything else

about Gemma's case? I don't think I can rest completely until we know who killed her. And Jesus, I've got cops and security all over me. I guess they might all think I'm next."

"I don't know anything about the case. I'm sorry."

Gemma Hollins dies in my apartment and suddenly people think I have some kind of in on the case. I did, but my in wasn't necessarily talking. What I knew didn't make much sense. What I knew is that the drink was meant for me. It was meant to provide a distraction from the heist. As to the rest of it, I hadn't a clue. Did Matthews have anything to do with it? Stella? Do either one of them have the jewels?

If they did, and Gemma was killed by them, even accidentally, they must be scared. They might be thieves, but killers?

"I know they're digging into my background." Zoe continued. "I'm sure I'm a suspect. But I'm not going to worry about it. I didn't do it. You saw me there. I wasn't close by or anything."

It didn't mean she couldn't have slipped something in one of the drinks.

"That guy I killed was in self-defense. And the judge agreed."

I shivered. "What?"

"Yes, I'm sure the police know this by now and the movie people are trying to keep it from the press. But I was involved with a murder a few years back. I didn't mean to kill him. But he attacked me, so I stabbed him, right in his dick."

Words failed me.

"It turns out you can kill a man that way. Who knew?"

CHAPTER 34

So I was back to thinking maybe Zoe had something to do with Gemma's death, even though it made no sense. Not yet.

It wasn't that she admitted to killing a man. I totally get killing someone in self-defense. It was the way she said it—with relatively little emotion. A flat note in her voice. It chilled me.

I was certain Den knew about this and didn't tell me. Why? Was she still a suspect? I assumed with all of the other stuff—my creepy IT guy, Matthews, and Stella—that the investigation shifted its focus from the actors to the collectors. Perhaps I was wrong.

But now I wondered what else Den knew and hadn't told me? I was aware of the ethics and the legal stance that he couldn't tell me what was happening with the investigation. But I was working closely with Zoe. it would be nice if he'd, I don't know, warned me or something. I sorted through my memories of us talking about her, but couldn't remember anything of the sort.

Where exactly was Zoe during the episode at the party? I

reflected back on that night. Gemma, Kate, Natalie, standing near me. Where was Zoe? The more I thought about it, I remembered that I didn't think she had shown up yet. But was she there?

The hordes of people at my party were mostly unfamiliar to me. I figured I didn't know everybody the studio invited. But security was supposed to be tight. People couldn't get in without an invitation.

I also remember a feeling of disorientation and irritation, because the crowd had gotten thick in my place, so she could have been there much sooner than I realized. People were crawling all over—Den had even mentioned that he found someone coming out Justine's bedroom, lost.

Surely if it were Zoe, he'd have known her and mentioned it. I dialed him.

"Yeah," he answered with a gruff.

I took a breath before launching into my questions. "How are you?"

"Exhausted. Sorry, what's up?"

"I was just talking with Zoe Noss on the phone."

"And?"

"She mentioned that she killed a man."

"Yeah, but that was a long time ago."

"Did you know we're working pretty closely together?"

"Yeah, but, like I said, it happened a long time ago. Special circumstances. I don't think you're in any danger from her. Why? Where's this going?"

"I just wondered if she might have something to do with Gemma's death."

"We wondered the same thing. But she checks out."

"Was she the woman you saw coming out of Justine's room?"

"Nah, it was an older woman. Tiny. Redhead. Sound familiar?"

"Not at all." I knew plenty of tiny women, but few redheads and even fewer tiny redheads. "But I didn't know most of the people at my party."

"Yeah. It was the strangest party."

"Hollywood in New York City."

He laughed. "Yeah. So are you sitting around thinking of murder scenarios?"

A rush of embarrassment moved through me. I had better things to do, of course. He was the cop.

"Not really. Zoe called with questions about Audrey and *Breakfast at Tiffany's* and, well, one thing leads to another."

"You, ah, don't quite trust her."

He was right. He read me so well. "No I don't. You will think I'm paranoid, but I saw this look in her eyes when she didn't know I was watching her."

"Look?"

"Yes, a cold glare. It reminded me of you-know-who. The name that will never be mentioned."

"Ah, yes. I see." He paused. "Well, I ain't going to lie to you. She's troubled. But I've not been able to find any evidence that she killed Gemma. So rest easy, okay?"

"Have you made any headway at all on the case?"

"Nah, not really. The leads are leading nowhere. Your girl Stella has a solid alibi. We can't find Matthews. The manufacturer of the drug hasn't led us anywhere, either."

"Those diamonds have to turn up somewhere."

"Have you been searching on the boards?"

My fingers pecked at my keyboard. "Off and on. But let me look now."

I glanced over the late finds on my favorite Hollywood collector chat room. Nothing.

I clicked over to the next one. Nothing there either.

Very quiet. Almost suspiciously quiet.

"I don't see anything."

"Maybe the thief just wants to keep them all to himself."

"Maybe. But usually, they sell soon after the heist."

"Maybe your crook is old school."

"What do you mean?"

"Maybe they don't use computers?"

My mind circled around that thought. "You're brilliant, Den."

He laughed.

I sometimes forget about old boots-on-the-ground research, given that the computer was such a useful tool, but I always came back to it. Every book. Every article. I had to actually get up and away from the computer to find something, to make a connection that led me somewhere.

"Now, wait," he said. "What are you going to do?"

"I'm just going to call Kate. And we're going to go shopping."

CHAPTER 35

Kate met me at Jimmy's, the largest gem pawn store in the city—and word on the street was the place took anything—didn't ask questions. This according to my Gram, who, as an antique store owner, kept up with such matters.

"I know you hate to shop. This must be important," Kate said.

I explained what we were looking for. Kate lifted an eyebrow. "No wonder you didn't want to tell me on the phone."

We walked into the store, which was clean, but jammed with stuff, an assault to my senses. We walked toward the back, where there were long glass displays.

"Good afternoon, ladies," a man came from out of the back.

"Hello," I said.

"What can I help you with?"

"We are looking for a set of diamonds."

"A set? What exactly do you mean?"

"Earrings, necklace, and bracelet. That kind of set."

"Sure,.Yeah. I don't think I've got anything like that. I've got rings and necklaces. Y'know, all separate items. We've had stuff like that come in, but not recently. Goes pretty quick."

A woman walked by exclaiming over a strand of pearls in the case. Another salesperson came up and helped her.

"Do you ever get in stuff from famous people?" Kate asked.

"Oh yeah, we've got a Hollywood section around the corner. And a Broadway section next to it. Check it out. Let me know if you need anything."

She turned toward me. 'Nice guy, but I'm not sure he knows what we're looking for. Let's check out the Hollywood stuff."

We walked around the corner, past several old guitars and violins and spotted the Hollywood case immediately—it was surrounded by small spotlights. There was a shelf of autographed photos. One of Jean Harlow stood out to me. I knew her signature by now and this photo was really signed by her —so many of them were not. I considered purchasing it. Afterall, I feel connected to Jean after writing about her, and I loved the photo, and something about the idea of holding it in my hand after knowing she held it in hers excited me.

"Look at that," Kate pointed to a wild-looking necklace that had once belonged to Cher. "I love it. But I'm not paying $2,000 for it. Christ!"

My eyes shifted away from the Harlow photo and the Cher necklace to a beautiful necklace, once worn by Elizabeth Taylor—the woman Audrey Hepburn wanted to look like, thought she would turn into. She was extremely disappointed that she never grew into the voluptuous Taylor.

"I don't see what we're looking for and we've got several other stops to make."

"I'm with you. Let's get out of here."

. . .

THE NEXT SHOP was nothing but jewelry. I'm always shocked by the crowd of people and what they are actually buying. Like, I'd never wander into a place like this unless I had business. But just to browse, or buy? Not on your life. Maybe I knew too much.

We examined the place thoroughly and didn't see what we had hoped we would. It might be worse than looking for a needle in a haystack, trying to find stolen diamonds in a place like Manhattan.

THE NEXT PLACE we went to was less crowded and soft music played over the intercom. I liked it immediately, even though I disliked pawn shops for the most part. They stank of unrealized dreams.

"How are you holding up?"

"I'm okay for now. But I'm going to need to rest a bit."

"Let's get a drink after this. I have a feeling we're on a wild goose chase."

"Could be."

A woman behind the counter looked up at us. "Can I help you ladies?"

We explained what we are looking for.

"Something like that came in a few days ago. I don't think it's on the floor yet. We're still examining and cleaning. Let me go and get it."

I tried not to jump up and down and squeal with delight. I looked at Kate, who was grinning.

The woman came out a few minutes later, holding a purple velvet box. Damn. That wasn't our box. But what was inside?

She opened the box—sparkling diamonds shone against the purple velvet. But they were not our diamonds.

"I'm sorry. Those aren't exactly what I was looking for."

"We're looking for Audrey Hepburn's diamonds," Kate said. I shot her a look. She shrugged.

The woman leaned closer to us. "I've heard they are on the market. But nothing has come in." She snapped the case shut. "Do you have a card? I'll let you know if they come in."

I dug in my bag and pulled out a card. "Please let me know."

"Hepburn collector?" She asked.

"Of a sort."

"Good to know." she wrote something on the back of the card and tucked it in her jacket pocket. "I've got a bit of a side business specializing in Old Hollywood. Here's my card. Just so you know, I love Hepburn. Anything Hepburn. I've got a bunch of her things and I don't think I'd part with them for any price. There's a woman in the club who's trying to get my nun's habit-— you know the one from *The Nun's Story*? Yeah, it's mine. She's not getting it!"

"Club?" Kate said.

Emily nodded. "We have our own Audrey Hepburn Fan Club. It's not official or anything. We get together and watch movies. Some of us collect memorabilia."

Kate's eyes lit up—she opened her mouth as if to say something, then closed it and smiled.

My heart raced. "Thank you, Emily." I took the card and tried not to skip as we left the place. Emily could be a very good connection—even if she knew nothing about the Audrey Hepburn jewels we were seeking.

CHAPTER 36

I plopped myself down into a booth seat, muscles screaming for relief. A break was just what I needed.

I sat my bag down next to me and pulled out my phone, sat it on the table. "Were you going to join that club?"

Kate leaned forward, her beads clanking on the table. "I thought about it." she grinned. 'You know how I feel about Audrey."

"So why didn't you?"

She shrugged. "It kind of felt silly or cheap after I thought about it. And I'm not sure I want to hang out with those folks."

"We've got a few more to go to today."

The servers approached us and handed us menus.

"Just drinks, I think." Kate looked at me. "Right?"

I nodded. "Do you have nachos? Wait. I can't have cheese."

"How about salsa?" The server asked.

"Sounds good. And I'll have Guinness."

Kate ordered a Chardonnay and the server went off. "We've got more places to visit?"

I nodded. "There's only three more I think."

"In the whole city?"

"No. There are places that you'd most likely take something like these jewels. You wouldn't take them to any old pawn shop, would you?"

Kate pulled out a mirror from her hand bag and checked over her makeup. 'This lipstick is great. I've not had to touch it up yet." she slipped the mirror back in her purse. "If I had those jewels, I'd keep them."

Our server came to the table with the drinks and sat them in front to us. 'Chips coming right up."

A group of loud women sat in the booth behind us, laughing, chatting.

"One of the reasons people steal is to sell stuff, right?"

"Yeah, but if a fan took them, they may just want to keep them."

"I've thought about that, believe me. I'm just trying to methodically figure out some things. Mostly, I want to know who killed Gemma. I don't really care about the jewels, except that I'd like to see the jeweler's family have them."

"That's awfully nice of you, but I'm betting Stella lied about all that, too." Kate lifted her glass to her mouth and sipped.

"If we find the jewels in one of these shops, we can get a description of who sold them, right? Then we turn it over to Den."

The women behind us were so loud that it was hard for Kate and me to communicate. I turned and looked at them, hoping to subtly tell them they were being obnoxious.

"I've been thinking. If the creepy IT guy had something to do with this, other than just wanting to spy on you for the party. Say if he's your crook. He's a computer guy. Maybe he'd be selling the diamonds on the darknet."

The server brought our chips and salsa and moved over to the table of noisy women.

Darknet! I hadn't considered it. True, I was in some of the sketchiest collector chat rooms, but the darknet?

"What do you know about the darknet?" I licked the foam from my stout off my lips.

"All I really know is you shouldn't go on it on your computers. It's dangerous, like it will infect you or something. But Roger has made a fortune from bitcoins and cryptocurrency."

Rich people were always making more money.

"So how can we get on the darknet?" I bit into a salty hip.

"I think Roger has computers just for getting on the dark web. I can ask him. But you know, I bet the cops know something about it."

I made a mental note to ask Den, who wasn't the most technically astute man I knew. But he did have access to a cybercrimes unit.

It made sense. A creepy IT guy who placed devices through my apartment would sell stolen goods on the dark web. If only I'd considered that sooner. But then again, the dark web wasn't in my purview.

"You're brilliant, Kate." I took a drink and sat my mug back down on the wooden table.

"Oh well, she said, grinning. "I try. Now let's talk about that outfit you're wearing. It looks great on you."

It was an outfit she had picked out for me, of course. My personal shopper. She saw it in the window of Macy's and said she knew it was for me. I'd never thought to wear anything except jeans, sweat pants, and maybe pants. But today I was wearing a Donna Karan dress and was comfortable with it. Since the trouble with the Jean Harlow book, I insisted on testing clothes to see if I could move in them. You never knew when you'd need to run or hide quickly.

"I like it. It looks good and it's comfy. Comfy is the important thing." I sat up straighter.

"The neckline shows off your boobs in a nice way."

"Can we please not talk about my boobs?"

"Why not? I love boobs. I love looking at them and my boobs are my favorite part of this body." She sat up and gestured.

"They certainly cost you enough." I grinned.

"Ain't' that the truth?" she laughed and took another drink.

WE FINISHED our drinks and continued with our search. We found nothing, except a pair of red pumps that may or may not have belonged to Marilyn Monroe, which Kate purchased, along with a scarf that may or may not have belonged to Elizabeth Taylor.

"Well, that was fun. You know how I love spending money," she said in the cab. "But it didn't lead us anywhere."

"Well, I do have the Emily connection now. And that might lead somewhere. Plus, investigation is often a process of elimination. We've eliminated all of those shops. Now, we need to look further into the dark web. And I need to keep working on tracking Stella and Matthew."

"Leave that to the cops, love. These people sound looney. You've got a book to write. Shopping is one thing, but all of this other stuff? Don't bother with it. You need to get well. Get stronger. What does any of it have to do with your life? Your book?"

I paused before answering. "I'm not certain, but there's a thread here. A thread leading me to more than Hepburn's jewels and Gemma's death. I feel like Stella was keeping something from me. There's something deeper going on."

We sat in silence a few moments as the cab rolled along.

People strolled on the sidewalks, moved across the streets in great heaps of humanity. Suddenly I thought I spotted someone who looked familiar. I batted my eyes, then squinted, leaned forward. "Cabby, turn right here, please."

"What?" he said.

"Turn right!"

"Okay, but this is not the way to L'Ombre."

"Fine, just do what I ask, please."

"What's wrong with you?" Kate asked.

"That man!" I pointed to him. He wore the same plaid coat and the same sad expression. "He's been following me!"

He stood for a moment on the street and turned to face us. He couldn't see us, but we got a good glimpse of him.

Kate gasped and paled.

"What's wrong? Do you know him?"

Her mouth dropped open. "Don't you? Holy shit, Charlotte. That's your dad."

CHAPTER 37

Kate's words reverberated through my body, as if I'd stuck my finger in an electric socket.

I was a child again, empty with the loss of my father, awakened in the middle of the night by my mom's sobs, afraid because every time a cop came to the house it was even worse news. I stayed in bed for days, hoping that if I slept long enough, I'd awaken to my mom and dad standing there both looking over me. Yes, I'd stayed in bed. And nobody noticed.

"Charlotte?" Kate placed her hand on mine.

I don't remember much about my Dad—just bits and pieces of images and feelings, none of them whole. His large rough hand held mine. Feeling as if nothing in the world could harm me when he was near. His police hat on the stool beneath the coat rack. Old Spice tempered with a hint of sweat.

"Charlotte!" She squeezed my hand.

He was my father and I hadn't even recognized him. Sure there were pictures of him when he was much younger scattered about the house. But the difference in his looks wasn't just age. Something had happened to my father. Anger roiled in my guts. I'd been angry since I learned he wasn't dead, as he'd ever reached out to us. Not once.

But what if he couldn't help it?

I heard myself gasp. "Something is wrong with him."

A shard of panic tore through my chest. "Follow him."

"Follow who?" The cabby said.

"The guy in the plaid jacket over there."

Heart racing. I searched the crowd.

"Where?" The cabby said.

I took in the crowd as we edged slowly through the traffic.

"He's gone," Kate said.

I searched Kate's face for some answers. She remembered him. I didn't. Not really. She knew who he was. "He's gone," she said again. "But it shouldn't be too hard to find him." she paused. "If you want to."

If I want to.

Now that he's come back, I could easily find him. But did I want to?

When my mom first told me that she'd gotten a letter from him, at first I was suspicious that someone else sent it. After all, my father was dead. Had been dead for 20 years. He'd disappeared, though, and we'd never found his body. As the letters kept coming and my mom communicated with him, my suspicions turned to anger. Here was a guy who took off and left his family and decided to come back twenty years later. Jesus.

"There's more to this than you know," my mom said to me.

"I bet there is and I don't want to know. As far as I'm concerned, any man who left his family, with no support, no word, for twenty years? I don't want to know."

"But Charlotte—"

"Please, Ma—"

What had she been trying to tell me?

A painful longing for Cloister Island, our cottage, and my room overcame me. I needed to go home. I wanted to go home.

"Charlotte," Kate elbowed me. "Open the door. We're here."

My trembling arms opened the door. I slid out of the cab, legs feeling wobbly.

My father was alive. He was in Manhattan. And he'd been following me.

Kate paid the cabby and wrapped her arm around me. I leaned into her. We walked into the fancy apartment building I found myself living in and made our way to my apartment

"Let's get you a drink," she said, after I was situated on the couch. "What's your poison? I saw some whiskey in the cabinet."

I nodded. "Yes. Just a shot might help."

'Over rocks?"

"Yes."

Kate bought two glasses of the amber liquid in. She sat down next to me. "I feel like I've seen a ghost." She shook her glass, the ice clanking on the sides.

"I'm thinking about going home for a few days."

I was sorry I mentioned home. Kate winced. She hadn't been home in years—since she told her family that she wanted to be a woman.

"You should come with me. You could stay at our place, like when we were kids."

She took a sip. "I'm not quite ready for that."

I let it rest. Kate was funny, upbeat, and caring. And she was the best friend I could ever hope for. But I knew the depth of her pain, too. Knew her abject sorrow.

"I feel like I need to see Mom and Gram."

"I get that. I wish I could go."

"You will. When you're ready." I lifted my glass. My hands were still trembling. I brought the whiskey to my lips and swallowed.

"They will be happy to see you. Of course."

"I need to talk with them and see what's going on. Mom said there was more to the story than what I know. But, Jesus, it's been over twenty years. I can't imagine any of what she has to say matters. Really."

"He looked, I don't know, beaten down."

"I got a good look at him the other day. Looked right into his face. And I think you're right. There's' something off."

My phone buzzed. I recognized the number. It was Zoe. I let it go into voicemail.

"I can't deal with Zoe Noss right now."

"You poor thing. I'm sorry you have to deal with her at all."

"Shit. I guess I'll have to call the studio and try to get a few days off. I'm not used to having a job."

"Just tell them your father has returned from the dead," she held up her glass in a mock toast.

CHAPTER 38

By this point, I'd had enough of *Breakfast at Tiffany's* to last a lifetime. I'd written the coffee table book, been involved in the reality TV casting show for *Golightly Travels,* and now I was actually in the studio again.

It was infectious—the Golightly look. If I saw one more pair of dark sunglasses, or black turtlenecks on the crew, I might scream.

"Why didn't you return my call?" Zoe asked as she came up to me. I was sitting in front of my computer, projecting my "don't bother me" look—which she was clearly not picking up.

"I'm sorry, Zoe. Something personal has come up. Today will be my last day for a few days."

She paled. "Are you okay? What will I do without you?"

Am I okay? Depended on what she meant by that. I was still in a bit of a state of shock.

"Just call me if you have questions."

"I called you yesterday and—"

I held up my hand. "I promise I'll answer your call next time."

That seemed to appease her.

She held a book in her hand. 'Have you read this?" *Breakfast at Tiffany's*. Of course.

"Yes."

"I like the movie so much more."

Of course.

"But they changed it so much, right? No wonder Capote was miffed."

"Capote was a brilliant man, but he was an egotistical asshole. I mean, come on. They are making your book into a move, dude. Just take the money, shut up, and be grateful."

Justine's face came into my mind. "Writers" a rolling of her eyes, a shrugging of her shoulders.

Zoe's carefully made-up face fell. "Bitter grapes?"

I bit my lip. Literally. "Don't you mean sour grapes?"

"No, I meant bitter." She crossed her arms. "People say actors are competitive. But we stop competing when one of us dies."

I shifted in my seat and shut my computer with a click. "What's really on your mind?"

"I'm trying to get into this character." She sat down. "So I thought I'd read the book and now I'm more confused than ever. She was much more edgy in the book."

"We sort of discussed this. You're not playing Holly Golighlty. You're playing Audrey Hepburn playing Holly Golightly."

"I don't think I can do it." her eyes downcast, cheek twitching. "This was Gemma's part. I can't get that out of my mind."

Gemma. Gemma was gone. Thoughts of her circled through my brain. We are no closer to finding her killer. All we knew was that the diamonds were gone. Stella Ross had been in the apartment and she was a known collector. Plus the creepy IT guy had planted spyware on my computer—as well as devices through my apartment. Den was working hard at putting the pieces together. And I was researching every chance I got. In between shopping for the diamonds, writing a book, taking my medicine in timed doses that seemed to take most of the day, and—did I mention?—writing a book.

"No point in going down that road. Yes. The part was hers. It's yours now. They have faith you can do it. I know you can." When did I become her cheerleader? Jesus.

She was dressed in 1960's garb. A pink mini dress. Made up to look like Holly, Zoe's face kind of freaked me out. It was Holly, but it wasn't. Not for the first time I wondered about the wisdom of taking the mini-series. Who knew how hardcore fans would react?

Audrey's fans were not as kookie as Harlow's fans. At least I wasn't being chased down the streets by any of them, nor was I investigating at drag queen shows. But Audrey was different. So her fans were different. Of course, the hardcore fans were crazy, but in a very different way than Harlow's. Their craziness took on more complexity. Stella came to mind. As did Emily.

Emily gathered with other fans monthly to talk about their passion. Stella, more subdued certainly, collected Jewish antiques, but the connection to Hepburn excited her.

When I thought about the money people spend just to have an item worn by a star, especially one in a film, it kind of made me cringe. But then again, I had a whole secret closet full of exactly that. Minus a few items. Most importantly, the diamonds Collette gave to Audrey. Stella had a set of pearls, there were the diamonds in my closet—how many other pieces of jewelry did Collette have? According to legend, she willed them all to Audrey. Maybe the connection isn't Audrey? Maybe it's Collette? Did anybody care about Colletteanymore?

Would someone want to collect her jewels? How to find out?

As I WAS LEAVING the office, I dialed Den. "Is it okay for me to call Stella?"

He paused, breathed into the phone. 'I thought you were going home."

"I am. But phones work at Cloister island, most of the time anyway."

"Ha. Ha."

"I don't want to screw up your case."

"Mighty kind of you."

"Well? Can I call her?"

"Sure. But please don't harass her. That's all I need."

"She doesn't know I know you, right?"

"Yeah, I guess."

Then I can harass her all I want to. "Okay. I'll be careful. I just want to talk with her." And I'd kinda' like to strangle her. She sat right there with the Jean Harlow biography, asked me to sign, and never mentioned she knew Justine. Intimately. Had been her apartment.

Den interrupted my thoughts. "How did your shopping trip go with Kate?"

"It went nowhere. Except we met a diehard Hepburn fan who works at one of the pawn shops. I got her card."

"Well, if it leads you anywhere, please let me know."

"Any word on Matthews?"

"We're not sure, but we think he left the country. Name is not Matthews."

"What is it?"

"Ah, let me see." Papers shuffled around in the background. "Igor Von Strasky."

"What? Is he foreign? He didn't have an accent."

"We're not sure yet. But some of these guys are really good at the no accent thing. Ya know."

These guys. He knew more than what he was telling me. "These guys? Who are you talking about?"

"Crooks," he said. "Getting more sophisticated every day. At least the smart ones are."

If only I believed him. There was something about his tone. Of course, we were on the phone and he had to be careful.

"Do you want to come by tonight? I don't know when I'll be back."

"I'd like that. I'll see what I can do. If you promise not to tie me up to force me to divulge my secrets." He laughed.

"I'll make no such promises."

CHAPTER 39

All women knew if they wanted to talk to their man, it had to happen before sex. After sex, they were useless. With some men, it was only during sex that they were useful at all. But that's another story. Another kind of man. Not Den. I had to be careful.

"Have you talked with Stella yet?" Den asked me, leaning back into the couch. Maybe this was going to be easier than I thought. He brought it up.

I swung a leg over his lap. He placed his hand on my thigh. Tingle. "No. I'm planning to call her in the morning before I leave. I want answers. I feel like she knows something."

"About the heist? I gotta tell you she has a solid alibi." He stroked my thigh.

"Well, maybe she wasn't here for it. Maybe she had nothing to do with it. But I'm thinking she has a background or a link to whoever took the jewelry and might be able to enlighten me."

He smiled, deep dimples, thick lips. "Well, good luck with that."

"She's sly."

He nodded. "I agree."

"Now, what can you tell me about Matthews?"

His chin angled toward me. 'I've already told you. We think he left the country."

"Think? I don't buy it."

"If that is his name, then he left the country. We're not sure. There were several names leading us around the city, then to port authority, finally to the airport. We're working to get some clarity." While he spoke, his gaze wandered around my place, then landed on me.

"You're not telling me everything."

"I can't. Not yet."

"But you know I'm a researcher, right?" I batted my eyes at him and smiled. "I'm going to find out whatever it is."

"You're a kick-ass researcher," he said. 'I know that. Are you just going to leave this alone if I ask you to?"

"Not a chance." I swung my leg off of him. "Gemma died in my apartment. Right here in front of me. The diamonds were taken out of my secret closet. And I was being watched. It feels very personal to me. So I want answers, which I'll get with or without your help."

"Okay," he said. "This guy has been on Homeland Security's radar for awhile."

"Is he a terrorist?"

"Of a sort. Brilliant hacker. He could bring down a city. Or a government. Hell, maybe even a country."

I wanted to laugh, but Den's tone scared me. "That seems like something out of a pulp fiction book, Den."

"I know it does. But HS is very serious about this."

"What would a guy like that want with me? Or the diamonds? I don't understand."

"Well, don't feel bad, babe, nobody else does yet, either."

"They weren't just any diamonds. They had a history.

Designed by Collette's Jewish husband. And we know Matthew, or whoever, is a neo-Nazi, or something. Could this have to do with war crimes? Are they trying to hide something? I don't get it. They are just diamonds."

Den cracked a smile. "Just diamonds. Worth millions. Just one of the reasons I love you." It was glib, off-handed, but there it was. Those three little words. We'd been dating over six months and I suppose it was about time. My chest felt as if a million butterflies were flitting about inside. I watched his face as he realized what he said.

"Really? I thought you loved me because of my mad bedroom skills." I tried to joke.

He laughed. "Well, there is that." Serious, again. "But I do love you."

Some people said those words after the third date, after a month. Some people say those words and even when they were being said, you knew, you just knew it was without gravitas. But when Den Brophy said anything, it was best to listen. When he said "I love you," he meant it.

"I know that, detective," I said, leaning into him, kissing his cheek and whispering. 'I love you, too."

AFTER, I drifted off in his arms and I watched him sleep. Soft snores. Mouth open. Still, just as cute as he could be. Fear gripped me and I willed it away. Stop being so afraid of having a relationship. This is it. You are in one. Right now. Take it as it comes.

I drifted off in a cocoon of love.

Den wrapped his arms around me, then his hand around my mouth, tightly. What the hell? I awakened. He was alert, placed a finger over his mouth and pointed to the door. "Stay here," he mouthed.

What was going on? Was he dreaming? A nightmare? Some kind of PTSD thing?

But then I heard the noise. A rattle. A thump. A moan. The same kind of noises I'd heard before. Den was out of bed, gun in his hand. Adrenaline coursed through me. I sat up. Placed my feet on the floor. Den was focused on the door. If there was someone in my apartment, woe be unto them. But as I breathed and began to awaken more, I realized there were the same noses I'd heard from time to time.

Maybe Den could solve it. He opened my bedroom door. It creaked with menace.

He carefully walked out in the hallway, gun in front of him.

I was behind him now, wrapped in a sheet. Feet on the cold marble. And listened. The noise was definitely coming from Justine's bedroom.

Creak. Hiss. Moan.

We moved toward her door, Energy flowing up and down my spine in the dark, with just shards of light from the night-light in the bathroom and kitchen.

Den opened the door to nothing. Nobody. One more low moan and then nothing but silence.

He moved into the closet. Nothing there either.

I switched on the light and he finished searching through the women.

"What the hell was that?"

"I'm not sure, but I think it was the ghost." I grinned.

"What?"

"The noises remind me of a ghost. It must be why Justine thought she had a ghost."

Den paled. "Look, I know you don't believe in ghosts. But I've seen some shit in my life. And come to think of it, those noises were . . . ghostlike."

"Come on, Den."

"No, you come on. Check it out. You've got a ghost."

"Put your gun away, Den. I think you've lost your mind."

CHAPTER 40

My man was not only hot, but he was steadfast, And interesting. Here was a tough-as-nails NYPD cop, who suffered from fear of large bodies of water, and from a belief in ghosts.

"I'm glad you're going away for a few days. I don't want you in this place alone."

"There's plenty of room here. Why don't you move in?"

"We've talked about this before. I'm not sure we're ready for that. I need to take this slow. And so do you. There's no rush, is there?"

"No. Except I still haven't made up my mind about this place. If I move, it may not be this large. We might be bumping into each other more."

He laughed, just as his cell phone buzzed with a text message. He read it over. "You're not going to believe this. Your friend Stella is heading out of the country for three months."

I sat up in bed. "What? I need to talk with her before she leaves. Where's she going?"

"Holland for three months."

My trip back home was slipping away. I desperately needed to see my mom and Gram. I needed answers about my father.

"Maybe I'll just call her and I can still get home today." I said it more to myself than Den, but he picked up on it.

"I know you need to get home. It would be good for you. I can't believe your old man has been following you. I don't like it." He rose from the bed and started for the bathroom to take his shower and I planned to move to the kitchen to make a pot of coffee.

"I do need to get home. But it can wait a day." I walked out of the room down the hall to make coffee.

As I made the coffee, I plotted my questions with Stella. Who knew if she'd even talk with me at this point? What, if anything, did she have to do with the heist?

She was a good liar. She had me fooled. She knew Justine and never mentioned it. But I did know she was lying. But I thought she had a secret about Hepburn. And perhaps she did.

Maybe if I were honest with her about everything, she'd open up. Honesty isn't always the best policy during interviews. I mulled it over as the coffee maker spit out coffee.

Den walked in the room, freshly showered.

"Did my name come up in the interview with Stella?" I poured him a cup of coffee and slid it across the counter.

"No. She asked how we found out about her relationship with Justine. She was curious, but nah, we never divulge our sources." He grinned. "Why?"

"I'm just trying to figure out how to play this interview. If she doesn't know I know about her, it will make it a bit easier."

Den drank from his coffee cup. "She's a smart woman, I'll tell ya that."

"Devious. She sat across the table from me and bald-face

lied. Got me to sign a book. Never mentioned she knew Justine. But I knew she was lying about something. I just had something wrong there. I figured it had something to do with Audrey Hepburn's past."

He rolled his eyes. "Audrey Hepburn was a saint, right? What should she be hiding about her?"

"I don't know. I don't think it's anything outrageous. I just think there may be an element to Hepburn's stories that's deeper than what we know. Maybe Stella knows whatever it is."

"I've got to run," he said, rinsing his cup and placing it in the sink. He kissed me on the cheek and found his way out of the apartment.

I searched through my phone files for Stella's number and dialed her. She answered on the first ring.

"Hi Stella, it's Charlotte Donovan."

"I'm so sorry, Charlotte, I can't talk because I'm heading out of the country on a research grant."

"How wonderful," I said. Shit. "Where are you going?"

"Holland." she sounded irritated. "I'll be there three months. I'm working with some specialists there, you see."

"What kind of specialists?" Trying to keep my voice light, interested, but not too interested.

"I'm looking to verify some documents I've recently found."

"Documents? I thought you were all about jewels."

She laughed. "I got involved in all of this because of the jewels, but it's so fascinating that it's taken over my life."

"Can I swing by your place with a pizza?"

She laughed again. "It won't do you any good. A car is coming for me in an hour."

I hated to let her go. I had questions. But if I was too assertive, it would scare her off.

"If you want to call or text in a few days, I fill you in. I may have found something more for your book on Hepburn."

My heart raced. "What? What could that possibly be?"

"I can't say anything else. Do take care." She clicked off the phone.

She was certainly in a rush to get out of the country. And she admitted she may have found something about Hepburn. What could it be? Her life was so well-documented. What could have surfaced?

What, if anything, did it have to do with my missing jewels and the death of Gemma Hollins?

CHAPTER 41

Now that Stella was leaving the country, I had to cross her off my list—or else I'd find myself in Amsterdam, instead of front of my computers, which is where I needed to be. The only thing I could do without her suspecting anything was to text or call her when she was gone.

Patience was not my greatest virtue. "Patience is highly overrated."

I stood and faced the length of the kitchen. If, by some chance, Stella had my gold velvet box with the diamonds inside, she's not be foolish enough to try to take it out of the country, would she? Or, would she have left it behind in her townhouse? Or maybe a safe deposit box somewhere? She was a smart and wily woman. What would she do with stolen goods?

My phone rang and startled me. "Hello."

"Where are you?"

"I got sidetracked, Gram."

"What's going on?"

"It's a long story. I'll be home later. " An image of our

cottage, beaten down by years of sea air, popped into my mind. Home. I ran my fingers about the clean, shiny marble kitchen counter. Would this place ever really feel like home?

She cackled. "Okay then. We miss you. I've got to get over to the shop, got some stuff coming in. Your Ma already has some soup on."

I could almost smell it—Ma's oyster stew.

"Let me ask you something. If someone brought stolen goods to you, what would you do?"

"How would I know they are stolen?"

"Uh, I don't know. Say they are expensive and there's no certificate of provenance."

She sighed. "I'd probably buy it at a very good price, then get my sources to figure out what it is and where it came from. If it was stolen, I'd get the police involved. Of course."

My Gram. She had sources.

"The business of antiques and collectibles ain't what it used to be. It used to take years to trace something. Now, maybe days."

I imagined her shrugging. "Okay, we need to talk about this when I get home." I hadn't told her about my closet. Like a curtain lifted from my eyes, my Gram and her knowledge shone a light.

"When you get home," she said with a level tone.

"I hear you. I'm packed. I just need to get moving."

"See you soon." she clicked off. Gram wasn't one for staying on the phone—not like her daughter, my mom, who could keep you on for hours—if you let her.

I rushed into my room to finish packing. Just a few more things. I mentally checked off what I'd placed in the bag and what else I needed to bring. I finished packing and zipped up the case.

Next I needed to get my work stuff together. Laptop, files

into my briefcase. Medicine was next. It was time for a dose, so I took care of that, then packed it up.

The face of the man who'd been following me popped into my head. The man who was my father. I shivered. What had happened? Where had he been all these years? Anger plucked at my chest, as usual when I thought about him, but it was tempered with something else—maybe empathy. But first to get home to Mom and Gram.

My phone rang. "Hello, Kate."

"Are you home yet?"

"Nah, Den came over and—"

"Say no more."

"I'm packed and just about ready to go. Den delivered some startling news. Stella is leaving the country."

"I don't blame her, do you?"

"What do you mean?"

"She was just dragged into the police station and questioned about Justine and stolen jewelry."

"And a murder. Let's not forget that."

"Yeah. So, she's running away. She's definitely hiding something."

"She said she may have more to the Hepburn story for me."

"Really? God. What else can there be?"

"Right?" I opened a file cabinet, searching for the file on *The Nun's Story*, the film that really made Audrey as an actress. "I'm going to put you on speaker."

"I hate that."

"I know. Bear with me, please," Something was caught in the back of the file drawer. I slid my hand back as far as it could go, felt nothing, and pulled my hand out. Then I yanked the drawer hard and heard something tumble along the back of it.

"Roger and I am going to the Hamptons for the weekend. Do you believe it?"

"The Hamptons?" I got down on my knees and opened the bottom file cabinet, only half full of Justine's old files. "You've come up in the world."

"Ha! Don't I know it. Some of his family will be there and I'm nervous about meeting them."

Still on my knees—and it hurt like hell—I crouched even further down and peered inside the drawer. It looked like there were a couple of old notebooks lodged in the back. "You'll do fine. Everybody loves you."

"Not everybody," she muttered.

"Come on. This isn't like you." I pulled the notebooks out of the back to the drawer.

"Well, I really like him."

"What the worst that could happen?" I sat down on the floor, back against the closed drawers. "He likes you. A lot. So I'm thinking his family will, too." I dusted off the notebooks with my hand and blew on them. I opened one and flipped through the pages. Handwritten. Justine's writing. It caught me. A pang of grief erupted from the center of me. I ran my fingers across the words.

"What are you doing? You're not paying attention."

"Sorry, I found a couple of old notebooks. They fell inside the back of the files cabinet."

"What's in them?"

"I'm not sure. It's written in another language."

"What?"

"German, I think. Maybe Dutch? Nothing but lists."

"Did Justine speak German?"

My stomach twisted. "She must have." I set the notebook aside and cracked open the next one. As I sifted through the pages, photos and handwriting flipped in front of them. "A scrapbook."

CHAPTER 42

I tucked the notebook and the scrapbook into my bag and called an Uber.

The trip to the pier was a long one from the Upper East Side, through the neighborhoods of Chelsea and lower Manhattan, and I had plenty of time to think while my Uber wove between cars. When we pulled up to the pier, where I caught my ferry to Cloister island, it was eerily quiet.

The Uber driver shrugged.

Finally, I saw the sign that said the trips were canceled today because a storm was expected. A storm? Damn. I hadn't checked the weather. What the hell? What a stupid move—I used to check the weather on a daily basis.

"Please take me back home." My driver was a tiny older woman and she just smiled and said, "Sure thing."

I checked my phone as we headed back uptown. Sure enough, a whopper of a storm was heading our way. Surprising that my mom hadn't called to tell me about it. But then again, she was expecting me to come home.

I dialed her.

"Charlotte! I've been so worried. Are you on the ferry?"

"No, a storm's coming. I guess I'll try tomorrow."

"I hoped you caught the last one that went out. But we'll see you tomorrow." she paused. "Everything okay, honey?"

I didn't want to tell her over the phone that I'd seen my dad. It didn't seem right. "Yes. I'm just missing you and Gram."

"Is the book going well?"

"Yes, I'm about halfway finished with it."

"How about the series?"

Zoe's face popped into my head. "As well as can be expected."

"Ah, well, the show must go on, and all of that."

So they say. But this show should have died with Gemma. "Yes, that's what they say. Look, I'm almost back at the apartment. I'll see you tomorrow."

The L'Ombre loomed large in front of us. Tucked between two larger buildings, it looked like an art deco cake between the nondescript newer apartment buildings.

"Back so soon?" Stan, the security officer asked me.

"Boat is not running today. A storm is brewing."

"Funny, the sky is as blue as can be."

"Maybe it will pass by."

"One can hope."

I grabbed my bag and hopped onto the elevator. That was enough small talk to last me for weeks.

I SAT down at my computer with the intention of working. I could crank out at least one more chapter before bedtime. But a photo of Gemma caught my eye. Would the cops ever find out who killed her? The case seemed to be at a standstill.

Did her murder relate to the heist?

As Den said, it would be unlikely that two crimes would

be going down in the same location at the same time and be completely unrelated.

One of the ways in which we cracked open the Harlow case was by luring people out and I couldn't help but wonder if there was a way I could lure these folks out of hiding. What might I have that I could sell that would appeal to Audrey Hepburn collectors?

Gloves. Tiara. Cigarette holder. None of that seemed to be on the same scale as the diamonds.

I made my way back to Justine's room, switched on the light, and opened the door to the secret room. I stood for a moment taking it all in. Boxes—velvet, floral, plain. Covered furniture and paintings. It was a mess. I still didn't understand why Justin had this stash of valuable goods.

I slid a box across the shelf so that I could get to the Audrey Hepburn things that I knew were there and when I slid it, I noticed there was something off. A tear in the seam. I picked it up and examined it. Pulled at the fabric, which had been glued haphazardly and not well. The fabric tore off and revealed nothing but a tight little space between the fabric and the cardboard. A space that could have held something. Money. Jewelry. Documents. But nothing was in there. Odd. I set it aside and pulled down the Hepburn box. Everything was just as it should be. No surprises here.

But I remembered Emily and how crazy she was about Hepburn. Like, maybe she, or someone like her, would find this stuff amazing. As far as I knew there were no mysterious variables that had gone missing pertaining to Hepburn, except those jewels, which most people thought were just a myth. There had never been any evidence that Collette had actually left Hepburn her jewels. Until Stella realized she had at least one set in her basement.

With Harlow, there were several items that had gone missing. The star sapphire ring. A painting. And many of her costumes. All of those items had been cloaked in rumor and mystery.

With Hepburn, that didn't seem to be the case. In fact, she held on to many of her things, which were later auctioned off to raise money for UNICEF.

Wait. Maybe I was missing the point. The items I hid in my hand were missing items, right? Even though most collectors would not know about them, some would.

But I had no idea where they came from or how Justine had gotten them. How could I sell them? I wanted to call Den, but I also didn't want to involve him in this. It wasn't illegal, not really, but it certainly sorted along this side of legal.

If a collector saw these items, it would certainly bring them out. But the question is, would they be the same folks who took the diamonds?

My head spun and the air seemed scant. I needed to lie down. I also needed to take my next dose of medicine. As I dug through my bags, my hands brushed against the notebook and scrapbook I slipped in there earlier. I was curious about what was in them. But I think I was more tired than curious. It'd been quite a day for me. My ankle still wasn't completely pain free and all the moving around wasn't helping.

I took my medicine and went to bed. It was early. But I'd long ago decided to sleep when my body told me to.

My phone awakened me out of what was a deep sleep. Den.

"Hey, did I wake you?"

"Yeah," I mumbled. "What's up?"

"How's things with the family?"

"I didn't make it. Ferry wasn't running. Storm?"

"Ah yeah. It's nasty out. Are you okay?"

"Just tired."

"I've got some news about your friend Stella."

"Oh yeah?"

"She never got on the plane. She's missing."

My blood rushed to the center of me. "Where can she be?" I sat up in bed and glanced at the clock. 11:30. Her plane was scheduled to leave at one. "When did you find this out?"

"We knew about it around two and have been trying to find her. It seems she's slipped right out of our hands."

CHAPTER 43

I begged Den to take me with him to her house. Now that she was missing, the police could enter it legally and search the place. I wanted to be there.

"I can't do that, Babe. You know that."

"You let me come with you when you search Justine's rooms at Club Circe."

"That was different. You were almost like her next of kin. Jesus, Charlotte."

"But what if she has the jewels?" I persisted.

He sighed. "If she does, I'll recover them for you. Don't worry."

I loved Den, but I wanted to get in that house. "I really want to see her place for myself."

He paused. "I can't think of a legal way to have you there. Sorry. I play by the book. You know that." Damned Den. Always playing it straight. "Unless . . . Can you be walking by and . . ."

"Yes,. Yes I can do that." I glanced at the clock. Five a.m. It would take at least an hour to get there. "What time will you be there?"

"Probably not until eight. You've got time."

"Thanks so much Den."

"What are you hoping to find?"

"I'm not sure. Anything related to Gemma or Hepburn, I suppose."

I wanted answers, not just about the murder. But about Justine. How on earth did Justine get involved with someone like Stella? Maude said she thought her apartment was haunted, which, given the strange noises I kept hearing, I could kinda' understand. But I believed there was another explanation and found it difficult to believe Justine was so gullible. But then again, even though she was dead, Justine kept surprising me. "I'm full of surprises. Snort."

Stella knew Justine. Had been in her home. Yet, she sat across the table from me at Layla's and didn't mention it, even though Justine's name was on the book she wanted me to sign. What was she hiding?

Why didn't she tell me she knew Justine?

As I readied for the rip to Brooklyn, I texted my mom and told her I'd be getting in later than I anticipated. I'd probably take the last ferry of the day.

She texted me back: "Are you sure you want to come home?"

That was the first thing I needed. I needed to go home. I needed to see the face of the woman who raised me. I needed to tell them about my father following me. About the broken expression in his eyes. I needed to know what they knew. And I needed the sea air, the sweeping vista out of my bedroom window. I loved Manhattan, but found myself feeling a bit claustrophobic. Sometimes, I just wanted sky and sea, rock and sand.

"Yes, absolutely. It's just that something has come up that I need to take care of."

"Okay. See you later."

I slipped on my jacket, as it was still raining off and on, grabbed my umbrella, tucked it inside my bag, and I was off into the wet, chilly streets of the city. The scent of rain on pavement greeted me as I walked out of the building and toward the subway. A woman wearing a fur coat, walking a tiny dog went by me. What the hell? It wasn't that cold.

I elbowed my way toward the subway platform. Rush hour filled the place with people scurrying off to jobs, schools, and whatever else they had going on. Even though most of the crowd was heading the other way, this side of the track still was crowded with people.

When the train came, I entered it and luckily found a seat next to a pleasant-looking woman dressed in a business suit. She smelled of Chanel and leather.

I blinked and squinted. The poster across from us was a *Golightly Travel* poster. Bright pink. "Whatever happened to Holly Golightly?" across the top then "Coming soon! Zoe Noss as Holly Golightly." A picture of her holding the cigarette, looking very much like Hepburn. God, I abhorred this production. I hated the idea of it. Capote must be turning over in his grave. Not that I cared about him really, just that he was a brilliant writer, and I hated to see the continuing commercialization of his idea, a kind of a twist on it. He was not someone I would have hung out with. But still.

The train came to a lurching stop. People filed off and filed on. It was the rhythm of daily life here.

I gathered my things and exited the train, found my way to the slick street.

I loved Brooklyn. In some ways I felt more at home there than I did in Manhattan. There were a lot of places here where people could actually afford to live.

I turned down the street and began walking toward the

park where I had sat that first night and spotted the cop cars. And an ambulance.

Ambulance? What? My feet felt heavy as I pushed myself to get there quickly. I searched the gathering crowd for Den's face. When I arrived at the ambulance, the crowd parted as they brought out Stella on a stretcher. Was she dead? My stomach roiled. Another dead body?

A hand on my shoulder startled me. I turned to see Den. "She's not dead. But she's in bad shape." His eyes told me there was more. "Whoever did this to her probably thought she was dead. But they left her, suffering." he paused. "I hope she pulls through. I want to nail this bastard."

Den's jaw stiffened.

"What happened?"

"She was raped and beaten. That's all I'm going to say, but there's more. Much more. Sick fucks in this world."

My chest squeezed. I heard myself gasp, then I dug my head into Den's solid shoulder. "Oh god."

CHAPTER 44

I don't know exactly what Stella was involved in, but she was in it deep. This attack was not coincidental. What was she really planning to do in Amsterdam? She had said she was interested in Hepburn and her family, and, of course, they had lived in Holland during the war. But her interest didn't seem that deep. She was more interested in Jewish collectibles and antiques and the Hepburn thing was a side issue, simply relating to what she collected.

I stood at the bottom of the steps to her brownstone and looked toward the door.

"You don't want to go inside. Not yet," Den said, standing next to me. "There's blood everywhere and we've got forensics inside. The cleaners will be here later."

"Thanks for the warning."

"Something I did notice, though, there was some Nazi shit inside."

"Make sense. she collected all sorts of things related to Jewish people."

"Nah, this stuff was new. Like, she was tied up with a Nazi flag."

My heart thudded against my rib cage and I remembered the Nazi flag on Matthews' wall in his tiny smelly apartment. I had stopped searching for neo-Nazis in New York because, frankly, it scared the shit out of me.

A uniformed officer came up to us then. "Detective, we have a guy who says he saw a man here this afternoon. He's working with Jones. They just about have a sketch ready."

"Great." Den's eyes lit. A lead. He liked nothing better than a lead. Wait. Yes, there was one thing he liked better.

We walked over to the van, the makeshift lab or office, if you will.

"Yeah, the man he was tall and thin and had one of those Ichabod Crane faces. You know what I mean. The chin was a little more pointy."

I was surprised to see the artist drawing on the iPad instead of paper.

"And the eyebrows are a little more heavy. Yeah. High forehead, though. Yes, that's it.

The artist mused over his work. The witness nodded his head. "Yeah, that's him."

The artist turned the screen toward us. "Anybody know him?"

I batted my eyes. It couldn't be. "Is that . . ?"

Den turned to face me. "It's Matthews. God damn it. I've got people looking for him and he slipped right in here. He's in Brooklyn. Jesus Christ!"

Officers sped into action. On the phones. I heard more sirens in the distance. I stood out of the way, off the sidewalk, and watched the officers spring into action.

I wondered if the cops were on the right track. If I was Matthews, I'd have taken her tickets and been in Holland by now. "Den," I said as he walked by. He held up a finger and kept going. I followed him. "Den. I don't think he's in Brooklyn."

"What? He was just here."

"Check her purse."

What? Why?"

"See if her tickets are there."

His face lifted. "Oh, shit! Who has the purse?" He looked around and spotted the person he wanted.

I wondered if they'd let him use someone else's ticket. Maybe if she's actually changed the name on them? I don't know. It was a lead worth checking out, though. She could also have e-ticket, which might have been easier to change than paper tickets.

"Her purse is already back at the station," Den said as he walked up to me. "Her phone, too."

"She could have used e-tickets."

"We'll find out. If he's on that plane, we'll have someone waiting for him on the other side."

I was beginning to feel like I was in the way. I wanted to get inside the house, but not now. Not with the mess. "What hospital did you send her to?"

Den's chin rose. 'You've got no business going to the hospital."

"What? I know her. Does she even have any family? She's going to wake up to nobody?"

"Look, I understand your concern. But they won't let you see her. You've got to be family. That's just how it is." he paused. "Don't you have a boat to catch?"

I knew he was right, but anger erupted from the center of my chest. He didn't get to tell me what to do. "It's kind of late now. I'll have to go tomorrow."

Probably best for you to go home, then." Was he telling me what to do, again?

"I'm a big girl Den. I do what I want."

His mouth dropped.

"Detective?" a uniformed officer came up to him. "We need your help over here."

"Be right there." He turned to me. 'I know you think I'm being an asshole. But I'm a cop. I'm working here. And I care about you. I don't want to see you get hurt. I don't know what's going on, but it ain't good."

"Okay, I'll go home." Whatever adrenaline had been sustaining me, was fading. My energy level was plummeting.

He kissed me on my cheek. "Catch you later." I watched him walk away.

I pushed my way through the crowd and walked toward the corner, which was almost empty, crossed the street. The wind was picking up, which made me wonder if more rain was coming. I stepped across a puddle and made my way toward the subway. As I walked along, a familiar face jumped out at me. Fitz Wellston, the producer of the new *Gigi* was heading my way.

"Charlotte?"

"Hey, Fitz."

"What are you doing in my neck of the woods?" He seemed genuinely happy to see me, but it was hard to tell with theater people. They were such a mixed bag of fakery.

His neck of the woods?

"Visiting a friend." *A "friend" who was raped and beaten and was hanging on for her life.*

He nodded. "I was just on my way to grab a bite. Best pierogi in Brooklyn. Would you like to join me?"

He was one of the most annoying people I'd met since starting the project—even Kate didn't like him. And I was getting tired, but for some reason, when he said the word *pierogi,* none of that mattered. Besides, my curiosity was piqued. I had thought he lived in Manhattan. But I wasn't just curious. No. I was a confirmed nonbeliever in coincidences.

He lived in the same neighborhood as Stella, who had connections with Audrey Hepburn—albeit tenuous—and he was the producer of the new *Gigi*.

"Best pierogi in Brooklyn? I can't pass that up. I'd love to join you."

CHAPTER 45

Sometimes when I was upset I couldn't eat. But pierogi were a comfort food for me and Fitz was right. These potato dumplings bathed in butter and onions were the best I'd ever eaten. Thick, but not too thick, and plenty of potato and cheese inside. It was almost as if the company didn't matter. Almost.

Fitz was just as annoying sitting across a table eating pierogi as he was elsewhere. In fact, maybe it was worse. He was a loud eater, smacked his lips and yes, let butter drip down his chin before wiping it off, leaving a disgusting sheen.

"How are rehearsals going?" I asked, hoping to take the conversation elsewhere—other than his life story. To say I wasn't interested would be an understatement.

"Good," he said. "It's going to be a great show."

"Jazz is okay?" She'd passed out at my party—probably because she's not eaten that day.

"She's fine. I make sure she eats."

"Dieting seems to be the thing for these women playing Audrey."

"Well, Audrey was thin," he said and took a swig of his water.

Even though Audrey had gained weight at one point in her life, she quickly lost it. She was very disciplined about her eating. Which was a bit ironic, when you considered that one of the things she stood for was body acceptance.

"Indeed." I paused. "People adore her, still. My best friend Kate considered joining one of these unofficial fan clubs. They get together once a month or so, watch movies, swap collectibles"

He looked up from his last pierogi. 'Not surprising."

"I'm not a collector, but I've inherited some Hollywood stuff from Justine."

He swallowed his bite of pierogi. "What are you going to do with it?"

The woman at the next table dropped the fork loudly on the table and laughed nervously.

His complexion had taken on a pinking tone. Was he blushing? "I'm not sure. What would you do with it?"

He shifted around in his seat. Why was this conversation making him nervous? The server came up to the table and handed him the check. I wasn't sure he was going to answer.

"I suppose if I were broke, I'd sell the stuff. If it had sentimental meaning, I'd keep it. At least for awhile."

"What do you collect?"

"Who said I collect anything?" A twitchy smile.

"You don't? I'm sorry. I assumed."

"I like things from the 1960s, but I wouldn't call myself a collector. I have a few things. But I'm a producer. This is my first big show. I'm not exactly swimming in money." For a moment, his slick self was almost invisible.

I reached for the check.

"Please. I can at least buy you pierogi."

"I've recently inherited a bunch of money. I can get this."

He shrugged. "Fine."

"So you live in the neighborhood?" I asked after the server took the check and a credit card.

"Speaking of inheriting, I've inherited my grandmother's brownstone. I'm not sure I can keep it. But I've been able to manage it so far." He paused, seeming to be reflecting. "I spent a lot of time there as a kid. My parents split up and Gram's place was the solid thing in my life. When she left it to me, well, you can't imagine how it moved me."

Yes, I could.

His head jerked back. "What. You've just inherited your apartment, right?"

I nodded, but I was thinking about him, his discomfort about the subject of collecting. The fact that he lived in the same neighborhood as Stella.

"Where are you off to after here?"

"Home, but I might stop at the hospital first."

"What? Why?"

"My friend that I came to visit is there."

"I'm confused. You said you came to visit her, but now you're saying she's in the hospital."

"I came to see her, but the police were at her place and she was being crated off by an ambulance."

His face paled. "That's awful. I'm sorry to hear it."

"Do you know her, maybe? I mean you are kind of neighbors?"

He smiled. 'I doubt it. Even though this is Brooklyn, it's still New York City. "

"Name is Stella Ross."

His mouth dropped. Then he caught himself. "Sorry, I need to go. It's getting late. You should go, too."

"I take it you know her?"

"No," he said with abruptness. He stood, looked around the place.

I followed his lead and the server arrived and brought my credit card back to me. I took care of business, signed the paper, figured out the tips, kept the right copy, turned around, and Fitz was gone.

Maybe he was waiting for me outside. I exited the place and looked both ways. Yeah. he was gone. And my gut told me he knew Stella. Maybe he was heading to her place when he ran into me. Maybe he had been there earlier. I shivered. I didn't like him, but it was hard to imagine him brutally raping Stella.

But of course, I wasn't sure I could imagine anybody doing that.

I took off down the street toward the subway station—dark, wet streets. Stella on my mind. Just who the hell was she? And who the hell would rape and beat and old woman like that? I knew rape was not about sex. I knew it was about power and rage. Was it just some random attack? Or was she targeted?

I dialed Den. No answer. Of course.

"Den, I'm still in Brooklyn. I ran into someone and we got a bite. Headed for home now. I'm called to see if you—"

"Yeah," he picked up. "Why the hell are you still over there?"

"I ran into a producer I know and got some pierogi. I'm heading home now."

"Good," he said, relief flooding his voice. "There's a rapist in that neighborhood. I want you out of there."

My heart thud against my rib cage. "Was Stella's rape targeted or just some random thing." I stood at the top of the stairs to go down into the station.

"We don't know. But what we do know is your IT guy is on his way to Holland."

"You don't know if he was the rapist?"

"Not yet. But there were at least two other people there, according to forensics."

"You mean . . . one was watching?"

"Jesus Christ. I don't know what I mean." He sounded tired. "This is one messed up case."

"It's not as messed up as you think if Matthews is on his way to Holland. They'll apprehend him over there, won't they?"

"Yes, I don't think he can slip away from us now."

I thought about him and the way he creeped me out. I didn't know why Justine liked him so much. Okay, most IT guys were quiet and kind of anti-social. But this guy looked and moved like a marionette version of Ichabod Crane, and was so persistent about patches and updates. Plus he infected my computer with spyware, along with a camera placed through my house. I was certain it was him—even though there was no proof of it being the same person.

What I wasn't certain about is what exactly he had to do with Stella and what they knew about the murder of Gemma Hollins.

CHAPTER 46

I don't know what was freaking me out more—my father showing up or Stella's attack. I searched through the apartment before going to bed. Checking in all the closets, under the beds, behind the curtains.

After an hour of tossing and turning, I rose out of the bed and downed a couple of Kate's sleeping pills, then sat down at my computer until they took effect.

I fired it up and keyed in "Neo Nazis in New York city."

Neo Nazi Rally Draws Crowd

Nazi Flyers Found Near School

Neo Nazis- Beat Up Twin Brothers over "Anti-Fascist" Sticker.

So, it was true that they were here. In the heart of "liberal" New York City. I shouldn't have been surprised, but I was. What surprised me more is that Justine hired this guy. Did she not look into his background before letting him into her home on a regular basis?

I wondered if he'd been apprehended by now. Cold crept over me. Did he kill Gemma? Did he take the jewels? If he hurt Stella, then one assumed he could have been hurting other women all along.

Why those particular jewels, when I had a closet full of other stuff?

People loved Audrey Hepburn. Sometimes people wanted to feel close to someone by owning their things. But Audrey barely owned these diamonds. She never even wore them. Huge diamonds were not her thing. She was into simpler things. Understated.

I knew how much she hated the Nazis, which made all this feel like it had to do with her past. But we had no proof of that. And why would neo-Nazis want something of Audrey Hepburn's if she was so anti-Nazi. And she was.

One of the most hidden things about her background was that her parents knew Hitler and they even attended a party where he was the guest. She didn't like to talk about it. But she was a child and had no say in anything her parents did. Still, she didn't want the association. I got that. I'm sure her mother's tune changed a good deal during the war when her brother was shot and her children were starving. Being interested in a movement intellectually and socially was one thing—but seeing it play out in your life?

I didn't know how to follow this thread or if I should follow it. Was there a neo-Nazi headquarters? Should I show up on their door and ask questions?

I'd done a lot for a story—snuck in places, eavesdropped, lured people out of hiding, setting myself up, gave people cash for information, and well, the list went on. "Anything for a story, Doll."

But I think this is where I stopped. Where the story stopped. It felt like giving this neo-Nazi bullshit attention was giving it voice. I didn't want to do that. I would not give the neo-Nazis a visit. I would not do "anything" for a story. Sorry, Justine.

No. I wasn't going to track down any of their offices and I wasn't going to write about any of this. I was going to keep moving ahead with the narrative. No sidetracks into Audrey's parents and Hitler.

My eyes felt blurring and heavy. The pills were taking effect.

I shut my computer off and made my way into the bedroom.

Thanks to the pills, I'm sure, I heard nothing and didn't wake up until it was past time for my first dose of medicine. My brain was clear, though, as if it had been swept away by cobwebs. The story. The narrative. Steering it away from Nazi bullshit. But there was a good element here and that element was Collette. Collette was Stella's interest. And the relationship between Collette and Audrey Hepburn could be explored a little more in my story. As far as I knew, nobody had focused on this at all.

After coffee, medicine, and breakfast, I sat at my computer and pounded out some thought and notes.

When my phone rang, it registered as nothing more than a pain in the ass. I let it ring. The words were falling out of me and I couldn't stop now. The phone rang again. I picked it up.

"Are you coming home or what?"

Oh shit. I'd forgotten.

"Probably tomorrow. I'm sorry. I should have called."

"You're welcome here any time, you know that. But I keep expecting you and you never show." Mom was trying not to show her anger. But I knew that voice.

"I'll explain when I get home." Waves. Rocky sand. Images that played in my mind. "I'm in the middle of this Hepburn book and I've just hit a vein."

She paused. "So when are you coming?"

I glanced at the time. 'Probably tomorrow morning. I'll let you know if something changes." And I would. I feel so bad that I didn't call yesterday and let her know I'd been delayed.

I wanted to get home. I needed to see my mom and Gram, women who raised me, who loved me. I needed to see their faces when I told them that my father had been following me. I needed to know what they knew about him.

When I thought he was dead, it was hard enough. But then finding out he was alive and had just ignored us all these years filled me with rage. But after getting a good look at him, I knew there was more to his story. I needed to know, not that I ever imagined any kind of relationship with him. At all.

My door buzzed. "Hold on, Ma, someone's buzzing." I walked over to the intercom. "Yes."

"Officer Den Brophy to see you." My heart rippled a bit.

"Please send him up." I hoped he had news for me. Hoped they caught Matthews. "I've gotta go, Ma."

"I heard," she said with a flat note.

CHAPTER 47

"Can I get a drink?" Den stood in my doorway, haggard, rumpled.

"Of course. Beer?"

"Yeah, that'd be great."

I walked to the kitchen, reached into the fridge for two beers, then walked back into the living room, where Den was pacing. He looked up at me. "This fucking case is going to kill me."

I sat the beer down on the table. He reached for it and lifted it to his lips, took a drink, sat it back down, and paced again.

I sat down. "What's going on?"

"It's just a mess. Nothing is connecting. Nothing is making any sense." He reached for the beer, drank, and took it with him as he paced. "My boss is on my ass. 'I want results.'" He used air quotes around results. "Snot-nosed Ivy Leaguer gonna tell me how to do my job? What the fuck?"

"Have you heard from Amsterdam?"

He stopped pacing, nodded. "Yeah. But it's not him. It's

not Matthews. Claimed he found the tickets on the street and has always wanted to go to Holland."

I laughed. "As if."

"Yeah right." He sat down next to me. "The thing is, I get the feeling we're being led around by our noses. Smoke and mirrors. Nothing is what it should be."

"And yet?"

"I don't have shit."

Heavy eyes, rimmed in dark circles, Den looked exhausted.

"That's not true. You're tired. Why don't you get some sleep and we'll talk about this all tomorrow? Can I get you something to eat?"

He shook his head no. "Not hungry. Can't sleep."

He was wired. I'd seen him like this before, when we were working together trying to figure out the Jean Harlow craziness, and I wasn't in love with him then.

"Can I help?"

His head tilted. "I'm trying to keep my personal and professional life separate. You know?" He slid his hands back through his auburn hair.

"Admirable. But impossible." I grinned. "You know cops go home every day with stories. That's just how it is." Did my father talk with my mom? His mother? Me? I couldn't remember. My memories of him slipped out of my mind years ago, replaced by day-to-day stuff, like trying to pay the bills, making sure we had food. Anger well up inside of me. Daughter of a cop. A cop who disappeared and was now back, following me, wandering the streets of the city.

I reached for my writing tablet. I kept them all over the place in case I had a thought about the book I was working on and needed to write it down.

"I can't get the image of Stella out of my mind. I've seen some shit, but that was hideous. It'll be a miracle if she survives." he drank from his beer. "But I don't know if she looked familiar. I don't know if I've seen her before. Or if she just looked like all the older ladies I've known in my life."

"You didn't question her?"

"Nah, this was this first time I'd gotten a good look at her."

I scribbled the word Gemma on the tablet. The word diamonds. Stella. Matthews. Neo Nazis.

"What do you know about neo-Nazis in the city?"

Den lifted an eyebrow. "They are nobody to mess with, but I've not run much into them. I know they've done some rallies, distributed flyers, stuff like that. This whole thing? It doesn't make sense they'd be involved. Maybe Matthews is working alone. He's not a part of the group."

"I know this is a stretch, but Audrey Hepburn was a kind of a spy during the war. Stella said she's a hero to some people."

"So what does that have to do with Gemma?"

I shrugged. 'Nothing. Remember, she was allergic to the medicine. Otherwise, she'd not have died. The working theory is she was a not the target and I was supposed to be the decoy."

He laughed. 'That's your theory. I still don't buy it. But let's roll with it. Say someone tried to drug you, you'd have gotten sick enough to provide a distraction from the real crime going down—the heist in your bedroom, which is unofficial, by the way. Off the books. So I can't officially use that as my theory in any case."

My face heated. "I'm sorry to put you in that position. I really need to figure out what I'm going to do with all of that stuff. Kate and I need to take stock and I need to talk with a lawyer or someone."

He quieted.

"So what's your theory?"

"What?" He downed his beer.

"Your theory about the case?"

"I'm looking into the Hollywood angle."

I wrote down Fitz Wellston. "Yesterday you know I had a pierogi with this guy, the producer of the new *Gigi*. I don't really like him. And Kate despises him. But he was in Stella's neighborhood and I thought it was suspicious. Turns out he lives there."

"And?"

"You might want to check him out. He seemed like he was nervous about something. We talked about collecting a bit. Said he collects things from the 1960s."

"But those diamonds are older."

"True, but they were Audrey Hepburn's and he's working on *Gigi*, a play of hers. I don't know if he'd steal diamonds, and I sure as shit don't know if he'd kill anybody. But I'm telling you, there's something not quite right about him."

He slipped his phone out of his back pocket and keyed something in, sent it off. "We'll get him checked out." He finished his beer.

"Another one?"

"You read my mind." He reached over and brought my face to his, kissed me, sending tingles through my whole body. Den.

I walked into the kitchen and grabbed another beer, opened it.

When I came back into the room, he was fast asleep.

CHAPTER 48

I woke up the next morning my favorite way, naked, warm, and with a hot, naked guy waking me up with sexy attention.

After, Den made his way to the shower and I made coffee. We met at the kitchen island, which was our usual thing. I had a usual thing with a guy. A guy I like. Hell, a guy I loved. I couldn't be happier. And more surprised. But life surprises you. Most of the time, it's not in a good way.

I set up my medicine regime.

Den walked in. "How is it going with the new meds?"

"Okay. It's hard to tell because I've not been taking them long. But so far, so good."

He poured himself coffee. "I've got a meeting this morning with my boss. I have a feeling he's going to pull me from the Hollins case and make like the Hollins case and Stella's are two separate things."

"He may be right." I downed my last bit of medicine.

Den sat down at the island. "Could be. The only connection is the jewels and I can't really mention them yet."

"You know what? I'm sorry. I really need to figure this

out. I'll call Susan Strohmeyer today and see what I should do about it. I mean there are so many reasons I don't want anybody to know about the stash." I was afraid I'd be inundated by potential buyers. I was also afraid being held responsible for stolen goods—as I'm almost certain that's what they are.

"Look, I know you want to keep Justine's memory pure and all that. I get it. But damn. I don't think she meant for you to have to deal with all of this shit. The Harlow thing. Now this. And I can't keep covering for you."

Justine had a solid reputation. Was well-respected. The fact that she was hoarding valuable stolen Hollywood memorabilia didn't make sense. But there it was. And I was afraid of what the press would do with this if it leaked. How it would affect her memory.

I drank my coffee, waiting for the caffeine to take effect, thinking I probably needed another cup.

"Did you hear that noise last night?" Den asked, reaching for a banana from the fruit bowls I kept on the counter. Fruit was safe. I could eat fruit.

"I heard nothing last night. What noise?"

"Same kind of thing from the other night. I think you've got a ghost. It woke me up again."

"Ghost? Come on, Den."

"All I know is what I heard. In the middle of the light. Coming from Justine's room. What the hell, Charlotte?"

I laughed. "This is an old building. There's all kinds of strange noises in here."

He peeled the banana and took a bite, swallowed. "Not like that. In fact, I'm afraid for you. There's something in here. I can't believe you didn't wake up."

I didn't wake up last night. But there had been nights I did awaken, frightened because of the noises. It was disturbing. But I was a fact checker, a researcher, along with being a writer, and I needed proof of everything. "Nobody can prove ghosts exist."

"Not true. There's plenty of proof." His phone buzzed with a text message. He picked it up and read it. "Stella is still alive this morning and she's conscious. Talking, even. Christ. I can't believe it"

My heart rippled with excitement. "I want to see her."

He sat up straighter. "I thought you were going home."

Oh. yes, there was that.

"I will. Just not today I feel a sense of urgency about this."

"I can't stop you from seeing Stella, but be careful." He flung his banana peel into the trash. "And also? Go easy on her." a sad look came over his face. It tugged at me. Den. I was in love with a good guy. Who would have thought? He downed the rest of his coffee. "Gotta run. Meeting with the boss and, yeah, trying to get a bead on this character in Holland. He should be getting back to the states today."

"So where is Matthews?"

"Beats me." he leaned in to kiss me. "Just as long as he's not around you anymore." His breath was hot on my skin. He kissed me and I wanted to wrap myself around him and never let him go. So unlike me.

When I thought about Matthews in the place, it bothered me more than the thought of a ghost. Matthews was corporeal, real, I could touch him. To me, that was more frightening. He was a neo-Nazi, which scared the shit out of me. Twisted thinking was dangerous—it lead to murder. Hell, it led to war. To have such hatred in my home unsettled me, but the truth of the matter was you never really knew how people felt about others. Deep down inside, were they racist? Were they homophobic? People wore masks—that much I knew. And, as far as I was concerned, one form of hatred was just as bad as the other. It was like cancer.

Did people leave traces of psychic energy behind when they'd been in a place? Not like a ghost. Just energy. If I allowed myself to dwell too much on him being here, I might want to get the place cleansed myself. Just to be safe. I could see the mental uplift from such an exercise.

MAYBE THIS WAS my way into Stella. Maybe I should tell her I knew about her relationship with Justine. Maybe I should ask for her help.

Bells. Whistles. Yes. That's exactly what I would do. Invite her here, once she was better. Invite her here to do another cleansing and see just what exactly the old woman was up to.

CHAPTER 49

The hospital was dingy and not well lit. As I walked through the door, a feeling of claustrophobic helplessness overcame me for a moment. What a lousy place. Who could heal in this mess? I held flowers in my hand, as I approached the chipped check-in counter. "I'm looking for Stella Ross."

The man looked up at me from behind huge owlish glasses, circa 1985. "She's on the second floor. Room 224."

No questions. He just told me where she was. What if her attacker came by for more? I shuddered.

"Thanks." I walked across the floor. I noted that they weren't dirty as I had originally thought, just old and faded, as was the wallpaper in the waiting area, peeling at the edges.

Why had they brought Stella here? She was a well-off woman. I was certain she must have insurance. The neighborhood she lived in wasn't exactly swank, but the old Brownstones went for millions. It must be a mistake that they brought her here. I'd been in a lot of hospitals in this city and had not seen one in this condition.

I pressed the elevator button, making a mental note to

make sure I washed my hands properly as soon as I could. The door opened and I stepped inside, pressed the 2.

When the doors opened, I was surprised to find this floor a little better lit and more modern. My stomach settled. This was more like it.

My eyes skimmed the room numbers. I turned and headed the other way once I realized I was going in the wrong direction.

I spotted a police officer standing outside of her door. This was more like it.

He eyeballed me.

"I'm a friend of Stella's," I said. Good-looking man.

"ID please."

Tucking the flowers in the crevice of my arm, I dug in my purse and extracted my license. He glanced at it, then back at me.

"Okay. go ahead inside. We're only allowing fifteen minutes."

"Has she had other visitors?"

His eyebrows gathered and he crossed his arms, not replying. Okay then.

I stood, girding my loins. Who knew what I'd find inside? I had only spoken to her three times, twice on the phone and once in person. She was going to be shocked to see me. And maybe on guard. Uncomfortable. Which was good, that is just where I wanted her. Yes, I felt bad for her—more than bad for her. But at the same time, her bald-faced lie to me . . . Just exactly what was this woman up to?

I walked into the room.

"Charlotte?" the woman on the bed looked small and frail. One eye was swollen almost shut.

Butterflies. Sinking stomach. My heart ached for her.

"Jesus, Stella, you look terrible." I handed the flowers to her.

"Oh!" she squealed. "You brought me flowers! Thank you."

She set them on the bedside table, not without some trouble. I noted her bruised wrists, where her attacker must have held her down.

"Oh yes, I'm sure I look bloody awful, but that's what happens when you're attacked by a mad man."

"I'm so sorry that happened to you." And I was. Deeply sorry. But I was glad she hadn't gone to Amsterdam. "I can't believe how you've bounced back. Yesterday, you were comatose."

"The miracle of modern medicine I guess."

"Don't let looks fool you." A nurse had wandered in. "Don't stay long. She needs her rest." She picked up Stella's wrist, taking her pulse.

After he left, Stella sank back into her pillow.

"What an awful thing to have happened to you."

She blinked a long slow blink. I noted a quiver in her chin.

"Stella, do you think it was targeted? Or was it just happenstance?"

She squinted through her one open eye.

"I don't know you well at all. But here's what I know. Since we had tea, I found out that you knew Justine."

She crossed her bruised arms. Black and blue, yellow circles. It wasn't as if I had no feelings for her plight, it was just that we all needed answers. "Well that was no big secret."

"But you didn't tell me."

She looked away from me again.

"What's going on here? I may be way out of line, but I think you're in some kind of trouble. I think the attack had something to do with it. You're lucky to be alive."

"Yeah, lucky, right," she muttered.

"Is there something I can do to help?"

Her eyebrows gathered and she shot me a glare, but didn't say a word.

We sat for a few moments in silence. She obviously was not going to tell me a thing. Whatever was going on, she was either too scared or angry to tell me. Besides, I might be the absolutely wrong person to open up to—since the heist and murder happened in my place.

If the direct approach didn't work, I had another up my sleeve.

"So, Maude tells me you cleaned Justine's place. You know I'm living there now."

She nodded a weary nod. She was getting tired.

"It seems like the place is still haunted."

Her chin came forward in my direction. "Impossible."

"I'm telling you something wakes me up every night. Moaning. Sobbing. Creaking. "

"The pace has been cleansed. Unless . . ."

"Unless?"

"If there are spirits in Justine's Turner's home, it must be her."

My heart raced, even though I knew it was impossible. "What? Justine??"

She nodded. One eyebrow lifted. "Unfinished business."

She was deadly serious. I bit my lip. How could she believe such nonsense? She was a medical doctor, for godsake. An intellectual. A collector of meaningful Jewish memorabilia. Yet, my stomach knotted.

"Well, you're just going to have to get better quickly to do another cleansing. I can't have Justine hang around."

She laughed a little, then winced. A look of relief washed over her face. If I was reading her correctly, she was quite pleased to be invited back into Justine's home. Which is exactly what I wanted.

"Welcome," said the spider to the fly.

CHAPTER 50

On the way back on the subway, I spotted another *Golightly Travels* sign. Zoe's face, looking very much like Audrey Hepburn, emblazoned across the poster. "Whatever became of Holly Golightly?" Whatever, indeed.

They certainly were promoting this series.

I allowed the train to lull me. Its constant low humming noise. The moment. And just a few people on this train. Quiet people. I closed my eyes, with thoughts of Hepburn, Zoe, *Golightly Travels,* and the swinging sixties on my mind. "Free love? What was that? Hippies? I don't know," my Gram had said. "I was a mom on Cloister Island. I missed all the fun."

My mom had responded. "We all did, Ma. You made sure of it."

Memories and dreams were colliding in my mind. When I opened my eyes, my heart nearly stopped. My father was sitting across the aisle from me. I closed my eyes. I must be dreaming. He can't really be here.

But when I opened them back up, he was still there,

watching me, with that expression on his face. Troubled. Haunted.

My heart marched like a drum. Sweat beads pricked to my forehead. He didn't look away.

Bastard. After all these years, coming around, following me, watching me.

I looked away, pretended not to see him. Even as the blood rushed through me. My neck popping with my pulse.

I should have gone home. I needed to see Mom and Gram. Needed to know what was going on with him. I really didn't recognize him. Kate did. But his face pulled at me like a misty dream. The more I tried to remember, like smoke, it vanished.

I had prepared myself for a long train ride, settled in. But now, I didn't care where the next stop was. I pulled my shit together and stood. Legs shaking. Why? Fuck him. I'm not going to let him scare me. Unsettle me.

He remained seated, but his eyes never left me. Cold sweat through my body, traveling up and down my spine with a shudder. I exited the train and found my way to street level. Central Park. Not too far from home. I looked around, breathing heavily, heart still pounding. He had definitely stayed on the train.

When I first emerged from the train station, I had a moment of feeling like I was lost. I knew the city, knew the subways, but my father's appearance sent my head spinning. I kept walking. I'd figure it out as I went along. I saw Central Park in the distance, got my bearings, and walked toward it in the crowd. Always in the crowd.

I sucked in air, like there was a shortage of it. My lungs hurt from the deep, rapid breaths. I entered the park and found a bench. When I sat, my shivering legs thanked me. You can talk yourself out of stress and fear, you can intellectualize and believe you are not afraid, but the body knows.

Just ask my shivering thighs, sweaty palms, and drumming heart. Get a grip.

I closed my eyes and counted to ten slowly. My father. What was going on with him? This man I thought had died. This man who was a cop. Suddenly there. All the time.

I opened my eyes; my heartrate had slowed to almost normal. The sound of a saxophone rang out and my attention drifted to the song. Some jazz tune, vibrating in my chest. The player was close. I looked around and spotted him standing off to the right of a long tree-lined throughway. On the other side, a photographer was shooting two men dressed in tuxedos, holding colorful umbrellas. Maybe it was a wedding picture. A Muslim woman walked by me, covered, with just her fresh-looking face sticking out of her hijab. Her long dress wafted around her as she moved. A man covered in tattoos walked by. As he passed, I noted a dragon on his calf.

My heartrate was back to normal. I drew in more air. Whatever was going on with my father was his issue, not mine. I didn't want any part of him.

A woman walked by with her corgi on a leash. The park was quiet here. Security is pretty thick. A woman security office built like a bulldog of a man walked by, vigilant.

But he was my father. He obviously needed help. Is this why he disappeared all those years ago? Was he sick?

Another man walked by with tattoos. A swastika on his arm. I squinted and blinked. Was that right? Was it a swastika? Yes, it was. He caught me looking and sneered, sending shards of fear through me. Either he thought I wanted him or he knew his disgusting display caught my attention--which is exactly what he wanted. I looked away. Quickly. Enraged at his audacity. Walking around with that thing on his arm, as if it was an okay thing to do.

My cell phone buzzed. It was Susan Strohmeyer returning my call.

"Hi Susan."

"Charlotte. How can I help you?"

How to find the words about Justine's secret million-dollar stash?

"I've got a bit of a problem."

"Okay."

"I found something in Justine's apartment."

"Your apartment." she corrected me. It was so hard to think of Justine's luxurious Upper East side apartment as mine.

"My apartment."

"Yes? You've found some things?"

"I think they might be stolen things."

Silence on the other end of the phone.

"Valuable Hollywood memorabilia."

"What makes you think they were stolen? Justine was a wealthy woman. Why would she steal anything?"

"No. I think she perhaps bought the stuff from people who stole it. Some of these items are things that have been missing for years--like Harlow's ring, for example."

"I see," she replied. "I'm still going through her estate. These items might be listed. But you have to understand that I've got pages and pages of things. And her will is . . . problematic, as you know. There are still these legal hoops and loops."

Justine. Always in control. Even after she died.

"Okay. You're the lawyer. Advise me on the best thing to do with this stuff."

"Just leave it there until I do my research."

"There is a problem with that."

"What do you mean."

"Something's been stolen. My cop boyfriend can't keep a lid on it forever without jeopardizing his case and his career."

A pause. "I see. A valuable item?"

"Yes."

A long drawn out sigh. "I'll get right on this."

CHAPTER 51

I felt better about things as I walked into the apartment. Just speaking with Susan helped lighten my psychological burden about the items in the secret room. Now if I could help nab Gemma's killer, I'd be very happy with myself. But a wave of weariness threatened to take over, I remembered my medicine. Such a pain in the ass. But, from everything I had read about it, the regime was getting great results. It was a little too hard for me to tell because it was early on, but I think it was helping. But maybe it was my diet.

I had never been a great dieter and was proud of myself for sticking to it. I don't know how these actresses kept so slim, but I had an inkling. Many of them were on drugs to help them control their appetite and some of them were completely anorexic. The whole weight issue is over *Golightly Travels* like a cloud. Audrey Hepburn was almost too thin, in my book. Yet some women used her as an example they tried to emulate. Which was sad for a few reasons, not the least of which was that Audrey herself had a lot to say about body image and being happy with the way you are.

The other reason is that Audrey had almost died from starvation. The war killed thousands through the lack of food. It came at a time when she needed food and nutrition the most and it affected her weight and health for the rest of her life.

True, she kept up the thinness by being disciplined throughout her life. But after having almost started and eating tulip bulbs to stay alive, that discipline may have seemed less like she was depriving herself. As Maude had said "when you almost starve to death, it affects the rest of your life in profound ways."

For Audrey, her near starvation, and the cruelty she saw during the war created a sense of gratitude for her own life and an overwhelming compassion for others.

Her compassion marked her as a person and an actress. It only added to her beauty.

I scribbled my thoughts down. I was considering a chapter on food. Audrey had spoken enough about it and it was on record how she had almost died.

My cell rang. I picked up.

"What exactly is going on with you, Charlotte?" Mom asked. "One minute you're coming home. The next you're not."

"I'm sorry mom. A friend of mine was attacked yesterday and I went to see her today. Now I'm exhausted."

"A friend? Who?"

"Well, not exactly a friend. An acquaintance. Stella Ross. that collector I met."

"You mean the woman you met for tea?"

"Yes." I didn't want to go into the whole sordid tale with her over the phone. A tale that might lead nowhere, though I had a feeling about Stella. She might hold the key to everything. But then again, maybe that was my imagination.

"But it seemed like, I don't know. It seemed like there was an urgency to your coming home. Like there was a reason for it."

"There is, but I don't want to talk about it over the phone."

"You getting married?" her voice raised, lifted.

"What? No! I'm not getting married."

She sighed. 'Okay, okay. I guess I can wait until you get home. Maybe tomorrow, hey?"

"Maybe. Let's see how Stella pulls through this." A tug toward home pulled at me. But Gemma tugged harder right now. As did the heist.

Going home. Getting answers from my grandmother and mom about what was going on with my father, in person, was near the top of my list. But my gut told me that something was about to crack with this case, and I wanted to be here for it.

"How's the book going?"

"Good. I'm so glad to be done with *Breakfast at Tiffany's* and *Sabrina*. But I've had enough of *Breakfast at Tiffany's* to last a lifetime."

"I never liked the movie." Her mantra whenever it came up. "It was a sad movie. It wasn't a life I could relate to at all. I don't know why people think it had anything to do with women in the sixties. I couldn't relate to it at all."

Mom's life was on Cloister Island. She was a teenager then, with a strict Catholic mom and community. She'd never thought to move into the city on her own. It just wasn't done. She grew up almost afraid of the city and all its evils. "I'm happy on my little island." another one of her mantras. I didn't know whose life more represented women in the 1960s, mom's or Holly Golightly, but I did know that lives were not that easily placed into pockets of meaning. Women's lives, in particular, were more nuanced than a movie or book could begin to portray. But the very island mom found comfort in, I had hated. I had wanted off the island. I had wanted to live in New York city, be a famous writer. But when my health took a dive, Cloister Island became a refuge for me. And now, with my Dad following me all over the city with that haunted sad expression, Cloister Island loomed in my heart.

"I like Audrey," Mom continued. "But the movie? Nah. I still don't know what the big deal about it is."

"We'll talk about that someday, Ma."

"If you ever come home."

I cracked a smile. "I will. Soon. I promise."

CHAPTER 52

I was exhausted, but I needed to speak with Den about a few things and run some ideas by him. I couldn't get through. So I left several messages and fell asleep.

The phone awakened me. I looked at the clock. 2:30 a.m. I picked up the phone, figuring it was Den, not bothering to look at the screen. "Yeah?"

A garbled cough. "Stay away from Stella." The voice sent shock waves through me. I sat up, wide awake.

"What? Who is this?"

"Stay away from Stella. I will kill you." Click.

My face heated and tears rushed to the brim of my eyes. Why was I crying? Fear? Sadness? Being awake at this time of night with a death threat?

I dialed Den. Two rings and he picked up. "What?"

"Someone just called me and told me to stay away from Stella or they'd kill me." I hated the waited I sounded. Needy. Frightened. I'd worked on self for years to not show those qualities, and yet here I was.

"Okay. Calm down. What did the person sound like? Man or woman?"

"Definitely a man, maybe kind of, um, robotic?"

"He was using a device to manipulate his voice."

Big words for a man just awakened in the middle of the night. But then again, he was used to it.

"I think you're right. That's exactly what it sounded like."

"Who knew you went to visit Stella?" I imagined him sitting on the edge of his bed in his boxer shorts and T-shirt, which was usually what he slept in.

"Just you, the cop at the door, and my mom."

"How about Kate?"

"I haven't talked with Kate. She's getting ready for Fashion Week."

"Can you bring your phone into the office tomorrow?"

My trip home was fading further into the future. "Sure. first thing in the morning?"

He yawned. "Yeah."

"Why haven't you returned my other calls?"

"The case has me reeling. Let's talk about it tomorrow, okay?" An edge of abruptness in his voice. "Okay?"

"Of course," I said. But my gut told me there was more going on here, so much more that he wasn't telling me about. I wasn't sure it all had to do with the case. "Just so you know, I spoke with Susan, and she's looking into things for me. You know, about the stuff in the secret closet."

"Good." He quieted.

"Good night, Den."

"See you in the morning."

I sank back into my pillow, heart calmer, but still racing. What the hell? Why would someone not want me to see Stella so much that they would threaten to kill me?

I rolled over onto my side. It wasn't my first death threat, but it was my most perplexing. Stella was an interesting character, sure. A collector. A ghost cleanser. A one-time medical doctor. All of these didn't necessarily add up. But lives needn't happen in a neat linear fashion sometimes. Not all doctors loved what they did, so they quit as soon as they possibly could. But to go from being a doctor to a ghost hunter was a long stretch. The ghost hunter thing sort of matched with the collector trait. I guessed.

Ghost hunter. Of course, the "Ghost Buster" song popped into my mind. I laughed. Then Scooby Doo drifted in and out of my mind. These images and sounds were keeping me from sleeping. So I got up. And went to my computer, typed in "Ghost Hunters in New York City."

Good God. Where to start? There were paranormal societies. Ghost Hunters. Investigators. They were everywhere.

What a scam. These people were making good money doing their 'investigating." Almost as if on cue, my own ghost began to moan. And even though I knew it wasn't a ghost, was troubling because, well, what was it?

I walked toward the sound, which was definitely coming from Justine's room. I flipped on the lights and took in the room, standing watch, as if waiting for someone to claim it. That would not be me. I had no desire to sleep in Justine's bedroom, even though it was beautiful and was bigger than two of the largest rooms put together in my family's Cloister Island home. Floor to ceiling windows, and a settee draped by a silky turquoise shawl, which was undisturbed since her death. Otherwise the room was stark white and cream, with blonde furniture. A king-size platform bed, flanked on either side by low, built-in wall tables. Above each lamp were huge inlays into the wall—each held a huge sleek, matching long vase. Hanging lights added even more elegance to the room. In the center between the two inlays was another one, exactly above the bed, which held a painting—an art deco version of a goddess? Nymph? Painted in tones of pink and flesh.

The high-pitched moan rang out again. I walked toward the sound and opened the closet door. Off to the left of it was an air vent close to the ceiling. Maybe that's where the noise was coming from. I pulled a chair over from Justine's dressing table, climbed up on it, and listened. The air vent was silent. I stood, still in my nightshirt and slippers, waiting.

Nothing.

I climbed down just as the noise rang out again. It was coming from the secret closet. Definitely.

I pushed the door and reached for the light. As I flipped it on, a shadow or a mist moved across the room.

What the hell was that? A bat? A bird?

Perfume tickled my nose. I sneezed. This room didn't smell of Topaz, Justine's favorite perfume. It held the scent of perfumes from countless stars. The scent clung to scarves and hats and whatever else was in this room.

I examined the room and it all looked fine. There was nothing in here--except whatever it was that flew off—and it had seemed to fly off. Or maybe there was nothing there. Maybe it was just my eyes getting used to the light. There wasn't a trace of anything else.

When I turned to leave the room, the velvet cardboard boxes caught my eye. Something about the way the light shone on one showed how wobbly looking it was, as is if someone had torn it open and then glued it back together. Its edges were not quite lined up. I picked it up and picked at the edge. The velvet came away without much effort. When I tore it off, I saw that there was a space between the cardboard box and the velvet, enough space for something to have been inside hidden. But there was nothing inside now. Had there ever been?

I checked out the other boxes it was sitting with. Each one also looked off. I tore them apart.

Whatever had been tucked inside the pretty boxes—if anything ever was—was definitely long gone. But it would have been the perfect hiding place for something.

I couldn't help but wonder if these boxes were like this before the heist. I had no idea. Maybe the person who took the box of jewels wasn't really looking for the jewels, but whatever was tucked inside a box.

I talked myself out of that theory. Come on. Audrey Hepburn diamond designed by Collette's husband. That's what they were after, not some clandestine something tucked in old boxes.

CHAPTER 53

I tossed and turned and dreamed and dreamed.

I dreamed I was at Audrey Hepburn's funeral, standing in line for the viewing. When I finally got there, I looked down at her and reached in to take off her skull and peer into her head. I was grasping, hoping, to find some thoughts. Some way of understanding her better.

When I awakened, I had to take a few moments to mull that over. What an odd dream.

I'd grown accustomed to the "biographer brain" where the person I was writing about almost became alive in my head. If I saw a piece of jewelry Jean Harlow would have worn, for example, I'd think, "Jean would love that," as though she were still alive. Same thing with clothes and art.

But this dream was a first for me. It was creepy and funny all at once.

Some dreams cling to you through the day. And this one was. Even as I walked into the police station carrying my overnight bag, the image of peering inside Hepburn's head clung to me. Hard to shake it.

I walked up to the woman behind the desk. "I'm here to see Den Brophy."

She nodded. "Just a moment."

The place was a typical police station. Utilitarian. Off-white bricks, Wanted posters, and less-than-friendly sorts hanging out in the waiting area. A man sat in a crumpled heap in a chair in the corner, nursing something in a coffee cup. I'm betting it wasn't just coffee. A woman stood against the wall, heavy make-up, sexy dress, maybe here to visit a boyfriend.

It stank of stale coffee, a hint of body odor, and cheap perfume. I held my bags close.

Den popped through the door. Damn, he looked good. I ate him up with my eyes, had to stop myself from reaching out to him and wrapping myself around him. But we were in a cop station. His station. That wouldn't be good. He smiled that crooked smile of his. Maybe he was thinking similar thoughts.

"Charlotte," he said. "Good to see you."

"I brought my phone."

"Follow me," he said and led the way to his office.

As we walked through, I felt eyes on me. Scanned the room and saw him. Lou—what was his last name? I'm not sure I'd ever gotten it. Lou with the beefy thighs. I turned toward Den, not allowing eye contact with Lou at all. My face heated.

We finally go to the office he shared with his partner and I took a seat.

"How's the case going?"

"We don't have much of a case right now at all." His face was tight with stress. I was sorry I had brought it up.

I dug in my hand bag and found my phone, handed it to him.

"I'm not sure how much good this will do." he sighed.

"These guys are IT experts. They know their shit. I'll tell you what, if this is what police work is becoming . . . I hate the fucking computers. I'm not sure I even like these things." he held up the phone.

"Well, we have to try, right?"

"Yeah, Rogers will be here in a minute. I see you've got your bag. Are you finally going back to Cloister?"

"Yeah, I really have to go. Some strange shit's been going on and I need to talk with Mom and Gram. Plus I need to head back into the studio in a few days. My time off is almost over."

I hated to even think about it. I didn't miss it at all. At first, it was new and interesting. But now, it bored me.

"What kind of stuff?"

Rogers entered the room and took my phone. "Be right back." He turned to me. "Hey," he said.

"Hey," I said and smiled. We'd been here before, Rogers and me.

"What kind of stuff?" Den asked me again.

"My dad's been following me."

Den's chin lifted. "Oh yeah? You sure?"

"Oh yes. How crazy is my life, Den. I thought he was dead. Twenty years later he resurfaces, wants to be a part of my life, and is now following me."

Den picked up a pen, tapped a few times on the desk. "Does he scare you?"

I thought about that question for a few beats. "Not exactly scary. He unsettles me. I don't really remember him. Just parts of him. But he seems broken. I don't want anything to do with him. I want him to leave me alone. I just need to know what Mom and Gram know, so I can figure out how to deal with getting rid of him."

"Why not give the guy a break and find out from him

where he's been?" Den tapped on the desk with the pen again. I quashed my urge to grab the pen and break it.

My face heated. "I don't think you understand. We thought he was dead. He disappeared. No word. No money. We struggled for years, Den. I mean, struggled. He turned his back on us. In the worst kind of way. What excuse could he have that would make his behavior even close to justifiable?" I took a breath. "I don't know about you, but I'm done making excuses for people. I don't have to forgive."

I wanted to leave the room, run off onto the streets. Den had struck a nerve and I wanted to smack him. He'd never understand. A Brooklyn boy with a huge and caring, stable family. He could never know what a hardscrabble life I had—sometimes we couldn't pay the electric bill and it would be shut off for months until we scrabbled together the money. Sometimes there was no heat. There never was enough for decent clothes. Some days the only thing we had to eat was bread and butter. All of that might be forgiven at some point, but his disappearance left my mom hollow. She filled her emptiness with booze. And that would never be forgiven.

I wanted to leave the room, but instead, hot tears pricked at my eyes. Angry and embarrassed for losing control.

"Hey," Den said, handing me a tissue. "I'm sorry. I just wanted to help."

His voice caressed me.

Just then, Rogers walked back to the room. "Cell phone number belongs to Stella Ross."

"So Stella was warning you to stay away from her?" Den grinned. "She must be feeling better."

CHAPTER 54

The next day, Susan Stohmeyer called with good news. I couldn't legally be held accountable for the things in Justine's closet. But she suggested I return them all to the rightful owners. Which would be more difficult than it sounded. I mean, who knew where to start? These folks and often their whole families, were long gone. So I need to mull it over.

The Hepburn items were a no-brainer. I'd return them to her family and they'd probably give them to her foundation to auction off. But someone like Jean Harlow? No living direct descendants. Same with Marilyn Monroe.

The thought of sorting through it all overwhelmed me. I was going to need help. At first, I thought Kate and I could manage. But it really was too much for both of us. What to do?

I went back to my computer and worked on the manuscript. I didn't need to be thinking about the Hollywood treasure in my closet. That could come after I finished the book.

I moved forward with the timeline, past *Breakfast at*

Tiffany's. I was thrilled with that. I'd had it with the movie and the culture of it, dreaded going back to the studio tomorrow into the madness of it all.

Several hours later, Den called. "Hey, good news. We nabbed Stella's rapist. He was the guy who took the tickets. DNA evidence."

"That doesn't make any sense. The description was of Mathews or Von whatever his name is."

Den sighed into the phone. "Yeah. The best we can figure is that he was there. Maybe he saw everything. Maybe a witness? And took off?"

"But what was he doing there?" I shut my laptop. It was getting late.

"That's a good question. We've got the rapist and, of course, he's lawyered up. He's one sick fuck. Has quite a record of beating up old women. We're not sure if this is the first rape or not."

Shots of anger tore through me. The only thing worse than beating up an old woman was beating children. It made me feel like I wanted to wrap my hands around his neck and squeeze the breath out of him.

"So we're trying to piece this all together. But finally there's a bit of a break. I don't know if it's got to do with anything else. But this guy's going down."

"Stella is involved in something. She's in trouble. I can feel it."

"Ah, well. If she doesn't open up to you, what can you do?"

What could I do?

"She's been in Justine's house. Knew her well. Seems like there's something I could do."

"Just be careful. She's already warned you off. She might slap an injunction on you if you don't leave her alone."

"Is she still in the hospital?"

"No, she's home."

I imagined her going back to her brownstone in Brooklyn, to the palace of her attack, and couldn't help but feel sorry for her. She was either in trouble or up to no good, but she was raped and beaten and had to go back to the place it happened. Or not. Maybe she went something else. She was a tough old bird.

"I'm a New Yorker. We keep moving until we die." she had said to me.

I respected that. But the more I thought about her, the more suspicious I became. What a mixed bag of emotions she stirred in me. She was a woman of a certain age and I'd been taught to respect them. And I did. She was smart, capable, and yet had quit being a medical doctor to chase ghosts and Jewish antiques.

I'd already researched her a good bit on the computer—but as was the case a lot of the time, it wasn't enough. I wondered how else I could find out more about her. The more I thought about it, the more I thought she had something to do with stealing the jewels and, by proxy, Gemma's murder.

But then again, there was Matthew who'd been in and out of the apartment. Creepy IT guy. How did this all fit together? If he was at her apartment that day, what was he doing there?

I didn't believe in coincidence. Well at least not much anyway.

"Do Matthew and Stella know one another? Seems unlikely. She collects Jewish antiques. He's a neo-Nazi."

"Still they may have bumped into one another over some collectible or something. They might have been after the same thing."

"Den! You're brilliant. Maybe they were after the same thing—the diamonds?"

"Eh, why would a Nazi go to all that trouble to get a necklace that belonged to a woman who was a hero fighting against them?"

Why, indeed?

"What else could it be?"

Silence on the other end of the phone.

"Maybe nothing. I can't see it. I can't see them wanting the same thing at all." I had just talked myself out of a theory. My brain was fuzzy. Time for another dose of medicine. "Look, I better go I've got to take my medicine and get some stuff done around here." Laundry had been piling up. The dishwasher needed unloading. This place was a lot to take care of. I could see why Justine needed a maid.

I needed to go back to work tomorrow and I hated it. Why had I let them talk me into this? I was a writer, not a consultant.

As I collected my medicine, then took them, my mind reeled at the possibilities. What was Stella up to? I walked over to the dishwasher and unloaded the dishes, sliding each dish and glass and utensil into place. My arm was sore.

I went into the living room, sat on the couch, found the remote, and flipped on the TV. I suffered for a while and stopped--there was Zoe Noss being interviewed.

"We all miss Gemma." Her face was drawn. Had she lost even more weight? "Probably me more than anybody. We were very close, behind the scenes, and I had a great deal of respect for her."

News to me.

The interviewer leaned forward. "Is there more pressure on you because she was the rumored favorite?"

The camera zoomed in on her and captured the look I'd seen once before. She blinked it away. "No," she finally said. 'I miss her. But I'm a professional. And remember," she grinned wide. "Nobody really knows who was the favorite."

Her saccharin smile sent chills through me.

CHAPTER 55

Matthews, or whatever his name was, was still missing. Stella was home from the hospital. And Den was nearing a nervous breakdown over this case. I was glad that I had the book to write. It kept me focused and sane. It was a touchstone. Words on the pages. Stories on the page. They had a pattern, made sense. There was a beginning, a middle, and end. Life rarely fell into a nice little pattern that made sense. At least that was my experience.

My work was my salvation. But having to go into the studio was not. It was one of those things that made very little sense. How did I get here? I just needed to make the best of it, put my time in, and figure out a time to get home.

I made my way in the rain. The streets were slick with rain and the sidewalks littered with people with umbrellas, poking into one another.

I'd barely gotten my coat off when Zoe approached me. "We need to talk." Her eyes were bright with interest.

"Okay. what's up."

"Have you heard Audrey's parents were friends of Hitler?"

My heart stopped. Where was this going? And how much more odd could a question could be on a Monday morning?

"That's not quite true. They attended a party where he was also a guest. That doesn't make them friends."

"My sources say they were Nazis."

"Your sources are wrong."

She placed her hands on her hips. "I doubt that. You're just trying to cover for them. And her."

What the hell? "I'm not trying to cover for anybody. Besides, whether or not they were Nazis—and I assure you they were not—has no bearing on this project. We are working on *Breakfast at Tiffany's,* not a war picture. So, what's the issue, Zoe?"

She looked off for a moment. As if she were trying to find the right words. "I'm just trying to get to know Audrey as much as possible. And I've been reading."

"Sounds to me like you've been reading trash," I said. "Be careful what you read and what you believe. Excuse me, I need to get to the bathroom."

Was she really that concerned about Audrey's parents? Why? What was going on with her? There was so much ridiculous clap-trap conspiracy-theory stuff out there, particularly online, that sometimes I wanted to scream. Any joe-schmo blogger could call himself a journalist and do some half-assed research and write up a blog post that some witless reader would take as fact. Maddening.

As I scrubbed my hands in the bathroom, I couldn't shake the weird feeling I'd gotten from her. She didn't seem to be quite be herself. I couldn't place my finger on it—but something was off.

I just needed to get through this day. Maybe I could avoid her as much as possible. I recalled Vincent's hint to me about her. That she'd killed a man, had spent time in a mental hospital. But that had happened so long ago. She seemed fine —most of the time.

Was she on medication? Maybe that's what I was picking up on.

I walked out of the restroom and made my way to the makeshift desk they'd set up for me. A photo of Gemma was on the wall in front of me. I wasn't getting anywhere with helping Den on finding her killer. Things were very confusing. I got why he was so upset about it.

But I still thought Stella knew more than what she was telling us.

Zoe walked into the office. "There you are."

I looked up at her. Jesus. I was never going to be able to stay away from her.

I took her in. She was made up, and in costume, resembling Audrey Hepburn so much that it was a little unsettling.

"They need you on set. Wanted to ask you about some color, if it was popular then? Or something like that."

I looked away and rolled my eyes. Is this what my life had become? I vowed to not get involved with a production again. This was not my thing. At all. I needed to call my agent and see how contractually obligated I was. This seemed to be a colossal waste of time, when I could be home writing.

"I'll be right there," I said.

She smiled. Once again, it was a smile that chilled me.

"Thanks."

"I'll walk over there with you." Jesus. She was really starting to annoy me,

We walked over to the studio in utter silence. But the tension between us was palpable. I couldn't say why. Was she upset because I told her that what she'd found about Audrey's parents wasn't true? Or maybe she really just didn't like me. And that's okay, because I didn't like her either and I really didn't want to be around her.

Vincent might be on to something. Though it didn't make sense with the heist. It made a kind of sick sense that she'd want to off Gemma. But that was a mistake. The crime was going down in the secret room. The drug was meant for me as a decoy. What would Zoe want with those jewels—and how would she have even known about them?

I tried to shake it off. But I knew it was no use. I knew myself. I was like a dog with a bone. I'd have to investigate her a bit more before I could let it go. I couldn't shake this feeling. I needed to follow it wherever it led me.

The rest of the day I was the worker bee on the outside. In my mind, I was formulating secret plans.

CHAPTER 56

I tapped my pencil on the table. Then I scribbled some words on the paper. Zoe. Stella. Matthews. Threads of a narrative of suspicion that I'd not been able to follow up on because I'd been so distracted by Stella. I wasn't giving up on Stella yet. But still, these others beckoned.

When the phone rang, I nearly jumped out of my skin.

"Hey," Den said. "What are you doing?"

"I just had a weird day at work with Zoe."

"Really? What happened?"

So I explained to him her sudden interest in Audrey's parents and their political leanings.

"That's a really dumb line of questioning," he said. "Like, my grandparents were the most racist people I ever knew. Does that mean I am?"

"Right?" I paused. "So what did you find out about her?"

He breathed into the phone. "I think I told you everything. She killed a man. Self-defense. But it messed her up, psychologically. She spent some time in a mental hospital."

"New York?"

"Yeah. St. Andrews."

A wave of shock pulsed through me. "Isn't that the same place what's his name is at now?'

A few beats passed. "Yeah, why? She was there a few years back. Their path's would not have crossed."

"Unless . . . she's still seeing the same doctor there?"

"I might be able to find that out. I can find out if she's seeing someone there, but not why, or any of the details. You know what I mean?"

"HIPAA. Yeah. I know. But there are ways around that."

"Not for me, Charlotte." His voice held a measure of warning.

"Okay, detective. Whatever you say. Do you want to swing by tonight?"

"I thought you'd never ask." His voice changed into a lion's purr. I liked the sound of it, more than the other. "I'll pick up some Chinese."

Memories of our day in bed eating Chinese food plucked at my insides, sending sinking sensations through me. "Fantastic."

I had my laptop open before we finished the conversation, pulling up St. Andrews on the screen. Our staff. Our doctors. My eyes scanned the list of doctors. None of them looked familiar or struck a chord, but then again, I'd never been there and had no way of knowing who Hartwell was seeing during his stay there, nor who Zoe saw during hers. I only knew one mental health professional, other than my mom's counselors—Maude. I rang her.

"Hello, Doll. How are you?"

"I'm well. I had a bit of a setback. But things are good." My ankle was the least of my worries. It appeared to be healed.

"Good. How can I help you?"

Maude was a lifetime retainer, set up by Justine's lawyer years ago. I had no idea how deep and far the agreement went. I'd just used her to help piece together personalities. She was helpful. I had no idea how she'd react to my asking a favor like this.

"More Audrey questions?" she prompted.

"No. I'm wondering if you know any practitioners at St. Andrews."

"Of course. I know several, why?"

"It just came up again. The name. Zoe Noss had treatment there."

"I was aware of that," she said, breathing into the phone. She was smoking. A lifelong habit and she was never going to quit.

"So the guy who threatened my life—Severn Hartwell—arch enemy of Justine, is there now."

"And?"

"It's a long shot, but I'm just wondering if the two of them might have the same doctor."

A long silence on the other end of the phone.

"You might not know this, but the drug that killed Gemma Hollins was meant for me. Her death was an accident. Not murder."

She gasped. "Someone was to poison you to death"

"No. They just wanted to provide a distraction from a theft going down in Justine's room. Well. That's the theory. In any case, this is police business and I'm confiding in you."

"Okay. I get it. So what you're asking is if I can find out if they had the same doctor. You're suspicious of Zoe."

A tingle traveled up my spine. I felt my suspension creep through me. "Yes, I am."

A long drawn-out sigh.

"I'm not asking you for private information. Just who the doctor was. Maybe they shared appointment dates? Maybe they are in group therapy together?"

"Okay. I can do that. But it can't go any further. I can find out who their doctors are and get you that information. But I can't tell you anything else."

"Fair enough," I said.

"How's the book going?"

"Great, I'm almost finished, except there may be more to add in the front of it, about her youth, and another thread about Collette, the woman who discovered her."

"Ah yes, the French writer."

I was pleased she knew who she was; many Americans didn't.

After we hung up, Maude promised to get back to me in a day or two, I hopped in the shower to get ready for my date with Den.

I thought about and missed Kate, but it was crunch time for her with Fashion Week coming up. I knew that I wouldn't hear from her much.

I thought about Mom and Gram waiting at home for me, now until Friday, when I promised I would try to get home. We needed to release this thing with my dad, once and for all.

As I closed my eyes, allowing the hot water to pour over me, I saw the face of Zoe Noss, with that cold look in her eye. My gut told me she was up to no good. Even if she knew nothing about the murder, she knew something, and I shuddered to think what it might be.

CHAPTER 57

"I'm sorry, babe, I can't make it tonight. I gotta work," Den said over the phone.

My heart skipped a bit. "A break in the case?"

"Yes. Before you ask, I can't talk about it." He paused. "Have you heard back from your therapist friend?"

"No, not yet. Is that the lead you're following?"

"Not really, but it'd be good to have a few, in case this doesn't pan out. I gotta go, Charlotte. Sorry about tonight."

"There's always tomorrow," I said. "Good night, Den."

Disappointed, I lowered the phone. Just as I clicked off, a call came in from Maude.

"You were right," she said.

"I was? Zoe and Hartwell had the same doctor?"

"Yes, and I had a hell of a time tracking her down," Maude said.

"Why?"

"Her name is not Zoe Noss. That's her stage name."

My eyes blinked hard, as if by blinking them, I could make sense of this revelation. How could I have not considered this? "What is her real name?"

"Ross, not Noss. Isn't that funny?"

My heart starts to pound. "Did you say Ross? Zoe Ross?"

"Yes, Ross. Not Zoe. Caroline. Caroline Ross is her name. I'm not telling you confidential information. That's a matter of public record."

I knew that. But why hadn't I considered that? Feeling stupid and ashamed were not emotions I had often. I swallowed. "Does the record say who her mother is?"

"Her mom is Stella Ross."

There it was. My head spun. "Holy shit," I said.

"Valuable information, I take it," Maude said. "Be careful. don't do anything stupid."

Funny that she used that word since that's exactly how I was feeling.

I had been played.

Zoe and Stella were in cahoots. It was Zoe who was on the inside and she was the one who probably killed Gemma. She was also the person who went into the secret closet, and took the Hepburn jewels. I tried to play things out in my mind, but I needed paper and pencil.

"Thanks, so much Maude," I said and hung up.

I drew circles—one was Kate, one was Gemma, and one was me. Where was Zoe before Gemma and I went to the bathroom?

A circle for Jazz, the other actress up for the roll. But Zoe? Where had she been? She entered the room just as Jazz was reacting to the news. She was not in the same room with us. So where was she?

She was in the bedroom. In the closet, of course.

I dialed Kate.

"Yes? What's up, Charlotte?"

"This is going to sound like a stupid question."

"From you?" She harrumphed.

"Maybe it's not stupid. But whatever. Think back to the party. Do you remember seeing Zoe before the incident?"

"Now that you mention it, no." She paused. "Why?"

"Zoe Noss is Stella's daughter."

She gasped. "What?"

"Are you up for a trip to Stella's?"

"No. I can't do it. Fashion week. I'm just completely booked. But you should just tell Den and let him deal with it. Don't put yourself in harm's way."

Made sense. But Den was busy on the case.

And I was afraid that the longer I waited, the more likely it would be that Stella and crew would either sell the jewels, or hide them so far underground that we'd never find them again.

"I don't plan to. But I do want to see her. And I want to see Zoe or Caroline or wherever the hell she is. I want to see her burn for this!"

"Just a minute." She covered up the phone and barked orders to someone. "I'm sorry. I need to go. These idiots need me to hold their hands!"

"Okay."

"But Charlotte. Don't do anything stupid. Promise me. These people are killers."

"I promise." I planned to be very smart. Very smart, indeed.

After hanging up with Charlotte, I dialed Den and left him a message. "Zoe Noss is really Caroline Ross, Stella's daughter. She has the same doctor as Severn Hartwell. They were in group therapy together. I'm heading over to Stella's tonight."

And I was. I wasn't sure what I'd say or do. But I needed to see her, face to face. I needed to let her know I had figured it out—well not all of it, but most of it. The most important part of it. She and her daughter stole those jewels and the killed Gemma. But why? Why those jewels in a closet that held so many others?

CHAPTER 58

She finally opened the door. "Charlotte?"

"I was in the neighborhood; thought I'd stop by and see you." I paused. "How are you, Stella?"

Stella's mouth smiled, but her eyes held confusion. "Do you want to come in, have a cup of tea?"

A cup of tea? Why yes, that would be perfect. It was the beginning of our relationship. This visit would be the end. A perfect wrap up. "Certainly. That would be lovely."

I followed her into the opulent townhome. It wasn't the first time I'd been inside, but the first time was when she was raped and beaten up and I wasn't looking at the Oriental rugs and Picasso paintings. My heart thudded against my rib cage. I'd formulated several conversations in my head on the way over here and now they escaped me. My hands balled into fists as we made our way to the living room. I wanted to hit her upside the head with one of the heavy vases, but I promised to not do anything stupid.

"I'll put the kettle on and be right back," she said, slipping out of the room.

I nodded. I found a chair and sat down, regretting it

almost immediately as it was so large that I sank into it. If I had to make a move quickly, it wouldn't do. I struggled to sit on the edge of it.

I took in a few long breaths, trying to calm my racing heart. I was in the home of a woman who was responsible for the death of Gemma. A woman whose daughter had engineered a way for herself to get the lead in *Golightly Travels,* The thing is, I had a feeling there was more. More treachery and secrets, as if these few weren't enough.

The room was tidy, with books lined neatly in built-in bookcases, fresh flowers in huge vases, and ornate heavy furniture. I scanned the room, trying to find something out of place. The box of jewels had to be here. Here in this apartment somewhere. But not in this room. There was no place to hide it.

Stella walked back in the room with a tray of tea, placed on the table in front of the couch.

"Why don't you sit over here next to me?" She gestured to the couch. "That chair is terrible."

"Okay." I moved to the couch and sat next to her.

The tea tray was lovely, but there was no way I was going to drink anything. That's how they killed Gemma, isn't it? Poison.

"It looks so lovely," I said. The silver tray held a black teapot cover in pink roses, along with sugar bowls and creamer to match.

"Shall I pour?"

"Sure." I squirmed on the couch. It was almost as unstable as the chair.

"How can I help you?" she asked after she poured.

I shrugged. "As I said, I was in the neighborhood. One of the production's producers lives in this neighborhood."

"Oh? How's it going with the production?" She dropped sugar cubes in her tea and stirred.

"The actress who's playing the lead now is a major fuck up." I watched for her response.

Her eyebrows lifted and she shrugged. "Aren't they all?"

I was betting that she knew that I had found out Zoe was her daughter.

"Gemma wasn't." I stirred sugar into my cup.

"She was lovely," Stella sipped at her tea.

"Do you mind if I use your restroom? Sorry but it's been a long day." I stood.

"Certainly. It's down the hall to the left."

I found my way down the hall and scanned the place. I walked by the kitchen, a few closed doors and one slightly open, off to the right. I pushed the door gently. It swung open. It was a bedroom, with a full-sized bed, made with a silk throw and cushions. I blinked. That was no cushion.

I stepped inside. My heart raced. I batted my eyes several times, squinted. My jewel box sat among the velvet and silk cushions. There was my proof, as if I needed any. Stella had the jewels. She killed Gemma to get them. Could it be that easy? To walk in the room, grab the box and leave? How would I sneak by Stella? I wondered about escaping through the window. It looked as it opened. I rushed over and grabbed the box, hoping the jewels were still inside, and moved toward the window, pushed aside the heavy drapes, unlatched it, and struggled to open it. Fuck! It was painted shut. It wouldn't open.

I'd have to find another way out. Maybe I could just walk down the hallway and out the door. Stella's back was to the hallway and entrance. As long as Stella didn't turn her head, I could sneak it out. Besides, she was a little old lady, and if I had to, I could get the best of her.

She had played me. And she had robbed me. I crashed the velvet box, my sweaty palms imprinting the fabric. I turned from the window and realized I wasn't alone in the room.

Matthew stood in front of me. He held out his hand. “Give me the box.”

I shook my head. “It belongs to me.”

He reached into his coat pocket and pulled out a gun. A gun.

Stella rushed into the room. “What are you doing?” I wasn’t sure if she was talking to me or him. But I held up the box and leveled a glare.

CHAPTER 59

Matthews pointed his gun toward me. "Why do you have to make it so difficult?"

My heart pounding in my chest, blood racing through my throbbing neck was the only answer I gave him. Here I was with Matthew and Stella. I had no idea if Den or Kate knew my whereabouts.

"I just want the diamonds." Finally I found the words. My mouth felt like sandpaper. But I found the words, a victory of sorts when a creepy guy was pointing a gun toward you. "I just want the diamonds. I don't care about any of the rest of it. You stole them from Justine. She's the rightful owner."

"She's dead," Stella said. "What does she care?"

"Please put the gun down."

"No. You need to drop the box and walk away." His cheek twitched. Nervous. This wasn't something he did every day.

"But it belongs to me."

The box felt heavy in my hands. Like it held more than diamonds. More than the jewels Collette's husband crafted for Audrey. "Sometimes what's valuable isn't the most obvious thing," I said, repeating back to Stella what she had said to me earlier. Mathews took a step toward me. Stella raised her arm to stop him. "Don't be foolish," she spat. 'Haven't we been through enough?"

Then she turned back to me. "What you have in your hand is valuable to us. Please just give it back."

Valuable to us. Who was she talking about? Diamonds were valuable to everybody. My legs quivered. A man had a gun on me. The only thing between him and me was a small lady, whose eyes were glued to me and the box I held.

Hard to think when a gun was on you. My thoughts dripped through my brain.

Think, think, think.

Valuable to us.

Not obvious.

Click. The gears of my brain were moving finally. What was valuable to them was in the box, but it wasn't the diamonds. What could it be? It was something both of them had risked their lives for. Both of them had murdered for—albeit accidental.

Something else was in the box. And it wasn't the diamonds.

A wave of dizzy rolled through. I sucked in air. I lifted the lid of the box.

"Charlotte, please, just give it to us," Stella said, with a pleading note.

The diamonds sparkle against the blue velvet in the box. Alluring. I felt around them, soft velvet, cool diamonds. I felt nothing underneath, but just in case, I dumped it.

Stella gasped. Matthews grumble, "What the fuck."

The diamonds spilled onto the marble floor. The necklace, bracelet, earrings, clinking on the marble. But nothing else spilled out of the box.

We all three stood and looked at one another. Stella crouched down to pick up the jewels. "Leave it," Matthews said. "Who cares about them? Just give me the box!" He held out his hand, long bony fingers.

There was something in the box. I tore the velvet from the inside. Nothing, I turned it upside down.

"Please, Charlotte. You don't understand. We're on the same side. I promise you."

"On the same side?" I nearly roared. "Your man has a gun on me. Before he shoots me, I want to know what this is all about. What is so important. If it's not the diamonds, then what?"

I plucked at the edges of the box, tore off a corner.

"Stop, please, you may rip a note."

"A note?" My heart stopped. She leapt toward me and knocked my hand across the box ripping it. I lifted it and as I did so papers wafted in streams of light, dust, flying and streamed down on the floor. Stella fell to her knees to gathered the paper. Matthews grabbed me. "What are we going to do with you now?"

A voice ranged from behind me. "You're going to let her go." Den and two other cops entered the room. Thank God.

"Step away from her," Den said. "Step away and nobody gets hurt."

Stella stood with the papers in her hand, tears streaming. "Let her go. It's over. Aren't we in enough trouble?"

He released me. I wanted to run to Den, but couldn't. My legs were still shivering.

The uniformed officer stepped forward and handcuffed Matthews. Stella shoved the notes into my hands before they handcuffed her.

Delicate paper with Dutch scribbled over it. "What is it?"

She lifted her chin toward me. "The notes from the bottom of Audrey's shoes."

Her words spun around in my mind. "Do you mean—"

She nodded. "Collected and verified by the experts. Those

notes you have in your hand were placed on young Audrey's shoes and she snuck them into Dutch resistance workers. She risked her life for others, even as child. The notes have become mythical. Some people claim she really had nothing to do with the movement. But imagine. You're holding the proof in your hands."

I knew more than just to take the word of one collector about the authenticity or value of anything. But the yellowed paper and the scrambled words looked real.

The cops shoved Matthews out of the room. But they were taking their time with Stella.

"But he's a Nazi," I said as he walked by me. "Why would he want this?"

"He's not a Nazi. It was only a way to throw you off. And it worked for a while, didn't it?" She smiled a slow, trembling smile. "He's the great grandson of a resistance hero."

How stupid could I be? How did I not see that? The Nazi thing frightened and blinded me. They were banking on that. My hands balled into fists at my side. If I could smack myself, right her and now, I would.

Den stood beside me. "You're holding evidence."

"It may be valuable, please be careful with it." I handed the small stack of yellowed paper to him and sucked in air, then found a chair, which I sank into. Relief washed over me. The room spun, melted and I let go.

CHAPTER 60

I sat up in bed. My own bed. How did I even get here. Thirst awakened me and I untangled myself from the blankets to find my way to the kitchen.

"Good morning," Den said. "I made coffee."

It wasn't shocking to see him sitting at the kitchen island. I knew he was beside me in bed and I knew he left. But it still made my heart race.

"Good morning." I leaned in and hugged him. "I've lost some time."

"You passed out. We brought you home after you came to. You've been sleeping for, oh, sixteen hours?"

"What?" No wonder I was so thirsty. I reached into the cupboard for a glass.

"What were you doing over there?" Den asked.

I filled my glass with water. My head felt cottony. But I remembered. "I wanted to ask Stella about her daughter, Zoe. I went there and as I was going to use the restroom; I spotted the box on the bed. On the bed, Den. The box of jewels they wanted so badly they killed Gemma for. It was just sitting there."

I drank my water.

"So? Why didn't ya leave and call me?"

I sat my glass down with a thud. "I have no idea. I just panicked, I guess. I grabbed the box and tried to leave through a window."

"A window? For chrissake." His jaw clenched. "I love you, but you need to stop this shit. I'm a cop."

"It's not like I wanted any of this."

He sighed. "I know that, but you're like a dog with a bone. You won't let it rest."

What could I say? That much was true. It was a good quality in a researcher and writer. Maybe not in the girlfriend of a cop.

"She died in front of us. In my apartment." I drew in the air. "How could I let it rest? She was a friend."

He stood and wrapped his arms around me. "I know, Babe."

His scent, familiar and warm, his arms enveloping me with all of his goodness, I unraveled, sobbing into him.

When we finally disengaged, he told me the rest of the story. That Matthew and Stella didn't mean for Gemma to get the substance. It was meant for me. But it still would've worked as a decoy tactic for her to have it—they had no idea she was allergic to it. They didn't mean to kill her.

Zoe would be implicated. She was the inside person. The person who actually placed the poison in the glass. The production had wrapped. But it was still up in the air as to what they would do with it, now with all of the bad publicity surrounding it.

None of it had anything to do with the diamonds.

It was all about those notes. All about what started as a good impulse to preserve a piece of history. But it festered in some collectors, like Stella, and became more than that. It became a personal mission and one she'd do anything to achieve.

We walked into the bedroom without coffee and I noticed his suitcase, which was unusual.

"I'm taking a few days off." He sat down on the edge of the bed. "I'm going to Cloister Island."

I thought he was joking. Den was afraid of water. He'd not been in a boat since he was a kid.

"I'm serious. I've been seeing a shrink."

"Oh." A shrink? My Den? "Boss make you do that?"

He smiled. "Kinda. Also, I want to get to know your family. I care about you and you need to visit the island. Your ma is . . . Well, this whole business with your long-lost father —you need to get home and I'm going to see to it."

I blinked back a tear. I didn't like to cry, especially in front of people. A welling erupted in my chest. I drew in a breath and looked into Den's face. There was no way out.

For me, the waterway between Manhattan and Cloister Island was a path between two worlds. Today, more so than any other time, with my Brooklyn cop beside me, shivering, but brave, and the Manhattan skyline behind me. The only thing missing was Kate and I would not push her. Her return to the island had to be on her terms.

As Cloister Island came into view, I exhaled. Home. The events of the past few weeks rambled my mind. Matthew's weird wiring through the apartment. Stella's attack. The floating notes. And most of all Gemma falling, dying in front of me. How to move forward?

The boat swayed. Den gripped my hand. With my other hand, I touched his waxy face, looked into his eyes, and found reassurance.

Together. We'd move forward together.

AUTHOR'S NOTE

Just before the first book in this series was released—the Jean Harlow Bombshell—I received word that the publisher was going out of business. I knew two things then: the first book was not going to get much attention or sales, and I needed to make a decision about The Audrey Hepburn Heist, which I was almost finished writing and would now not have a publisher. Should I continue and try to find a publisher for both books? Or should I walkaway and find another project? I decided to finish the book and try to seek a new home for it and the first book. At that time, no publishers were taking on series that had started with another publisher. I had no option but to publish it myself. Art for art's sake is all well and good, but there are bills to pay and mouths to feed. I needed to make my effort count.

The publisher had selected which actress my next book should focus on. They chose Audrey Hepburn and, at first, I was less than pleased. Much like Charlotte Donovan in the story, I admired her greatly, but she was a bit too perfect for me to sink my teeth into. Or so I thought.

I found that she just had a perfect image— she, of course,

was not perfect. But what grabbed me about her was her upbringing and her underground efforts during the war. Some say the story of her taking messages to the resistance on the bottom or her shoes is true; others claim it is not. I chose one side for this story. Even though it's a very dark story, I like to think it has hope in that scene where we find out why folks have risked their lives. Not for jewelry, but for little slips of paper.

Historically speaking, much of the book is accurate. Colette and Audrey did have a long-lasting relationship. But there were no jewels given as a gifts, as far as we know.

This book was written several years ago, so none of the current events have worked their way into it. I like to think of Charlotte and Kate holed up in that grand apartment, having a great time together, despite the Cover pandemic.

As for the question as to whether there will be more books in the series, the answer is I don't know. I'd love to write more. It seems like it could go on forever. But I'll reserve my time and energy until I see if my readers like the book and if it earns back what resources I've spent getting it published. Feel free to drop me a line at molliebryan@comcast.net. And, please, if you like the book, leave a review.

Special Thanks

I'm very grateful to the editor of this book, Mary Martin Sproles a good friend and a fabulous editor. I'm also grateful for my agent Jill Marsal, who tried her best to sell this book to the publishers. (And, if she can't sell it, nobody can.) I also want to thank my readers for sticking through thick and thin with me. Onward!

ABOUT THE AUTHOR

Mollie Cox Bryan writes cozy mysteries with edge and traditional mysteries with heart. She's the author of several bestselling mystery series, also writing under the pen name Maggie Blackburn. Her books have been selected as finalists for an Agatha Award and a Daphne du Maurier Award and as a Top 10 Beach Reads by Woman's World. She has also been short-listed for the Virginia Library People's Choice Award. Goodnight Moo, the second book in her Buttermilk Creek Mysteries was short-listed for a people's choice award by Fresh Fiction. Mollie is the mother to two amazing young women both pursuing careers in music. She makes her home at the foothills of the Blue Ridge Mountains in Crozet, Va.

ALSO BY MOLLIE COX BRYAN

ALSO BY MOLLIE COX BRYAN

The Buttermilk Creek Series

Beach Reads Mysteries (as Maggie Blackburn) The Cora Crafts Series

The Cumberland Creek Mysteries

The Jean Harlow Bombshell (A Charlotte Donovan Mystery , #1)

Sign up for her newsletter here! https://view.odesk.com/pages/6002f5f19b717a420f23b7d6